DARK SECRETS OF THE OLD OAK TREE

DOLORES J. WILSON

Medallion Press, Inc.
Printed in USA

Dark Secrets
of the
Old Oak Tree

Dolores J. Wilson

DEDICATION:

To my "bestest" friend, Jeannie Dickson,
who was the first to believe I could make the writer's journey.

Published 2010 by Medallion Press, Inc.

The MEDALLION PRESS LOGO
is a registered trademark of Medallion Press, Inc.

Cover design by James Tampa

Typeset in Adobe Garamond Pro
Printed in the United States of America
Title font set in Optimus Princeps

Library of Congress Cataloging-in-Publication Data

Wilson, Dolores J.
Dark secrets of the old oak tree / Dolores J. Wilson.
p. cm.-- (Southern Tree series)
ISBN-13: 978-1-60542-106-3 (alk. paper)
ISBN-10: 1-60542-106-5 (alk. paper)
1. Divorced women--Fiction. 2. Secrets--Fiction. 3. Murder--Investigation--Fiction.
4. Georgia--Fiction. I. Title.
PS3623.I5784D37 2010
813'.6--dc22

2009041001

10 9 8 7 6 5 4 3 2 1
First Edition

ACKNOWLEDGMENTS:

With special thanks to:

Professor Jeff Olma for the beginning spark for this story.

Two people I can't thank enough, Vickie King and Marge Smith.

And, most of all, thanks to my wonderful and supportive husband, Richard.

CHAPTER 1

IT COULD HAVE BEEN ANYTHING MAKING ITS WAY THROUGH THE Georgia underbrush. The loud crunching of dried leaves and snapping of brittle twigs called the tiny hairs on the back of my neck to full attention. I sat perched on a huge oak limb on what was left of the floor of my childhood tree house. Fear of the unknown caused my body to tremble.

Beyond the stand of trees edging the meadow between me and my home, the early evening sun was still bright, but shadows shrouded the small clearing beneath me. The thrashing in the bushes was too close and coming too fast for me to climb down and escape to the safety of my house. I was so high up in the leaves, I felt I could stay hidden, but my sweat-soaked clothes smelled of fear, and my heart pounded so loudly, any animal would sense my presence.

Whatever I was expecting to pop into the clearing—an armadillo, a raccoon, or even a bear—would have been welcome compared to the reality of what appeared below.

The huge form of Jake Harley broke through the palmetto bushes and briar thicket. Across his broad shoulder, he carried a nude body. He threw a shovel down, and then, with no more effort than if he'd carried a bag of chicken feed, Jake shifted what I was pretty sure was a dead woman and dropped her to the ground with a thud that rocked my teeth. Chills crawled the entire length of my body.

Jake disappeared beneath my perch in the tree and out of my line of sight. Trying to see him again, I slowly leaned forward and peeked over the side. Terror drummed through every inch of my being, and bile climbed higher in my throat. I swallowed several times, hoping to keep from throwing up.

The scene below me played out like a horrible nightmare. The corpse lay on its side. Leaves and twigs matted the woman's long, dark blonde hair and hid most of her face. Dried blood from the corner of her mouth formed a trail across her cheek and disappeared into her stringy hair.

As Jake dug shovels full of dirt from the hard ground, I watched in horror. He made it look easy, leaving me no doubt that I couldn't possibly defend myself against the powerful man. From the mounds of dirt, broken roots pointed like gnarly fingers to my hiding place. I prayed with all my might that Jake wouldn't look my way.

I glanced at my watch—7:05. I'd now been trapped in my hellacious hiding place for over forty-five minutes. During that entire time, I'd sat with my legs folded. Any sense of normal feeling had long ago deserted me, and I felt nothing but painful needles stabbing every inch of my flesh. I didn't dare move. I barely dared to breathe. But what I really wanted to do was cry. Cry for the poor dead soul lying on the hard ground, waiting for Jake Harley to finish digging her grave.

I shivered. The painful pounding in my head was rivaled only by the raw aching in my heart. A family was missing a loved one, and I knew where that person was, but I couldn't get to a phone to tell anyone. Even if I hadn't left my cell at my house, it would have been too noisy to use it to call for help.

Earlier, when I had first made my way into the clearing, all I'd really wanted to do was have a moment of peace and quiet. Once there I'd wondered if I could muster the strength to climb the two-by-four planks still joined to the tree to form a ladder where Dad had nailed them. The sides of the tree house were mostly gone, but the floor, although smaller than I remembered, was still sturdy.

Oh God, I wished with everything inside me that I hadn't tried to prove something to myself by climbing the tree. Had I done it because I'd turned forty that day or because my husband of fifteen years had traded me in for a red corvette and his legal assistant? Was I trying to prove I was still young? Given where I was at that moment, only one thing was for certain—I was too young to die.

I needed to take another glance at the things going on under the tree house, but it had grown too dark to see anything. Panic gripped my throat, making it hard to swallow. I could hear Jake moving around. Suddenly, a light brightened a large part of the clearing. Jake had turned on a flashlight and set it on its end with the beams shining up into the trees. I leaned back out of the glow, which kept me from seeing what was happening below.

Jake's grunting accelerated. An alarm went off in my head. Was he climbing the tree to where I was? My pulse raced out of control. With the beams shining through the slits in the wooden floor, I glanced around for a weapon, but found nothing. I looked down again and sighed with relief when I saw that Jake wasn't climbing the tree. He had dragged the body to the hole. A second later, he rolled it into the grave.

The dead woman landed on her back. With her mouth and eyes frozen open, she stared up at me. Uncontrollable anguish shook me to the core. Tears flooded my eyes, blurring my vision, but not enough to close out the grotesque image. I wrapped my arms across my chest to steady my body's violent shaking. I wanted to wake up and deal with the horrific nightmare, but that wasn't going to happen and I knew it. I'd never experienced such torture from a nightmare.

I squeezed my eyes shut to clear away the tears. When I dared to look again, Jake was shining the flashlight into the hole. I saw her face clearly and knew for sure the woman was Denise Farrell. A pain stabbed so deeply into my heart, I almost screamed. I hadn't seen her since we'd graduated from high school and I'd left Hyattville to go to college in Chicago, but that hadn't mattered. Twenty years and death didn't matter. I would have known her anywhere.

Sleeping legs, painful stiffness, sweat, and terror pounding against my tightly strung nerves weakened my whole body. Weighted with an overwhelming need to sleep or faint, I had to fight against the sensations. I had to stay alert in case Jake discovered me.

As he buried Denise, I didn't watch, but I couldn't close out the sounds of the heavy dirt hitting her body or the sour smell of the damp earth. Through the branches I could no longer see the meadow. Nightfall had claimed everything around me. Everything but the private little world surrounding the big oak tree.

Many times Denise and I had sat on the very boards that were keeping me hidden from Jake. The branches around me had heard our life's dreams and secrets. A place that once held pleasant and happy thoughts was now a keeper of deadly, dark secrets.

Remorse mixed with fear. It all had to end soon. I couldn't take much more. Suddenly, I realized I was hearing dried leaves rustling. Was Jake leaving?

I stole a glance. No, he wasn't leaving. He was getting handfuls of dried leaves from the edge of the clearing and dumping them onto Denise's grave. When he had enough piled up, he scattered them evenly over the ground, camouflaging the freshly spade dirt. I would never again hear the crunch of dried leaves without remembering this night.

Finally, Jake picked up his shovel and flashlight. Before he made his way back through the overgrown thicket, he said, "Bye bye, Denise." His deep, masculine voice contrasted starkly with the childlike words.

More tears made their way to my eyes. How had this mild-mannered man with the mind of an eight-year-old come to this juncture? If asked before this, I'd have bet my new boutique that Jake Harley would not be capable of something so heinous. But regardless of what my heart said, my eyes told a completely different story.

The road was quite a distance from where I sat praying Jake was gone, but I faintly heard a vehicle start. Once I was sure he was out of earshot, I stretched my legs and tried rubbing them back to life. I had to wait a while before I felt ready to climb down from the tree. I needed to have my body working properly so I could run home to call the sheriff, and I had to make sure Jake wasn't on his way back into the clearing. I waited. Hoping to hear nothing. Hoping to hear help coming.

No help came.

I would guess I'd been sitting in that tree a good thirty minutes after Jake had left the clearing. Time was wasting. I had to get someone out there right away. Of course, nothing could bring Denise back, but the earlier the authorities were alerted, the faster they could get her out of that dark hole and make her ready for a proper burial.

I was stalling, and it wasn't because of the weakness in my legs. I was scared half out of my mind, and I couldn't force my body to cooperate. Except for a small glint of moonlight hovering over the meadow, everything was hidden by pitch-blackness. Anything or anybody could be waiting at the bottom of the makeshift ladder, and

I would never know until I landed in their arms on my descent from the tree. But I couldn't just stay up there.

Somewhere in the back of my mind, I heard my Grandma Carson's sweet voice whispering in the wind that lightly rustled the leaves. "The unknown is always scarier than reality."

True.

Silently, I counted to three and then started down the ladder. In a matter of seconds, I was out of the tree. As soon as my feet hit the ground, I started running.

I'd only taken two steps when my foot sank into the newly spaded dirt. I landed face down, sprawled across Denise's grave. My skin instantly turned to gooseflesh, and chills shivered through me.

As I struggled to stand, I kept apologizing. "I'm sorry, Denise. I'm so sorry."

Was I losing my mind? As fast as branches and briar bushes allowed, I ran toward the moonlit meadow. Once there, I could see my home standing stately on the other side of the field. I ran in the direction of the two-story farmhouse left to me by my father, who'd died two years before. It looked forever away. The high, meadow grass wiped its evening dew on my jeans, and I fought to keep from screaming. I imagined someone was chasing me. I could barely breathe, but I was afraid to stop.

Miraculously, I was able to hit the latch and shove the gate open all in one fell swoop. The tall house hid the moon and cast a black shadow from the fence to the front porch. Tall, thick branches fortified with sharp thorns snagged my clothing and tore my flesh. Blinded by darkness, I had stupidly run through Dad's rose garden.

"Aw," I cried and grabbed at my arm only to get my hand locked around the barbed stalk. "Damn." I slowly unhooked myself from the rose bush and then cursed the rest of the way to the front porch. How could I have forgotten about the garden? It had been in that very spot all my life.

I bounded up the porch steps, flung the screen door open, and sailed into my house. After slamming the heavy front door, I slid the safety chain into place and collapsed against the wall. My eyes were closed tightly. I was gasping for air, giving thanks, and, since I hadn't locked the house before my walk across the meadow, praying I was the only one there.

When I opened my eyes, I found it dark and scary. As fast as possible, I flipped on a table lamp and then scanned the room. Everything looked just as it had when I'd left. After grabbing the telephone, I called 9-1-1.

"Hyattville Sheriff's Office. Deputy Douglas speaking." The familiar voice startled me. At that moment, my old friend Lonnie Douglas, class clown, was the last person I wanted to talk to.

"I need to talk to the sheriff. It's an emergency," I spoke quickly, hoping Lonnie wouldn't recognize my voice.

"Evie? Is that you? It took you long enough to give your old buddy a call. How ya been?" he asked with his mouth obviously full of food.

"What part of *emergency* don't you understand?" I choked out in heart pounding fear mixed with instant aggravation. "Denise Farrell is dead, and Jake Harley buried her in the woods on the other side of my meadow. You gotta get the sheriff and get out here," I demanded.

"Jake buried Denise? Slow down, Evie. You've got to be mistaken. Jake is just now backing out of a parking space in front of our office. He's been in with Sheriff Beasley for the past ten minutes."

Lonnie's words buzzed in my head like I'd been zapped with lightning. Had there been enough time for Jake to get to Hyattville and spend ten minutes with the sheriff? Evidently there had, because he'd done it.

"Did Jake confess?" I asked. "Why is he leaving? You have to lock him up?" Panic stole some of my voice. I wasn't sure Lonnie could even understand what I was saying. I certainly couldn't understand anything that had happened in the past . . . how long had it been?

As if it heard my thoughts, the grandfather clock standing in the corner of my front parlor began to *bong*. I jumped so hard, I nearly dropped the phone. It was eight o'clock.

"Evie? Evie?" Lonnie shouted through the phone. "Are you there? Are you okay?"

"No. Yes. I don't know, Lonnie. Please come quick," I pleaded, all the while trying not to sob uncontrollably.

"Okay, we're on our way."

I slumped into the overstuffed sofa and pulled Grandma Carson's afghan around me. I shook so hard, the decorative crocheted roses danced. I couldn't keep my mind on one facet of the last two hours. It kept jumping from one detail to another. I'd always been the cool one in troubled situations—but what was I thinking? I'd never been in a situation remotely like this one.

For fifteen years, I'd been the wife of a high-flying prosecuting Chicago attorney. One who loved to toot his own horn by telling me and everyone in earshot what pieces of evidence he'd brilliantly used to bring down a killer. Some of that had sunk into my brain. I threw the blanket aside. I raced to the window facing the meadow and stared at the oak tree outlined by the glimmer of the moon.

When the sheriff arrived, he would have questions for me. Mentally, I started to outline what they would be. I grabbed a notepad and pen from Dad's roll-top desk. While it was still fresh in my mind, I scribbled down the timeline. I wrote what Jake was wearing, but then scratched through that info. Since he'd gone directly to their office, they already knew what he was wearing.

What else could I tell them? Nothing other than that Denise was dead.

The grandfather clock sounded again—8:15. Lonnie and Sheriff Johnston Beasley should be arriving any minute. I turned on the front porch light and waited by the front window. A thick row of trees separated my front yard from the highway. I heard the sirens first, and then I saw the display of flashing lights from two sheriff's department vehicles, a fire truck, and an ambulance.

Hurrying out to meet them, I reached Lonnie first. Once he had been lanky, but life, or maybe a few too many doughnuts, had filled him out. On him, it looked good. He put his thick arm around me and kissed my cheek.

"Welcome home, Evie," he said sarcastically.

"Yeah. Some party, huh?"

Sheriff Johnston Beasley took longer to get to us. He pulled his hat from the passenger seat and positioned it on his head; then he finally made his way to Lonnie and me.

"Miss Carson." He tipped his hat. "What's going on?"

"Jake Harley buried Denise Farrell over there in that wooded area." I pointed at the woods beyond the meadow, and then I noticed the EMTs. "You won't need them. She's dead." Sadness lodged in my throat. I must have staggered a little. Lonnie put his arm around me, led me to the porch, and urged me to sit down.

"Thanks." I forced a wobbly smile.

"What happened?" Lonnie asked.

I told them everything I'd witnessed. My written timeline was inside, but I didn't need it. It was blazoned in my mind forever.

"What's the best way to get over there?" Beasley asked.

"You can't drive across the field. Too many potholes. You'll have to go down Miner's Road. That's how Jake got in there."

"Do you think you can show us?"

"Yes."

"You ride with Lonnie, and we'll follow."

I grabbed my house keys and locked my front door. In Lonnie's car, he and I rode along in complete silence. Our parents had been best friends, so he and I had grown up almost like brother and sister. Even though I'd been back in town a month, I hadn't seen him since Dad's funeral over two years before. There was much we could have talked about, but the tragedy surrounding us had shoved idle chitchat aside.

The official vehicles formed a caravan, each shining spotlights erratically swirling over the impregnable span of trees. They resembled Hollywood searchlights announcing a movie premier. But this was not Hollywood, and it wasn't a movie. It was real life with consequences that would change lives forever.

Large live oaks canopied the road, and in some places, joined above us like locked gnarled fingers. Splashes of gray Spanish moss dripped from the branches, deepening the eeriness of the journey.

I didn't have to point out the arched opening that would lead us to Denise's grave. Lonnie pulled to a stop right in front of it. He knew those woods as well as I did, if not better.

It wasn't until I'd gotten out of the squad car that I realized we'd been joined by several other vehicles. A state police SUV and patrol car, plus another Hyattville deputy, had parked on the opposite side of Miner's Road. Quickly, they all congregated around me.

"You come with me, Miss Carson." Sheriff Beasley took my arm and helped me jump the ditch. "The rest of you stay here until I call you."

I looked at Lonnie. I wanted him with me, but just then, his wife,

Kitty, had pulled up next to the cars. She rolled down the window and yelled to Lonnie, "Can you come here a second?"

Lonnie handed his boss a massive portable light with an extremely high beam. He went to talk to Kitty, and she and I acknowledged each other with a curt wave. We had grown up together, but our opinions were too opposite for us to be friends. She thought she was better than everyone else, and I didn't.

Beasley and I walked to the archway to Denise's tomb. The bright beams lit our path well. Night creatures skittered away, including a small green snake, which crossed our path. When we got into the cleared area, I stopped. "There." I pointed at the scattered leaves directly under the tree house floor. "Jake buried Denise right there."

The sheriff handed me the light. He knelt and shoved some of the leaves aside. Lifting a handful of the soft dirt, he let it sift through his fingers. When he stood, he removed his hat and looked up into the tree. I shifted the light to shine up there.

"That's a long ways up for a kid's tree house," he said.

"It wasn't that high when Dad built it. The tree has grown. Some of the branches knocked the roof and sides down, but the floor is still sturdy."

"Thank heavens for that. You might have ended up buried with Denise."

I clutched my fist to my chest. Beasley spoke the truth, but hearing it said aloud sent new tremors of fear flooding through me. Denise was the best friend I'd ever had. From an early age, we were inseparable, we thought alike, and our dreams were the same. She had encouraged me to be the best at everything I did. She was afraid of nothing, and she helped me overcome my fear of things that go bump in the night. Mostly, Denise made me laugh. We had sworn to do everything together. Ironically, had Jake discovered me, we would have died together. A shiver climbed my spine.

"Can you get her out of that dark hole? Please?" I begged.

"We have things to do first, but it'll be done as soon as possible. I promise. Over here, guys," he bellowed into the night.

Quickly, the men waiting back at the roadside made their way to the cleared opening. The ground vibrated, and their movements caused a loud eruption of jingling and clanking. The clamor of their shovels, their gun belts, even the change in their pockets magnified several times in the dead of the night. I covered my ears, trying to close out the disturbing sounds.

There were so many people. Where had they come from? I was shoved away from the immediate area. I found a fallen tree, hardened, almost petrified from the elements.

That's where I was sitting when Lonnie found me.

"Are you okay, Evie?" He sat beside me.

"I don't know if I can ever be okay again. Poor Denise. I'd never believe Jake capable of doing something like this. And why Denise?"

"Too early for all those questions. The sheriff has gone down to the lake to get Jake. I'm sure he'll tell Johnston everything we need to know."

"I saw Kitty back at the road," I said, but never took my eyes off the inner workings of the crime scene being cordoned off. Floodlights were set up to make the area as bright as daylight. A camera clicked and flashed taking pictures of every inch of the gravesite.

"When I was on the way here, I left her a message on her cell phone. She'd gone to a movie over in O'Brien. She stopped by to get some of the details so she can start spreading the news."

Under normal circumstances, Lonnie would have laughed and I would have joined him, but that didn't happen. He shrugged and stood. "I need to check with Johnston over the radio, and I'll be back shortly to take you home."

Once I was alone again in the shadows, I thought about the irony of the situation. Earlier, I'd sat on a tree limb watching my dear friend being buried, and hours later I was on another limb watching the process of getting her out of her makeshift grave. The men dug a large hole resembling an archeological dig, exposing a cross section of Denise's grave. The officials measured each layer of sand and clay, then gauged the depth of the cavity housing her body.

Watching them reminded me how, as we became teenagers, Denise and I would measure our breasts hoping they would someday be as big as Kitty McGovern's, who later became Mrs. Lonnie Douglas. By the time we graduated, Denise had gotten her wish. I, on the other hand, never quite made it.

By the time Lonnie returned, I welcomed the distraction to keep from dealing with all the dreadful thoughts that kept swimming around in my mind.

"I'm going to take you home. We're going to be out here for several more hours." He took my arm.

"I want to wait until I'm sure Denise is out of here and on her way to Benso Mortuary."

Lonnie sat and put his arm around my shoulder. "She'll be going to the county morgue first. They'll have to do an autopsy."

I knew that, but still the words squeezed my heart. The thought of Denise's beautiful body being cut was hard to imagine, but it would have to be done to determine any injuries she'd sustained, the cause of death, and if she'd been raped.

"Oh, Lonnie, I feel so helpless. Why has this happened? And why Denise?"

He pulled me to him until my head rested against his chest. "I don't know. After her divorce, she separated herself from any of the old gang. Her husband was only gone a couple of months when she found out she was pregnant. I always figured raising a baby without its father, plus the hurt from her husband abandoning her . . . well, it changed her, Evie. It changed her a lot." He paused for a long moment, then finally said, "Come on." He rose and urged me to my feet. "Let's go. I have to get back to the station. There's a flood of calls coming in, and the duty clerk needs help answering them. Word does travel fast, even in the middle of the night."

"Won't I have to make a formal statement to the authorities?" I followed Lonnie to the path leading back to the road.

"Yeah, someone will come by in the morning and talk to you. We don't have a lot of manpower, so right now working the scene is the most important thing."

We were a few feet down the path when we were met by a small group of people. Lonnie shined his flashlight on them. Denise's mom shaded her eyes from the bright light. I stepped ahead of Lonnie.

"Mrs. Farrell." My voice trembled.

My dead friend's mother, Judy Farrell, leaned out of the beam so she could see, but she didn't appear to recognize me.

"It's me. Evie Carson."

"Evie?" Her hoarse tone was choked with sadness.

She was being held up by her younger sister, Sarah Dupree, on one side, and on the other side by a young girl who looked a lot like Denise did when she was a teenager. Denise's daughter.

"Is it true, Evie? Is she dead?" Denise's Aunt Sarah asked.

All I could manage was to nod my head.

Lonnie reached out and took Mrs. Farrell's hand. "You shouldn't be here. This is no place for you." He looked at her sister. "Take her home, Sarah. Let us do our job, and then we'll talk to you."

When she started to argue, I spoke up. "He's right. You have to leave. Please come to my house, and we'll wait there."

The three women hesitated a few moments and then returned to their car. It was decided I would ride with them, and Lonnie could get back to town. He promised someone would come to my house as soon as they were through at the crime scene.

Sarah drove. Denise's daughter, Merrilee, rode in the front with her. I sat in the back with my arm around Mrs. Farrell. Occasionally, she sighed on the wings of a ragged breath. That was the only sound that intruded into the dead silence inside the car. Being locked in that consoling embrace reminded me of another time Mrs. Farrell and I had comforted each other at the loss of a loved one—her friend, my mother.

At my house, while I made strong coffee, the others settled around the kitchen table. With the coffee brewing, I walked to the table to join them. Until then, no one talked about the circumstances that had brought us together. I believe we were all in a state of shock. In my case, I didn't know how much or how little I should say about what I'd witnessed.

"Who would ever want to hurt our Denise?" Sarah was the first to speak.

I swallowed hard and decided to find out how much they knew. "How did you hear the news?" I asked.

"Goldie Douglas came to the house. Her daughter-in-law, you know, Kitty, had told her and she felt, as my longtime friend, she should be there when I found out," Mrs. Farrell said. I hadn't laid eyes on her in twenty years, so naturally she would have aged, but the lines on her face were etched in agony, making her appear much older.

"Is she the only person you've talked to?"

"Yes, and she really didn't know any more than that Denise was . . . dead and buried on your property." Her voice trailed to a whisper.

"What can you tell us, Evie?" Sarah asked.

My world stood still. I didn't want to tell Denise's family what I knew about her death. To that point, her daughter, Merrilee, had not said a word. She'd only sat stone silent, staring into her folded hands. Now she looked across the table at me. Her ice blue eyes melted, and tears streamed down her face. "How did my mom die?" she asked.

I took her hands. They were cold, and I rubbed them. "I don't know what happened to her. I worked at the boutique all day. When I got home, I needed to go for a walk to clear my head and, truthfully, to deal with some of the loneliness I've been experiencing."

Sarah placed her hand on my back. "Divorce is hard. It'll get easier, honey."

Suddenly, guilt slammed through me. "I'm sorry. My problems are insignificant compared to the developments of the last few hours. Let me just tell you what I know."

Coffee was ready, so I used that as an excuse to not have to look at Denise's family so lost in sadness. I pulled mugs from the cupboard and filled them with hot coffee and then set a glass in front of Merrilee along with a quart of milk and the sugar bowl. While everyone fixed their beverages, I started again.

"When I got to the old tree house where Denise and I used to play, I wondered if I could still climb up there. I did it and had only been up there a few minutes when I heard quite a racket in the bushes. That's when Jake Harley came into the clearing below where I was sitting." I swallowed hard.

"He had Denise over his shoulder. He put her down on the ground and then started digging a hole." I didn't see the need to tell them he'd dropped her in with a *thud*, but I had to shake my head to dispel the image. "I was trapped up there on the few boards still left. It seemed like forever. I was afraid to move or even breathe. I didn't want to die, too."

Mrs. Farrell sucked back a sob. "I'm glad he didn't find you. One death is enough," she said.

"It was actually two deaths." Merrilee swiped away her tears. "Mom was pregnant."

CHAPTER 2

MERRILEE'S ANNOUNCEMENT THAT HER MOTHER WAS PREGnant electrified the air around my kitchen table. Denise's mother released a whimper. My heart broke again.

"How do you know that?" Sarah asked her niece.

Merrilee hung her head and sat quietly. Finally, she looked at her aunt. "I did something terrible." She cradled her head in her folded arms and sobbed.

Mrs. Farrell rubbed her distraught granddaughter's back. "It's okay, honey. Tell us."

Merilee swiped her tears with the back of her hand. "I was coming down the stairs when I heard Mom on the phone in the hallway. I didn't want her to see me, because she'd told me to weed the flower garden. I hadn't done it. So, I was sneaking back up the stairs when I heard her tell whoever she was talking to that she was pregnant and didn't intend to raise another child alone."

As the ex-wife of a criminal attorney, I knew how important this information would be to the investigation into Denise's murder. Was Jake Harley the father of Denise's unborn baby? No, that couldn't be right. She would never be interested in Jake in that way. No matter how much she had changed, that was something I would never believe. But who?

"Do you know who your mom was talking to?" I asked.

Merrilee drank the last of her milk. "No, but I'm pretty sure it was a man. Mom told him if *he* didn't tell *her* by last night, she would—" Merrilee's lower lip quivered. I feared she would break down again.

"Your mom didn't give any indication who she was talking to?" My voice shook with sorrow for the beautiful, heartbroken teenager.

She shook her head. "I shouldn't have been hiding from Mom. What she wanted me to do wasn't a hard thing, but I was too selfish. I would rather hide and intrude on Mom's privacy than to chance her asking for a little help. It all seems so stupid now. I'd do anything she wanted, if only she was still here." Merrilee went to the sink and rinsed her glass and then filled it with tap water.

Her words stabbed deeply in my gut. I had no problem understanding how she felt. I wished with all my heart I would have come home more often from Chicago to visit my dad. I'd foolishly let David and his commitments tie up my time. There was always a client to entertain, dinner with the partners of his law firm, and God forbid we should miss a Saturday night at the Percy Hill Golf and

Country Club.

I'd finally left all that behind, but not until after Dad had passed away. I would regret that for the rest of my life.

"Merrilee, you have to let that thought go."

She came back to the table and took a seat.

"Whether you pulled weeds or not wouldn't have changed what happened." I reached across the table and took her hands. "Just concentrate on the things you did do with your mom. They will get you through all this."

"That's right, honey." Mrs. Farrell pulled her granddaughter into her arms and gently pressed Merrilee's head to her shoulder. "I wish you had known Evie's grandmother."

Warm thoughts of Grandma Carson brought a smile to my lips. She was quite a card.

"Her name was Anita Carson. She had a saying for everything. One I think appropriate in your case was *If you step in dog doo, don't walk around with it smelling up your life. Wipe it off and move on.*"

Merrilee looked up at Mrs. Farrell. "That's funny." The teenager managed to smile, but it soon faded. "I did something else wrong."

"What was that?" Mrs. Farrell asked.

"I waited until I heard Mom's car start before I came out of my hiding place. I went to the phone and hit redial to see who Mom had called."

We three ladies stared at Merrilee, all of us wanting to know whom Denise had been talking to. The frightened girl took her time, and at one point, I thought she wouldn't tell us who had been on the other end of the line. "It was the sheriff's office."

In the silence of the room, you could almost hear our brains laboring to absorb the data Merrilee had given in the past few minutes. Denise was pregnant, she'd issued an ultimatum to someone on the phone, and when her daughter had checked the redial, the call had been to the sheriff's office.

"Was Denise dating a police officer?" I looked to Mrs. Farrell for an answer.

"Not that I know of, but she never talked about her private life with me." She nodded in Merrilee's direction. "She was as close as anyone could be to Denise, but I doubt she confided in her daughter about anything that intimate."

"Do you know who she would have called at the police department?" I asked Merrilee, trying to soften my question with a smile.

"She never mentioned having any dates. Normally, she'd just say she was going out for a while. Sometimes I asked where, but she would just say she needed her alone time."

Aunt Sarah rose and went to help Mrs. Farrell to her feet. "Why don't you and Merrilee go to the bathroom to freshen up?" Sarah glanced at me. "That's okay, isn't it?"

"You know where it is, Mrs. Farrell. There are towels in the linen closet next to the door." Normally, I would have shown them the way, but I had a feeling Sarah was trying to get rid of them so we could talk.

Once they disappeared down the hall, she sat close to me. "You wouldn't have known Denise. She'd changed so much during the past two or three years. The two of you used to be so close. You laughed and found the best side of every situation. Lately, she'd lived a life that Judy knew nothing about. Disappearing for long stretches of time, sometimes overnight. Leaving her mom and Merrilee to worry about where she was."

"Do you know where she would go or who she was with?"

"No." Her voice carried a ton of disappointment. "I should have made it my business to find out. Something just wasn't right. We all knew it, but we never dreamed anything so horrible could happen to our family. She was always so sensible, we trusted she'd get it worked out.

"Denise was a grown woman. Judy and I had discussed that many times. Denise had to make her own decisions and live with the consequences of her actions, but I can't imagine anything she did warranted being killed over." Sarah buried her face in her hands. "Oh, Evie, why didn't I try harder to find out what was wrong?"

I grasped her shoulders and forced her to sit up. "You were right when you said Denise was a grown woman." The word *was* nearly choked me. "She made her own decisions. Neither you nor her mom could make them for her. You and Mrs. Farrell are not to blame. Get that notion out of your head right now. The person responsible for Denise's death is out there." I pointed into the darkness just outside my kitchen window and tried to control the shiver crawling down my spine. "Out there, Sarah. Not here in this house."

I wrapped my arms around Sarah and heard her softly cry on my shoulder. I wanted to join her, but Mrs. Farrell and Merrilee were coming down the hall, and I didn't want to upset them further. Sarah heard them, too. Quickly, she rose and took the milk to the refrigerator. With her back to us, no one would know that forever-in-control Sarah had just fallen apart.

The sun would be up in an hour or so. I insisted Mrs. Farrell and Merrilee go to Dad's bedroom and rest. Sarah stretched out on the sofa. Since I couldn't see the meadow from my bedroom, I went to the upstairs guest room and pulled a rocker next to the window. Light filtered through the trees, flickering as officers moved around the crime scene under my beloved tree house. Too far away to see much more than shadows, I tried to figure out what stage of the investigation they were in.

A few minutes after I'd taken my post, I closed my eyes and imagined the steps they were taking. Several officers lifted Denise out of her grave and placed her on a black body bag. In my head, I could hear the clicks of the zipper closing, imagine Denise being plunged back into the darkness within. Why had I let our friendship lie dormant for so long that I'd lost the best friend I ever had? Now, it was forever. I pressed my balled fist against my rolling stomach. It pitched with more anger than I'd ever known. How dare some vicious person decide it was time for my friend to take her last breath? How dare they play God and decide when she was to die?

It was then that I realized I was not thinking of Denise's murderer as Jake Harley. Even witnessing what I'd seen, I couldn't bring myself to believe Jake had actually killed her. But if not Jake, then who? And why?

I looked up into the sky beyond the first streaks of yellow and pink sunlight. "I'll find out who did this, Denise. I promise."

I awoke with a fog in my head and an ache in my heart. It only took a few seconds to remember where the heavy feelings came from.

Denise was dead.

The sun streamed through the window, warming my chilled body. I rose from the rocker where I'd fallen asleep and looked across the meadow. It appeared that the throng of officials was gone, but the yellow tape still wrapped the part of the clearing I could see from my house.

There was movement downstairs, and I heard a door open. Hurriedly, I ran down the steps and found Sarah talking to two state troopers at the front door.

"Evie, these gentlemen want to talk to you." Sarah stepped aside.

The men introduced themselves as James Mitchko and Oscar Thomas.

"Please come in." I led the way through the living room and into the kitchen. Both officers were tall and muscular. Mitchko was the youngest, and his face was heavily marked with acne scars. Thomas needed a shave.

"Please have a seat. Are you here to take my statement?"

Thomas sat while Mitchko stood near the door. Ominous looks on both their faces caused me to put up my defenses.

"We need you to tell us in detail how you came to be in the woods at the precise time the body was buried," Officer Thomas stated.

"Can I get you something to drink?" I offered. Sarah disappeared down the hallway to Dad's old bedroom, where Denise's mom and daughter were resting.

"No, ma'am. Just tell us what you saw last evening."

As I gave the officer a blow-by-blow description of my terrifying ordeal, he scribbled in a small, spiral notepad. When I'd finished, Officer Mitchko stepped forward.

"Do you usually go for a walk in the woods in the evening?" His question set me on edge.

"No, when I get home from work I've been too tired, and it's been too late for me to do anything more than fall into bed."

"So why last night, of all nights, did you go over there?"

"I got home earlier, and it sounded like a good idea at the time."

"So, you estimate you were in the tree for approximately two hours. Is that correct?"

"As close as I can figure. It was still daylight when I went into the clearing, but the moon was already up when I came out. Two hours sounds about right."

"And all that time, you were able to stay so quiet that Harley never heard you?"

"That's—"

"You didn't move, or cry out, or breathe hard enough for this man who was only a few feet below to hear you or sense your presence? Is that what you want me to believe?"

As the ex-wife of a criminal attorney, I recognized the officer's insinuations. He was trying to maneuver me into saying I had lied about being up the tree or that I was involved in Denise's murder. That was almost as crazy a notion as the truth of how I knew, but I didn't let him jar me.

"I told you exactly what I saw and how I came to be there. I'll tell you something else—I made a promise on my dead friend's body that I would make sure her murderer is found. So ask me all your ludicrous questions, if they make you feel better, but make it quick and get back to looking for the real killer."

Officer Mitchko's bushy eyebrows furrowed into one long one. "That brings us to another point I'd like to talk about. You yourself have told us you watched Harley bury Miss Farrell, yet several of the other officers who have talked to you say you don't think him capable of murdering anyone. Why is that, Miss Carson? Do you by any remote stretch of the imagination have an idea who would do that?"

That guy torqued my cheeks, but I answered his question as calmly as possible. "I've been gone from Hyattville for twenty years. A lot has changed, but I don't think anything could make Jake kill someone. I'm sure you've learned by now he's not the brightest person in town, but he's always been kind and gentle. It's just hard for me to believe he could take someone's life.

"And, no, I don't know who could have done such a thing, but you need to talk to Denise's family. They have knowledge of things about her that I'm sure you will find interesting. And whoever it was is close enough to Jake to ask him to do such a thing as bury the body for them. That is a definite avenue you need to pursue. Do you have any more questions for me?"

The two officers exchanged glances and then shook their heads in unison.

"Well, in that case, are you ready to talk to Denise's mother and daughter? They're here."

"I think that would be a good idea." Trooper Thomas stood.

I went and got them. Once they were seated, along with Sarah, around the kitchen table, I excused myself and went upstairs to shower and change clothes so they could talk privately.

When I'd finished scraping dirt and dried blood from my scratched skin, I walked to the window of my bedroom, pulled back the old, lace curtains, and looked down on the yard in front of the old farmhouse Grandpa Carson had built from timber he'd cut right here on the land I now owned.

I didn't remember him, but I remembered Grandma Carson. They raised their three sons in the house. By the time my mom and dad married, Grandpa was gone and Grandma was getting up in years. My dad was the only son who stayed in Hyattville, so my parents moved into the big house. Mom and Grandma worked side by side harvesting and canning crops they grew in the garden in the meadow. Mom made my clothes. Grandma crocheted.

Mom died of cancer when I was sixteen. Grandma mourned Mom's passing as much as I did. She may have been her daughter-in-law, but to Grandma my mom was her daughter. Grandma took care of me until I left to go to college in Chicago. She died about six years later, leaving Dad all alone in the house.

When he passed away two years before, I inherited the house, furnishings, and ten acres. I was torn between selling it off and keeping it, with the hope that someday I'd get to come back to the place I loved. Just when David almost had me talked into putting it all on the market, I came face-to-face with his infidelity.

Once the initial shock wore off, I looked at the end of my fifteen-year marriage as an answer to my many prayers. Armed with a huge settlement and a degree in fashion design, I decided to open my own boutique in my own little piece of heaven—Hyattville, Georgia. And regardless of what Thomas Wolfe said, I did go home again.

Waiting there for me was contentment, peace of mind, and a happiness I hadn't known in a very long time. It lasted a whole month, and then I made my trek across the meadow and landed in a nightmare.

From my bedroom window, I watched the two officers get into their car and drive down the dusty lane to the main highway that runs in front of my homestead. Swirls of dust rose behind their car. We needed rain.

After returning to Denise's family downstairs, I asked Mrs. Farrell, "Did you get any sleep at all last night?"

Her sullen gaze and dark circles around her eyes had pretty much answered my question even before I'd asked it. "Not much."

I suspected she had gotten none at all. I felt a sharp pang of guilt that I had slept at least a couple of hours. "I'm not sure what I have around here for breakfast, but I'll check it out." I opened the refrigerator.

"No, Evie, that won't be necessary." Sarah closed the refrigerator door and gave me a hug. "We have things to take care of. I'm going to take Judy and Merrilee home."

I didn't know what to say or what I could possibly do to ease their suffering. Lost in misery, I held Sarah tight. When we parted, I had to ask, "What did the police have to say? Did they know anything new?"

"No." Mrs. Farrell rubbed her temples with her bony fingers. "We told them about Denise being pregnant and the things Merrilee overheard. They seemed very interested in all that."

"They said we can't have Mom's funeral for a few days because there will have to be an autopsy." Merrilee shivered.

Poor baby. I remembered the hurt of losing my mother, but she had died from a disease no one could stop. I had warning she was going. I got to say good-bye. Merrilee didn't have that. Her last memory was hiding so she wouldn't have to lend her mom a helping hand. In her young mind, that was a terrible act. One that her mom would forgive instantly, but it would take a while before Merrilee came to terms with it.

"The officers said they'd come to Judy's if they had any news for us. We're going to go. Besides, we all need showers." Sarah led the way to the front door.

I knew they had to leave, but selfishly I didn't want them to. I didn't want to be alone. I stood in the doorway and watched them drive away while loneliness banded painfully around my chest. Rubbing my arms against a sudden chill, I wondered who had killed Denise, and, at that moment, where the murderer was.

I shook my head to dispel some of the fearful thoughts rattling around in my brain. I wouldn't be opening the boutique that day, but I wanted to go into town and place a black wreath on the door. There would probably be many homes and businesses doing the same thing in memory of Hyattville's first and only murder victim.

During the hour I hung out at my boutique, called the Victorian Sampler, I placed a large black bow and streamers on the front door but didn't open for business. I intended to rearrange the window display, but my mind wouldn't focus on the blouses and jewelry displayed to give customers a peek at the summer fashions inside. Mostly I stared through the plate glass at the minimal activity on Burnt

Magnolia Street.

In the few minutes I watched, only two people went into the Hyattville Bank. Three or four pedestrians strolled along the sidewalk. A couple of cars coasted down the street going about their own business. Not nearly the amount of traffic as on regular weekdays when the main topics of conversation were whether it would rain or if the temperature would reach one hundred degrees. Surely the topic that day was Denise's murder.

Outside the Victorian Sampler, located in the middle of historical downtown Hyattville, time appeared to stand still. Everyone waited to hear any news about the town's tragedy. Knowing Jake Harley would not be able to keep a secret and would surely spill his guts about how Denise died, they all wanted to hear what Jake had to say. I shared their curiosity and prayed we'd know very soon.

After I watered the live plants, I made my way out the back door to my Mercedes, another benefit of my divorce, parked in the alley. I couldn't decide if I should go to Mrs. Farrell's house and be with Denise's family for a while, or if I should go on home and try to straighten Dad's rose garden, which I had wreaked havoc on the night before.

It was a beautiful day. Not a cloud anywhere. Once I left the city limits, my car sailed briskly over the county road, void of center lines. On either side, dairy cattle speckled the flat, grazing land. Snowy cowbirds tagged after the cows and occasionally hitched a ride on a Guernsey's rump, ridding it of insects.

Some of the fields were no longer used for farming but had been divided, generation after generation, into parcels big enough to hold only a single-story ranch house or a double-wide mobile home. I loved living in the country. Everything looked fresh and green.

Not much farther and I'd have to decide if I was going to Mrs. Farrell's. I hated having to refer to the house on Artisan Lane that way. All my life I had called it *Denise's*, but that would never happen again. Just that minor detail represented one of the dramatic changes her death would bring. For the umpteenth time, the wretchedness of Denise's death sliced through my heart. Not just for Denise alone, but also for the baby she carried inside her.

Automatically, my hand went to my stomach. For the first few years of my marriage to David, I'd wanted a baby of my own. Unfortunately, a child wasn't on my ex-husband's to-do-list. That would be an interference in his life.

He had appeased me by saying we would have a baby when the time was right and that I would have to trust him to know when that time would be. Somewhere around our tenth anniversary, I silently accepted the fact that time would never come, but nothing eased the wanting in my heart.

Maybe that particular moment was not a good time for me to go see her family. I didn't feel completely in control of the ball of emotions rolling around in my stomach.

A short distance ahead, two birds of prey played tug-of-war with an unrecognizable roadkill. The wide-winged buzzards flew out of range of my car, and until the coast was clear, they soared overhead.

Through the rearview mirror, I saw the hideous birds violently attack the remaining shreds of flesh. I guess we all do what it takes to survive. And if that's what it took, I'd do whatever I could to comfort the people at *Mrs. Farrell's* house.

As I started to make the turn onto Artisan Lane, I heard sirens behind me and glanced into the mirror. There appeared to be at least three vehicles approaching at a high rate of speed, lights flashing. I pulled to the right side of the road. Two Hyattville deputies' squad cars and the county coroner's wagon sped past me. They went by the lane that led to my house, and then made a right turn onto Miner's Road.

The sinking feeling deep in my gut told me something terrible had happened. The road they'd turned down dead-ended in Jake Harley's yard, which was located next to the boat ramp on Folger's Lake. With tears stinging my eyes and nausea twisting my stomach, I was an emotional mess, and I didn't even know what was wrong. The only way I could find out was to follow. The decision between going to Mrs. Farrell's and going home was replaced with the mission to find out what was going on down on Folger's Lake.

As I parked my car next to a ditch along the road, I was surprised to find a mob of people. Hyattville authorities were just arriving, but the state police, the fire department, and a flatbed diesel wrecker were already there. Yellow crime scene tape cordoned off the area from Jake's front porch to a weeping willow on the other side of the boat launching ramp. They were all staring out into the silver water of Folger's Lake.

Old car parts and burn barrels overflowing with trash filled the yard between the Harley house and the ramp. Warped boards lined the dock. The place appeared to have been totally neglected since Jake's father had died ten years before. Until then, Frank Harley had taken great pride in maintaining the boat ramp and dock for public use. He'd collected only small monthly fees for mooring and even smaller fees for launching.

Time, and Jake's inability to handle such an enormous responsibility, had left the place in shambles.

I tried to blend into the crowd. Bits and pieces about Denise's death buzzed through the group of spectators. I hoped no one noticed me. I didn't want to be asked any questions about the loss of my old friend. Twenty years was a long time, and with any luck I could be just another face in the crowd, but suddenly my concern for myself dissipated.

A person near me called to one of the officers, "Is it Harley's truck?"

When the policeman answered, "Affirmative," my knees buckled and I would have hit the ground if not for the trash barrel I latched onto.

"Why was Jake's truck in the lake? Where was Jake?" The crowd's questions echoed my unspoken ones.

A red wrecker had backed halfway down the ramp. The rhythmic chug of the diesel engine vibrated the concrete where it sat. At that moment, a scuba diver broke the surface of the water, swam to shore, and walked up the ramp.

Evidently, he'd dived to the submerged vehicle to anchor the wrecker winch. Once he was clear, he motioned to the driver and called, "She's tied." The diver turned to watch the show. Across the back of his black wetsuit, yellow letters spelled out "Hyattville Fire Department."

The wrecker's engine revved. Its winch growled and squeaked, laboring to pull the full-sized pickup from the calm, shimmering water of Folger's Lake. Through the rear window, I saw someone's head buoy. Water gushed from every possible opening of the truck.

Just as the body slumped into the seat, I fought a strong urge to throw up. I moved away from the crowd and managed to steady myself against a tree. I watched a state trooper approach the passenger door of the rusty, blue pickup. He stuck his hand through the opened window and appeared to roll the body to a different position.

After a few seconds, he bellowed to his fellow officers, "I'm pretty sure it's Harley. It's hard to tell, though. His face is blowed off."

Chapter 3

I chose not to wait around for Jake Harley's body to be removed from his truck, which had been fished out of Folger's Lake. In the past twenty-four hours, I'd seen enough dead bodies to last me a lifetime. Not to mention the fact that my heart couldn't sustain many more blows. Poor, miserable Jake never stood a chance against some deranged person whom I felt surely had manipulated him into doing the atrocious chore of burying Denise.

Since Jake was now dead, that left no room to doubt he was not a murderer. It was just as my gut feeling had told me. He'd buried my friend as a favor to his friend. But what friend? It had to be someone Jake cared for greatly. Someone who would have shown special favors to him. That was the way poor Jake's mind had always worked. Even all these years couldn't change that fact.

In a town the size of Hyattville, it shouldn't be hard to find out who that was. Jake was about ten years older than me, making him nearly fifty, but his mind was like an eight-year-old's. Sheriff Johnston Beasley was Jake's father's best friend. When Frank Harley had died, Jake had become Beasley's ward. From what Dad had said during one of our Sunday evening telephone calls, Beasley paid all of Jake's bills, made sure he ate properly, and saw to it that he showed up at work on time.

According to Dad, that was never a problem because Jake loved his job at the local gas station. Even though Beasley was his guardian, most of the people in town looked after Jake, and he'd do anything to return their favors. He could do anything as long as it didn't require more than a third-grade reading level. I wasn't sure if it was because my emotions were raw, but just the thought of Jake dying so tragically broke my heart.

He was as much a pleasant memory of my youth as Denise was. They, along with my dad, were gone. Grief overwhelmed me. By the time I got back to my car, I was in a full-fledged meltdown. Draping my emotionally beaten body over the steering wheel, I buried my face in my folded arms and sobbed loudly, trying to pull all the sadness from deep within me. Since last evening, after calling the police, I'd only been able to release a few tears, but there in my car, I cried my heart out. Even if I'd wanted to stop, I couldn't.

Cleansing tears washed the layers of two years' worth of misery from my soul. My dad's death, the hard and tragic end of my fifteen-year marriage, Denise's death, and then Jake's. It was all too much for me to handle by myself, yet there was even another layer.

I was totally alone.

Lost in my own world of self-pity and drowning in tears, I was startled by the sharp knock on my car window. Without bothering to wipe my tears or my nose, I looked into a set of mahogany eyes shaded by a state trooper's hat. I glanced around for something to dry up my waterworks, but finding nothing, I was forced to pull the neckline of my white blouse over my face and mop up the remains of my crying jag.

I rolled down the window.

"Are you okay?" the officer asked.

I cleared away a frog in my throat. "I'm fine."

"Are you related to Mr. Harley?"

I shook my head. "I've known him all my life. I'm sorry he had to die, too."

"I'm Lyle Dickerson with the Georgia State Police." He extended his hand.

I dried my hand on my jeans and then shook his. His touch was so warm, I didn't want to let go. I didn't pull away till he did.

"What's your name?" He used his forefinger to push his hat back. The sunlight made his eyes dance. *Good heavens, Evie. If you have to drool over the first good-looking man you run into, you are more than lonely. You are pathetic.*

"Evie Carson," I managed to say without biting my tongue or doing any other stupid thing.

"Oh, yes, Miss Carson. You're the tree lady."

I looked to see if the corners of his mouth pulled to a smile, but they didn't. "Tree lady?"

"Don't take offense. It's what the other officers have taken to calling you. Sometimes making light of the serious things we come up against helps get us through them."

I sniffed loudly. "I'm happy I could be of service." There was a strong edge to my tone. I personally couldn't find anything in the events of the past two days to be lighthearted about.

"I probably shouldn't have said that. You've had a morbidly active couple of days." Trooper Dickerson took off his hat, allowing the sun to streak through his jet-black hair, highlighting the silver running through it. He leaned down his six-foot-plus frame and rested his arm on the car door. I had no choice but to look the handsome man directly in the eyes, realizing my own had to be bloodshot by now.

Trooper Dickerson kept my gaze as if he were delving into my soul. Could he tell instantly if a suspect was innocent or guilty? I'd bet money he could.

"Do you know what happened to Jake?" I asked, glancing back at the lake. The crowd had grown and now blocked my view of the truck. I wasn't sure if they'd removed the body yet.

"It's too early. The only thing we know is he was shot at close range, probably right here while he sat in his truck. As soon as we can, we'll make a formal announcement to the media."

I wanted to be with Mrs. Farrell when she found out about Jake. The way news traveled through Hyattville, I would have to hurry. I glanced back at the officer. “I’d better be going. It was nice meeting you, Trooper Dickerson.” I started my car and pulled the gearshift into *drive.*

“Call me Lyle. Everyone does.” As he walked back to the crowd surrounding Jake’s truck, I noticed he looked as good from the back as he did from the front.

Guilt stabbed me for the frivolous thought. Granted, he was very handsome and I was very lonely, but there was so much sadness surrounding me . . .

Quickly, I drove away from Folger’s Lake and would have made a beeline to Mrs. Farrell’s house, but remembering I had used my blouse front as a handkerchief, I made a short stop at my house to change clothes.

The phone light blinked, letting me know I had messages. The first one was from Cora Bass from the *Hyattville NewsLedger*, the local newspaper, which comes out Tuesdays and Saturdays. They wanted to interview me about my return to my hometown, my new boutique, and the murder of my childhood friend. Two days ago I would have jumped at the chance to do the interview. It would mean free advertising for the Victorian Sampler, but since I was sure she’d only gotten interested in me because of Denise, I felt I’d be cashing in on tragedy.

I placed a call to Cora. Thankfully, I was sent to her voice mail. "Hi. This is Evie Carson. As much as I'd like to be interviewed for the *NewsLedger,* I'm afraid I have to decline at this time, but please give me a call back after the recent unfortunate stories have died down. Again, thank you."

After placing that call, I checked the next voice mail. It was from my ex, David. David Holmes, to be exact. I'd readily given up his name at the time of the divorce. I'd wanted to go home and be Evie Carson again, so I'd done just that. From my answering machine, I heard David's most legal eagle voice say, "Uh, Evie, it's me. David. Uh, I can't seem to find the key for the safe-deposit box at Mariner Bank. This is the first time I've needed to get into it since we separated, and I realized I've never known where you kept the key. Give me a call as soon as you can. I need to get in there as soon as possible. I hope things are going well for you and you are enjoying your little venture. I'm sure it will give you something to occupy—"

I pushed the delete button and shut David up. I wasn't interested in his evaluation of my situation—one he'd pushed me into by having an affair with his paralegal. (Evidently they'd had a lot to talk about over his briefs.) Once the shock and humiliation faded, the feeling of independence raised me to a higher lever of self-esteem. Little did David know, I didn't need him anymore.

I was a new, independent woman. I loved owning my boutique, stocking it with the newest fashions. I had a degree in fashion design and during my fifteen-year respite, I'd stayed abreast of the industry.

God knows I had plenty of time to do that since David had insisted I not work outside the house but keep his sterile home shiny and entertain clients and partners with big, elaborate affairs. During that time, I longed to have a baby. I had so much love to give and more than enough time on my hands to devote to a child of my own.

Now I was totally alone and free to make and execute my own plans. I was confident that, so far, my decisions had been solid—except for possibly one. I opened the top drawer of Dad's desk and pulled out a bank envelope containing one safe-deposit key. The jury was still out on whether I'd made a good decision by not giving it to David before I'd left Chicago.

I put the key back and then ran upstairs to change my blouse. The residue of hearing David's voice lay heavy in my stomach. Suddenly I realized that two weeks ago I would have been reduced to tears, but being up close and personal with two murders had changed everything. I realized how precious life truly was and how important it was to be with people I loved and who loved me.

David wasn't on that list.

Five minutes later, I was on my way to Mrs. Farrell's. Just like my house, hers was set back from the main road. A small, dusty lane led the way to the Farrell's front yard. When I arrived, there were three other cars and one state trooper's SUV parked with no rhyme or reason on the grass.

As was always the practice at the Farrell's house, the front door was wide open, and the storm door was always unlocked. Those who knew them walked in without knocking. At least that familiar pattern hadn't changed. I went into the front room, where Sarah sat on the sofa. She was talking to a man and woman I didn't know. From the kitchen, I heard other voices. Sarah moved closer to her husband and motioned for me to sit by her.

"Evie, this is Reverend Stirling and his wife, Brittany. As soon as we get the word, he'll officiate at Denise's funeral."

Her referral to the inevitable jolted me. I needed a moment to recover before I shook hands with the Stirlings. "I'm Evie Carson."

"The Stirlings moved here about a year ago from Indiana," Sarah said.

"We wanted to get away from the high crimes of the big city." The young reverend's wife smiled widely, showing bright white, perfectly straight teeth. I'm not sure why that one feature stood out, because the rest of her was just as perfect. Big brown eyes, flawless complexion, and dainty hands folded in her lap.

No one responded to her comment. From the kitchen, the scraping of chairs being moved and voices coming closer drew our attention. Mrs. Farrell and Merrilee entered the room first, followed closely behind by Trooper Dickerson.

I joined them near the front door.

"Hello, Evie." Lyle's mouth curved to a teasing grin.

I smiled back. Putting my arm around Merrilee's waist, I pulled her to me. She rested her head on my shoulder. "How ya doing, sweetheart?" I asked quietly.

"Okay." Denise's daughter sounded very much in control of her grief. Was the realization of her mother's death still rattling around in her brain? Had it not yet fully slammed into her heart?

The surrealism of the past two days was too bizarre to believe it could happen at all, let alone to someone like your own mother. No, it hadn't completely come to life for Merrilee and probably wouldn't until after the funeral when everyone went home and she and her grandmother were left alone in their house. Then the quietness would crash around her and make it all real.

Merrilee went back to the kitchen, and I stepped onto the front porch where Lyle and Mrs. Farrell were talking. He had a wooden box tucked under his arm.

"This gentleman told me about poor, pitiful Jake." Mrs. Farrell's voice cracked. "He's with his daddy now, and I bet they're up there," she said, pointing to the clear, blue sky, "in a boat, floating across a magnificent lake and fishing their hearts out."

"I know you're right about that," I said, swallowing down a sob, "and those are the thoughts we need to hang onto."

I looked at Lyle. I didn't mean to, but my gaze traveled from my eye level, which was right at his chest, up to his chin, his mouth, his nose, and finally his eyes. He was staring at me, and probably with good reason. I was allowing my body to react like a moonstruck girl's, but since I was calm on the outside, maybe he wouldn't know that.

Surely he had some idea how alluring he was, especially in his gray trooper uniform.

"Do you have any suspects?" I asked, trying to disguise

my distraction.

"Not yet." Lyle edged a little closer to the steps leading into the yard.

Mrs. Farrell thanked him for coming and then went back into the house.

"I stopped by to make sure Mrs. Farrell and her granddaughter didn't hear about Harley through the grapevine. Who knows how far the story would have been stretched out of shape?"

"I'm sure they appreciate your keeping them informed." Warm air swirled around us. "We certainly could use some rain." *Evie, stop with the idle chitchat. The trooper has work to do.*

"Later tonight. That's what I heard on the radio on the way over here." Lyle shifted the wooden box from one arm to the other.

For the first time since I'd arrived, I took a good look at the shiny, mahogany box with an inlaid mother-of-pearl rose. "I know that keepsake box. Denise's father made it when he was in the Philippines during World War II. She loved it and always kept things in there that were important to her." I ran my fingers over the top and marveled at the contrast of the warm wood and the cool mother-of-pearl. "For a time she kept our cigarettes in there." I couldn't hold back a smile, but it soon faded as I remembered Denise was gone and she and I would never share those kinds of secrets again.

But Denise had left with a secret, a deadly one. Hopefully, she had filed it away in the box, and when Lyle finished searching for clues inside it, we would possibly know who would want her dead.

"I've got to get going," Lyle said as he bounded down the porch steps. "If we learn anything new, someone will let you all know."

For the rest of the day, no police officers had come by, so we'd assumed they had no news. I'd stayed at the Farrell house until well after dark. Now as I drove into my yard, I wished I had left a light on. The sky was black. No moon; no stars; and no streetlights like the ones outside the townhouse in Chicago where I'd lived for fifteen years. I was surrounded by nothing but mysterious, country darkness.

The air smelled fresh and crisp. Rain was close by. Curling up in front of the television and waiting for the pattering of raindrops against the windowpanes ranked high on my list of things to do for the rest of the night. I switched on the eleven o'clock news out of Savannah. The Hyattville murders were their lead story.

Sheriff Beasley was squinting into the bright lights outside the Hyattville County Courthouse. "We have no further information at this time, but let me assure you, the Hyattville Sheriff's Office and the Georgia State Police are hard at work solving these two murders as well as protecting our citizens against any further crimes."

I processed the sheriff's words. The eeriness of night and the fact that the murderer was unknown had caused me some concern, but not until I'd heard him say those words had it really registered with me that others may die before the killer was caught.

With a heavy jolt, a terrifying thought slammed through me.

What if that person thought I knew more than I did, or that somehow I'd foiled what they thought of as a perfect crime by learning about Denise's murder even before she was placed in her grave? Was it because I had witnessed Jake burying Denise that he had died, too?

The horrifying questions sent chills through me. The only way to answer them was to wait and see if someone tried to kill me, too.

I made a thorough check of all windows and doors to be sure they were secured. My butt had just hit the sofa again when a disturbing thought sent me back to my feet. What if someone had come into the house before I'd gotten home? What if someone was waiting till I fell asleep to kill me?

This time, I went to Dad's gun cabinet inside the closet in his bedroom. I punched in the combination code and took out a .38 pistol. Once I confirmed it was loaded, I made another round, looking in every closet in all the bedrooms and bathrooms, upstairs and downstairs. Finally, I felt at ease that no goblins hid in my home. By that time, the rain had arrived and was doing its happy dance on the living room window, the one that faced the meadow. Not expecting to see anything, I looked through the glass out into the darkness. The rain fell hard enough for water to form sheets across the pane and distort what looked like flashlights in the stand of trees where Denise had been buried.

I strained to focus the image, but I couldn't see anything but a flickering light. "Probably kids out for a morbid thrill," I said aloud to calm my racing heart. Surely the police would not want anyone messing around the crime scene. I certainly didn't want anyone on my property—especially at 11:30 at night.

I'd just rounded the sofa and was about to pick up the phone to call the sheriff's office. Someone knocked sharply on the door. I hadn't seen the headlights of any vehicle pulling into the front yard. I jumped inches off the floor, but somehow I managed to keep from screaming.

Armed with Dad's gun, I pulled back the curtain and flipped on the porch light.

Lyle Dickerson waved to me. His trooper hat was protected by a form-fitted plastic cover, and he wore a yellow slicker. I stuck the gun into a drawer in the long sofa table, and then I opened the door.

"Hi. Come in," I said and pushed the screen door open.

"No, I can't. I just wanted you to know that we had to come back to the crime scene to check a couple of things before the rain washed everything away. I didn't want you to see lights over there and be frightened."

"Too late. I was just getting ready to call 9-1-1." I made a feeble attempt at straightening my hair, which I was sure was a mess. "Still no news, huh?"

"We made a discovery a few hours ago. We dug a bullet out of the headliner of Harley's truck. It was in the right trajectory to have gone through Harley's jaw, out the other side and then lodge in the headliner."

A new wave of sadness washed through me. Jake had to have

seen the gun and the person who used it. I wondered if he'd realized what was about to happen. He had to have known, and he must have been horrified.

"Poor Jake. I assume they are sending the bullet to ballistics to determine the type of gun it came from."

"In some cases, that would have to be done, but this is a Black Talon. At one time it was widely used by police departments. They've been phased out for other types."

"Evidently, someone still uses them."

"The only one we know of is Sheriff Beasley."

The rain was really coming down hard. The sound of it pounded against the house's siding, making it hard to hear.

"Does his whole force use them?" I leaned closer to Lyle so I wouldn't have to shout.

He leaned closer to me. "No, just the sheriff. Things are usually peaceful in Hyattville. He seldom carries his revolver. Just the shotgun he keeps in his patrol car, and that he only uses for unruly animals and reptiles, should the need arise. He never changed the type of ammo when everyone else did."

"Could someone have used his gun without his knowledge?"

"It's a slight possibility, because if Beasley isn't using it he keeps it in his office. It's been sent to the lab to find out first if it is even the gun used and, if so, whose fingerprints are on it. It's very unlikely anyone got it away from the sheriff, but we're leaving no stone unturned."

"What about Denise? Was she shot, too?"

"No. We won't know how she died until the autopsy is complete, but she didn't appear to be shot."

"When will you have the report?"

"I don't know. The coroner will let my boss, Lt. Moore, know as soon as he has his report compiled." Lyle checked his watch. "I've got to run. We'll probably be over there for a couple of hours."

After he drove away, I decided to go straight to bed. With several law enforcement officers under a thousand feet from me, sleep should have come easily. Unfortunately, the officer with the beautiful, dark eyes kept sleep at bay. When I finally did drift off, my dreams were filled with Trooper Dickerson arresting me for not turning over the key to David's safe-deposit box.

The next day was Saturday. On my way to work, I passed the Far Rail Diner, a small café located by the rail yard just before the city limits of Hyattville. Mrs. Farrell had owned the eating establishment since the early sixties. My dad and his cronies met there every Wednesday morning and called themselves the Geritol Gang. Every Sunday, when Dad and I would talk, he'd bring me up to date on the latest gossip he and his friends had shared.

Several years before Dad passed away, he had told me that Mrs. Farrell had become ill, and Denise had taken over running the Far

Rail. When Dad had said anything about going to the diner, I would tell him to tell Denise I said *hello.* So much easier than picking up a telephone and calling my friend myself. Quickly, I applied a lead foot to the gas pedal with the hope that I could outrun the stab of guilt chasing my heart.

I arrived at the Victorian Sampler well before opening time. Since Hyattville was close to the trendy tourist spots along the coast, weekend traffic in the historic section of our town was normally very heavy. But in the few weeks since I'd opened my boutique, I had never seen as much as there was that day. Stop-and-go traffic crept along Burnt Magnolia Street in front of my shop. The sidewalks were lined with so many people, I could easily imagine I was back in Chicago.

From my display window, I looked down the street to the only building in downtown Hyattville to have been built in the last half of the twentieth century. The original courthouse had been destroyed by fire in 1953 and was replaced by our very own skyscraper. Granted, it was only four stories high, but it towered above the other historical buildings. Most days, the shiny Georgia marble surrounding the first floor of the courthouse glistened in the sunshine; that day, it was blocked by spectators.

Over the heads of the crowd were satellite dishes mounted on trucks from several television stations waiting to do remote broadcasts at a moment's notice. Several people stopped to check the hours listed on my door. I opened the boutique early, and by noon I'd had quite a run on my inventory.

A majority of the women who came into the Victorian Sampler made comments about the black wreath on the door and wondered if I was related to the man or woman who had been murdered. Some tried to reassure me with a gentle touch, while others ranted about why the authorities didn't have a suspect in custody.

By early afternoon, I didn't want to talk about it anymore. I knew no more than they did, and the speculations were mind boggling. Despite the fact that the streets were still bustling, I decided to close for the rest of the day. I locked the front door and went into the back room to unpack new merchandise that had been delivered the day before. I steamed the wrinkles from the beautiful garments and hung them on racks near the front window.

Someone tapped lightly on the glass. It was Kitty Douglas, Lonnie's wife. She was the former Kitty McGovern, whose father owned the only department store in town. We never saw eye-to-eye on anything, and I was pretty sure we wouldn't start at this late date. As I walked to the door, I noticed Kitty had not aged gracefully. She was no longer the Hyattville Panthers' petite blonde cheerleader. I wondered if her sour disposition had sweetened with time, but quickly decided no one had that much time. I unlocked the door.

"Hi, Evie. Do you believe what's going on out there? The town has gone crazy." Kitty never missed a beat. She walked directly to the rack of the new summer line I'd just put out. "These are nice, Evie. I've wanted to stop by and check out your stuff. Connie Maida said you've done a good job, and I can see she was telling the truth."

"That's nice to hear." I chose to move slowly around Kitty. I remembered well her ability to set a person up with flattery one minute and then smack them down the next. After sifting through several items, she pulled two pairs of cropped pants and matching blouses. She placed them on the counter and announced, "I'll take these."

I rang them up and found a spark of hope that maybe she had grown into a rational adult with manners and everything. After I bagged her stuff, I thanked her for her business. "I hope you enjoy your new outfits."

"Oh, they're not for me. These are for my niece. You remember my brother, Skip. They're for his oldest daughter. She's leaving for college in a few weeks and doesn't really need anything extravagant." She tossed her head, flipping her medium-length, bleached-blonde hair over her shoulder. With her blue eyes sparkling, she lined me up in her sights.

"I buy all my clothes in Atlanta at Nordstrom's and Saks Fifth Avenue." Her barb bounced off me. The difference between that moment and twenty years before was that Kitty McGovern Douglas couldn't wound me deeply anymore. She may not have grown up, but I had.

As I led her to the door, I used my sincerest tone to say, "Good for you, Kitty. I'm really happy things are going that well for you and Lonnie." By that time, she was standing on the sidewalk and my telephone was ringing.

"Yes, we are doing—"

I closed and locked the door in the middle of Kitty's sentence. Maybe I still had a little childish behavior left deep inside me, too.

"Good afternoon. Victorian Sampler," I answered.

"Are you busy?" Denise's Aunt Sarah asked on the other end of the phone line.

"No, I've decided to close for the rest of the day. Things are crazy here in town. Do you need me to do something for you?"

"Judy wanted me to let you know they've finished the autopsy and released Denise's body. Her funeral will be Tuesday at eleven."

I closed my eyes and said a silent thanks that Denise's family could at least get that part of the grieving process over with. "How are Mrs. Farrell and Merrilee doing?"

"They're having a tough time right now."

"Have they been told what the autopsy revealed?"

"Just the main cause of death. That's all we really wanted to know." Sarah sounded tired, understandably. I didn't think it appropriate for me to ask her the details of the autopsy over the phone.

Or maybe I didn't ask because I didn't want to hear the details while I was alone.

"I'm just about locked up here. I'll be there in about thirty minutes." While I emptied the cash and checks from the register, I juggled the phone between my ear and shoulder.

"Thanks, Evie. I appreciate that. Judy will, too."

We hung up, and I quickly made out my deposit slip. I went out the front door and walked across the street and down one block to the bank. I dropped the bank bag into the night deposit slot. Just as I headed back across the street, a clamor rose from the throng of media people gathered in front of the courthouse. To check it out, I had to work my way through the thick crowd.

Once up front, I found Sheriff Beasley, along with a lieutenant with the state police and Trooper Lyle Dickerson. A mass of microphones was duct taped together and attached to a portable podium.

The man who identified himself as Lt. Moore introduced the other officers and explained to the reporters that he wanted to bring everyone up to speed, as much as he could, with the investigation of the Hyattville murders.

"The autopsy has been completed on thirty-nine year old Denise Leigh Farrell," he began. "Cause of death is now known to be blunt trauma to the throat, crushing her windpipe. Estimated time of death listed at approximately 3 p.m., on Thursday, July 24." Lt. Moore's matter-of-fact words hit me hard. My body shook. I steadied myself against the cold marble on the front of the building and forced my brain to concentrate on what the lieutenant had to say.

"Forty-nine-year-old Jake Frank Harley was shot point blank while seated in his truck at the Folger's Lake boat ramp. The bullet entered Mr. Harley's left jaw and exited his right temple. The estimated time of his death is 10 p.m. on Thursday, July 24. I'll field your questions as long as they aren't intrusive to the investigation. Yes, sir." Lt. Moore pointed at a reporter close to the podium.

"Was Miss Farrell sexually assaulted?" the reporter shouted.

CHAPTER 4

"I DON'T FEEL THAT IS ANYTHING THE PUBLIC NEEDS TO KNOW," LT. Moore snapped at the reporter who so callously asked if Denise had been raped. Sighs of disappointment echoed through the crowd gathered for the media briefing in front of the courthouse.

Silently, I gave thanks that whether she'd been sexually assaulted or not, that information wouldn't be announced in front of a group of people craving bad news like piranhas on a feeding frenzy. I wanted to scream, *She's dead. That's all that matters.*

"How she died and approximately what time she died is the pertinent information we wanted to get out to the public." Lt. Moore mopped perspiration from his forehead and then returned his handkerchief to his back pocket. "Hopefully, someone will remember seeing her or perhaps anyone she may have been with around that time. If anyone has any information, no matter how minor you may think it is, please get in touch with me.

"We've set up an office at the Hyattville Sheriff's Office. It will be manned twenty-four seven by the state police, and we will be working alongside Sheriff Johnston Beasley and his deputies. Please come forward with any information you may have. We must stop the individual or individuals who have murdered two of Hyattville's citizens in cold blood."

"How long can we expect the state police to be stationed at the temporary office?" a reporter called from the middle of the crowd.

"As long as it takes." Lt. Moore put on his hat. "That's all. We have to get back to work."

The other officers followed the lieutenant back into the building. I remained propped against the cool marble building and stared at a crack in the sidewalk. It curved along with smooth valleys and jagged peaks.

A lot like my life.

As a woman passed in front of me, she caught her high heel in an uneven sidewalk crack and stumbled slightly. She stopped and looked back to see exactly what had caused her to trip.

That, too, was like life. Only after we stumble do we look back to see why. Seldom do we look ahead to avoid the unfortunate incident from happening.

If Denise had it to do over again, would she do things differently, or did she absolutely not see what was about to happen until it was too late?

Curiosity being my best and worst character trait, I'd spent a lifetime pondering unanswerable questions. Prior to my trek across the meadow, I'd been overwhelmed wondering why David hadn't loved me enough to stay faithful. What had I done to chase him away?

Deep sadness shook me, and my mind came back to Denise. I wondered what her last thoughts must have been. Surely, the devastation of leaving her teenage daughter, Merrilee, and losing the new baby growing inside her had squeezed the life out of her heart long before oxygen had left her lungs.

I wrapped my arms across my chest to thwart the chill coursing through my veins. Blazing sun or not, my whole body shivered. The eerie sense of being watched waved over me. Grandma Carson would have said someone just ran across my grave. I looked around but didn't see anyone. Since I couldn't shake it, I hurried across the street, back to the Victorian Sampler.

Before I'd gone to the bank, I'd secured everything. Now I let myself out the back door into the alley. With a foreboding notion that someone's gaze was trained on me, I quickly got into my car and locked the doors. Several dark or curtained windows lined the alley. I looked from one to the other, but saw nothing suspicious. Surely, the unspeakable events haunting Hyattville must have been playing tricks with my mind.

Going to Mrs. Farrell's to hear about plans for Denise's funeral probably wouldn't relieve my uneasiness, but at least I'd be with loved ones. I desperately needed that.

During the three days prior to Denise's funeral, the rain came down in an unrelenting torrent. The soggy grass surrounding her final resting site sloshed under the feet of the large group of mourners approaching the casket. Pink carnations blanketed the bronze box, reminding me that two years ago I'd sat next to Dad's casket with sadness strangling every fiber of my heart. I closed out the sharp memories and focused on the scent of Denise's flowers. Unfortunately, the sweet aroma mixed with the murky smell of damp earth caused my stomach to undulate. I swallowed hard.

I sat with Denise's family. Along with Reverend Stirling, we huddled under a green canopy. White words advertising *Benso Mortuary* embossed the flapping valance. Those who could not push under the heavy canvas sheltered themselves under a sea of black umbrellas furnished by the Benso brothers.

Seated opposite the majority of the congregation, I could easily study the faces of those who chose to brave the rain and the unusually cool summer wind to pay their last respects. Several city officials attended the ceremony—Mayor Pritchard, who'd been called home from vacation in the Bahamas, Judge Thompson, and Clerk of Court Sikes.

Surely their presence at the funeral of the first murder victim in Hyattville would make the public aware they were on the job, showing their concern for the terrible things taking place in our fair town. It certainly wouldn't hurt at election time.

Reverend Stirling pounded his Bible with his closed fist. "Why was such a loving mother and devoted daughter ripped violently from the ones who love her? Whether it is part of God's divine plan, or the evil work of Satan's hands, Denise's soul now walks with our Lord."

I scanned the crowd one more time. What was I looking for? Did I think I would see something on a person's face that would tell me who killed Denise? I recognized so many of the people gathered there. None I would ever believe capable of murder.

From the front of the group, Lonnie Douglas, the brother I'd never had, winked at me. He was sworn as a deputy to uphold the law and was definitely too kindhearted to take someone's life; I quickly passed him by. His wife, Kitty, stood directly in front of him. Her medium-length blond hair lightly touched the collar of a long cardigan sweater I was sure cost a fourth of what Lonnie made in a week. When we'd been in school together, although most of my classmates and I had bought our clothes from McGovern's Department Store, Kitty's mother would take her to Atlanta for all her shopping. And as a spoiled teenager, she'd always made sure we knew how much her latest items had cost.

I would've bet she'd choke to death if she knew David had insisted I wear expensive clothes the whole time we were married. He'd provided me with closets full of designer couture.

During our school days, Kitty tried to act as if she was better than the rest of her classmates, but even then I knew she was insecure. Still, I took way too much joy in giving her a hard time. Especially when her words cut one of our classmates to the quick, and the girl would decide to knock her block off. I'd have to hold in a laugh when Kitty would run crying to the teacher. Funny how some memories stick with you forever. Now that I was a grown woman, the thought entered my head that I should try to understand her and possibly even make an effort to be her friend.

Precisely at that moment, Kitty shot her holier-than-thou gaze in my direction and tilted her chin in an air of supremacy, quickly chasing my thought of befriending her completely out of my head. Even if she was only trying to hide her insecurities, I really didn't want to get close enough to her to delve into that matter.

Mrs. Farrell grasped my hand with her cold fingers. Her sudden touch reminded me that life was too short to engage in jealousy and pettiness even if Kitty had always brought that out in me. Suddenly, having the upper hand against Kitty McGovern Douglas didn't seem as important as it once had.

Also in the bank of people, I saw Lt. Moore and Trooper Lyle Dickerson stationed at opposite ends of the congregation. Their eyes were hidden behind shaded glasses, a strange sight since clouds and rain completely hid the sun. I'd watched enough *CSI* programs to know that, behind the dark lenses, the two men were watching expressions and movements of everyone in the crowd, looking for the slightest implication that the murderer had dared to show up to watch the burial of the person whose life they'd taken. Since the officers hadn't moved from their posts, it appeared they hadn't found any more than I had.

Also among the mourners stood Sheriff Johnston Beasley. Fifty-something, tall, lean, and head held high. His muscular face showed age from hours in the wind and sun. Seeing him there brought a few jumbled facts into clear focus. First, Merrilee had mentioned that Denise had issued an ultimatum to someone at the sheriff's office over the phone. Second, being caught in an affair would ruin Beasley. And third, after burying Denise, Jake had gone directly to see Sheriff Beasley. Was it to report he'd finished a job the sheriff had asked him to do?

I was sure I wasn't the only one who'd had those thoughts, but when I looked at him I couldn't imagine him being involved in the murders. Suddenly I remembered that the authorities were checking to see if the bullet that killed Jake had indeed come from Sheriff Beasley's gun. If it had, I shuddered to think what that would mean for Hyattville.

My heart ached for the woman standing next to him—his wife, Clara. Her lovely, slender face showed no signs of anxiety or worry. Was she hiding her feelings like a true Southern lady, or was she simply oblivious to the fact that fingers of evidence were pointing at her husband to connect him to the murder of the very person we'd all gathered to bury?

What had happened to my peaceful town in my absence? Why had it waited until I'd returned to appear to rotate off its axis?

A man standing away from the mob caught my eye. He didn't have an umbrella, but the hood of his jacket was pulled over his head. Rain had slowed to a drizzle, yet water streamed down his face. He swiped his sleeve over the unmistakable trail of tears. Redness rimmed his eyes. I'd never seen the man before, but his expression showed the depth of his pain.

Before I could speculate how the man was connected to Denise, Merrilee rose from her chair. Supported on either side by her grandmother and her Aunt Sarah, she placed a long-stemmed red rose on her mother's casket. She removed one pink carnation from the blanket of flowers. As she touched it to her lips, sobs racked her body. Weeping sounds, soft and low, rippled like a wave through the mourners gathered. I sniffed several times, trying to keep my own waterworks at bay.

I looked around for the unknown man who had cried so openly. He had disappeared.

As everyone dispersed, I lagged behind. I'd driven my car to the cemetery and hoped I'd have a few minutes after the service to visit Mom's and Dad's graves. Since they were only a few rows from Denise and the rain had stopped, I chose to walk, leaving my car next to her grave.

After pulling a few weeds from inside the granite border surrounding the Carson family plots, I picked up the artificial flowers strewn by the recent wind and rain and stuck them back into an iron vase attached to Dad's headstone. Mentally I made a note to come back soon and give the family plot the attention it needed. Take care of it just as Dad had done until the day he died.

But that would have to be at another time. That day I needed to get on to Mrs. Farrell's as quickly as possible. The food had been taken care of by the church, but I'd promised Denise's family I'd be there to help in any way I could.

As I walked back to my car, I noticed someone standing next to Denise's grave. He turned slightly, and I realized it was the man I'd seen crying during the service. I moved closer to him.

"Hi. I'm Evie Carson."

He glanced at me, but remained silent.

"Were you a friend of Denise?" I asked.

"Sort of. A long time ago, I was her husband." He turned away, but I plainly heard the guttural sob he tried unsuccessfully to suck back.

"Kevin Trammell?"

He nodded and slowly turned to face me.

"She talked about you often, Evie. She said you were the best friend she ever had." Kevin smiled slightly.

"We were dear friends, and I'm not sure how we let that slip away."

We both grew quiet. After a short period of time, Kevin broke the silence. "I live in Atlanta now. An article about the Hyattville murders appeared in the paper there. I couldn't believe it."

"How long had it been since you'd seen Denise?"

Kevin shrugged and continued to stare into the grave, not yet filled with dirt. "About three months after I left with another woman, I realized I'd made the mistake of my life. I came back here and begged Denise to forgive me. She wouldn't even give it a thought. She sent me away, telling me to never contact her again."

He looked upward and exhaled loudly. "I never did."

"Not even to see your daughter?" Learning Kevin had run out on Denise and never come back to see Merrilee should have been enough to make me walk away. But something about the way his body shook urged me to stay. I looked at him and waited to see if he intended to apologize in some way for his actions.

His gaze locked with mine. "She's not my daughter."

I'm not sure what I expected him to say, but that certainly wasn't it.

"I'm confused. It's my understanding you left around the time she became pregnant with Merrilee. Just because you weren't present when she was born, that doesn't erase the responsibility of fatherhood."

Just when I thought I couldn't be any more disappointed with mankind, Kevin Trammell stacked the heap a little higher. Before I could leave, he stopped me. "Denise was my second wife. Before we married, I'd had a vasectomy. She knew I couldn't give her any kids. I thought she was okay with it. She gave birth nine months after I left, so I guess I wasn't the only one who had strayed from our marriage bed."

Without another word, he left the gravesite. Bewildered, I watched him get into his car and drive away. Why hadn't Sarah mentioned that Kevin wasn't Merrilee's father? We'd talked about every other aspect of Denise's life? Was it possible Sarah never knew? With baffled thoughts spiraling, I made my way to my car. I had to get to Mrs. Farrell's house along with the other gathered mourners and try to lend moral support. Hopefully, between the cemetery and her home, I'd find the strength to do that.

More importantly, with curiosity surging through my veins, I would have to find a diplomatic way to broach the subject of who fathered Merrilee.

The Ladies' Auxiliary of Hyattville's First Baptist Church spread quite a feast on Mrs. Farrell's dining room table. The aroma of fried chicken, ham, and apple pie permeated the damp air. The rain had stopped, allowing a slight streak of sunlight to inch its way into the farmhouse parlor. Every room of the Farrell home bustled with people gathered to offer support and comfort—family, friends, and mere acquaintances.

I circled each room, making sure all the guests ate and were comfortable. The police officers from the gravesite were not present. I'm not sure I expected them to be there, but I wouldn't have minded running into Trooper Dickerson. Learning any new information he might have was only one reason. Getting to look into his dark eyes also made the prospect appealing.

I made a quick check of the area for Merrilee. When I didn't find her, I climbed the creaky stairs to her bedroom. I found her in Denise's old room. The one I'd spent many nights in during the sleepovers she and I had whenever possible. As I watched the beautiful, young girl from the doorway, I marveled at the angelic picture she made. Seated on a window bench and surrounded by white and violet flowered curtains, she stared out a large bay window. Her face glistened with tears.

Sunshine, finally in full array, shined through her long, light brown hair with a semblance of a halo.

"Can I get you anything?" I whispered, not wanting to startle her.

She looked first at me and then down at the yard below. "No, thank you."

I waited quietly.

"Mom loved to work in her flower garden. She pulled weeds and dead flowers with all her might. Hard and fast, like she was mad at them. Once I asked her why she did that, and she told me it was the only thing she had real control over. So, if it wasn't to her liking, she'd just rip it out and throw it away. Then she'd plant beautiful flowers where the dead ones had been and smile like she'd healed the world." Merrilee's sigh shuddered past her lips, sending chills through my soul.

Suddenly, she leaped from the window seat and ran into my arms. Her body shook with heartrending sobs. Holding her tightly, I stroked her silken hair, trying to soothe her heart. But my own heart shattered, too, for the child with no mother and for me with no child.

"I want my mom here with me." Merrilee's voice broke. "I don't want her to walk with the Lord on the golden streets of heaven, like Reverend Stirling said. Why doesn't anyone understand? I want her here with me."

All I managed to pull through my constricted throat was, "I know."

Eventually, Merrilee moved from my embrace to get a tissue from a box on a dresser. "During the services today, I started thinking, I'm an orphan now. I have no mom or dad. I'm alone. I don't belong to anyone."

I remembered well the acute sense of loss I'd experienced when I came to the same realization following Dad's death. As I was already suspecting David of infidelity, the depth of loneliness couldn't be measured on any scale. Although Merrilee wouldn't realize it for a while, she had a huge network of family and friends she would always be able to lean on.

"You'll never really be alone," I said. "You have your grandmother and your Aunt Sarah, who love you very much. And all your friends who are downstairs wondering where you are."

Merrilee blew her nose and wiped her red-rimmed eyes. Her finger traced the outline of a framed picture of Denise smiling at a baby cradled in her arms. I picked it up to study it closer. "My mom and dad are gone, too." My throat ached. "But I have wonderful memories that'll never let me be alone." I slipped my arm around the beautiful teenager's shoulder and told her sincerely, "I'd be honored if you'd consider me a friend."

Her blue eyes sparkled, and her face brightened with a smile. "Mom would be happy you're here with me." Her smile widened even further. "She told me about things you two did when you were my age. I'd be grounded for life if I pulled some of those stunts."

Those memories were etched in my heart, and the happiness in them would help me through the grief of losing my best friend. I nudged Merrilee toward the hallway. "Wash your face, and let's go check on your grandmother."

"Wait." Merrilee took my hand and led me to the window seat. From a bookshelf, she removed a beautiful mahogany box and handed it to me. I recognized it as the one Lyle Dickerson had taken in as evidence shortly after Denise's murder.

"It's beautiful," I said.

"My grandfather made it. Mom always kept pictures and newspaper clippings in it. They're little things that meant a lot to her. She called them reminders of the best parts of her life."

As I ran my hand over the top, the coolness of the mother-of-pearl and the smoothness of the polished mahogany sent a slight shiver up my arm. Holding the box tightly, I wondered if it held the culmination of Denise's memories.

Merrilee handed me a small key attached to a piece of blue satin ribbon. I took it and opened the tiny padlock hanging from the tarnished brass clasp. As I lifted the lid, a sickeningly sweet smell overwhelmed me. I took out an empty perfume bottle lying on top of several pictures. The handsomely shaped atomizer was covered with gold flecks and had a cream-colored spray bulb attached. I didn't have to put it near my nose to recognize the scent. Honeysuckle. When I studied the label, I found it was a special mixture prepared by Garnet's Emporium in Atlanta.

Laying the bottle aside, I dug through the newspaper clippings, yellowed, folded sheets of paper, and pictures. They took me on a major jump back in time. Faces from color and black-and-white photos smiled at me from twenty years in the past. There were pictures of me and Denise in poses of teenage antics. Pictures of old classmates. Some, I could remember their names; some, I could only remember their faces.

Nestled among newspaper clippings and photos I found a watch. I wasn't familiar with the brand and couldn't estimate its worth. The inscription on the back read "All my love, L."

"Who gave this to your mom?" I held it out to Merrilee.

"We don't know where it came from. Grandma gave the box and the watch to the police, and they returned it, saying they didn't find anything useful for their investigation. We figured it must have meant something to her, though, because she kept it in that box."

For a moment, I tried to imagine how my friend could have come to get the watch and what would make it dear enough to Denise for her to keep it. At one time, she and I were so close I would have known the answer. But too much time had passed. I knew nothing about the woman whose life had ended tragically.

I started to put the watch back in the box.

"Hi, Evie." Kitty Douglas's loud voice startled me. I nearly dropped the box. The watch hit the floor. I quickly scooped it up, stuffed it back among the pictures.

"Kitty, you scared me to death." I tried to hand the box to Merrilee. She wouldn't take it.

"No. Grandma and I talked about it, and we decided you should have this because there are a lot of pictures in there of you and Mom. She would want you to have it."

I hugged it to my chest and squeezed my eyes shut against the tears welling there.

"Is there a bathroom up here?" Kitty asked. "The one downstairs is occupied."

I guess almost everyone who grew up in our part of the country had a Southern accent. In most cases, it was so natural no one noticed. But Kitty exaggerated hers ad nauseam. She broke every one-syllable word into two. Patience. I needed patience.

"Sure, Mrs. Douglas," Merrilee spoke up. "It's down the hall on the right."

Kitty didn't move. "You got back in town just in time to stir up a hell of a mess, didn't you, Evie?"

Her callous words stunned me. Before I could find my voice and reply, she continued.

"Well, you know what I mean, with you finding the body and all." She made a feeble attempt at a smile.

Merrilee released a whimper. Kitty's words had jarred me to the pit of my stomach. I could only imagine how they affected Denise's daughter. Like a bear protecting her cub, I quickly took a stance between her and Kitty.

"I see you still haven't learned to think before you speak." I glared at Kitty and pointed down the hallway. "The bathroom is that way."

She smiled. I got the feeling she had no idea how hurtful her comment was, nor did she care. I turned to Merrilee, whose face was ashen.

"Let's go downstairs, honey. You have *friends* waiting for you." Gently, I nudged her into the hallway, holding desperately to the last shred of my control. What a pity Kitty's arrogance from our childhood days hadn't mellowed with age. I'd always been pretty good at putting her in her place, but I didn't want to upset Merrilee any further.

I tucked the precious mahogany box under my arm and followed Merrilee down the stairs.

For the third night in a row, darkness beat me home. The night cast its curious reflections on everything in its way. There's something eerie about going into a house alone, especially when all day long you're reminded a murderer is still out there. Somewhere. Perhaps behind the huge oak tree across the meadow. From the porch, I could see it. The one with its branches draped with Spanish moss, bathed in moonlight, waving to me. The one where I watched Jake Harley bury Denise. That place, so dear to me as a child, could never be special again.

I slipped out of a gray, linen suit I'd worn since early morning and allowed my oversized pink chenille bathrobe to wrap me in a consoling cocoon. Slowly, I sipped hot chamomile tea, inhaling the aromatic bouquet as it rose to me. Finally the tautness of each muscle began to relax, one by one. Snuggling against the overstuffed cushions of the sofa, I drifted off.

The phone shrilled, jolting me up to full attention.

"Good Lord." I picked up the receiver. "Hello?"

"Did I wake you, sweetheart?" David asked.

"No, you didn't, and you lost the right to call me *sweetheart* when our divorce was finalized."

"Okay, if you say so. Did you get my message? I need to get into that safe deposit box you opened for me sometime last year." Ice cubes being dropped into a glass, followed by a splash of what had to be Scotch, David's favorite, sounded through the phone.

Still a little groggy from my very short nap, I couldn't think fast enough to lie. "Yes, I got your message."

"Well?"

"Well what?" Sometime during our divorce, I found it was fun to yank David's chain. Something I would have never done as a devoted and obedient wife.

"Where is the key? I need to get into the box to get that envelope I had you put in there."

"You mean the envelope with that large amount of cash you hid for your client who was accused of laundering money? That envelope?"

Although stone silence came across the miles, I could almost hear the static electricity buzzing around David. I definitely heard the double *glug* of Scotch splashing over ice cubes.

"Yes, Evie, that one. My client will be released in a week or two, and I need to be in a position to return that envelope to him." David forced sweetness into his words.

I struggled to keep from laughing out loud.

"Gee, let me think." I waited a few seconds. "No, I don't know where it is." He'd told me so many lies when he was supposed to be a loving husband, I didn't have any qualms telling him a little white one. "I guess you'll just have to ask the bank for a duplicate," I said knowing full well he couldn't do that because he'd had me open the safe-deposit box in my name and then insisted he was too busy to go have his name added to it. I suspected he didn't want his name associated with that box or that money in case any of it ever got connected to his client.

Amazing how clear things became when I took off the rose-colored glasses and looked closely at David Holmes. Every move he made was for himself, and heaven help anyone in his way.

"But—" David started.

"Sorry I can't help you. Gotta go. Bye." I hung up on him and wondered if I should give up the key and cut the only tie David and I had left. Quickly, I decided it wouldn't hurt him to suffer a little. I would get around to sending it to him before his client breathed free air. Maybe.

The phone rang again. Listening to any more of David's crap

that night wasn't in my plans. Irritated, I picked up the receiver. "Now what?"

Silence.

"Would you like to have dinner with me tomorrow night?" An unexpected male voice stopped me cold. I glanced at the caller ID, which read, *Dickerson, Lyle.* "That is, unless that 'now what' was meant for me then I have to assume the answer is *no*."

In another lifetime, I would have been embarrassed. But not that night. Elated that I'd just one-upped David and relieved that Denise had been properly put to rest, I erupted in a nervous giggle. "Sorry about that. I thought you were a ruthless attorney from Chicago who is a real pain in my backside." That summed it up.

"Your ex?" Lyle asked.

"Yeah. What's this about dinner tomorrow night?"

"I thought maybe we could get together over a pizza."

For a short moment, I wondered if I should feel guilty for finding Trooper Dickerson's offer tempting. I never would have met him had it not been for Denise being murdered. Why did I always try to find the logical side of every decision I made? My desire to do that had shriveled up when I realized I'd been a fool for fifteen years. I had rationalized that trailing behind David, adhering to his every wish, would warrant me a faithful husband.

No, doing only what was expected of me hadn't worked out. Maybe I should throw caution to the wind and do whatever sounded like fun.

"I'd love to."

"It certainly took you a long time to make a decision. Do you usually give everything that much thought?"

"Actually, no, I don't."

Through the phone, I heard a young voice call out, "Mom, I'm thirsty. Can I get a drink of water?" followed by a woman's voice calling, "I'll bring it to you, but then you have to go to sleep."

Of all the unmitigated gall, I thought, but said, "Is that your wife?"

Chapter 5

"Wife?" Lyle sounded surprised I would ask such a question. Since he'd just asked me for a date, and at the same time, I heard a woman and child in the background, it seemed a very logical question to me.

"Yes, I heard a woman there with you. Is she your wife?"

"I haven't had one of those since Christ was an altar boy. That person you heard . . . wait a minute. Sandy, come here," Lyle called.

A woman spoke to me. "Hello?"

"Tell her who you are," Lyle said, and I could hear him laughing.

"I'm Sandy, and as much as I hate to admit it, this person here who is acting like a child is my big brother."

"Oh . . . well, it's very nice to meet you, Sandy. I'm Evie Carson." A smile tugged at the corners of my mouth.

"Nice sort of meeting you, too," she said, and then she was gone.

Lyle came back on the line. "Sandy and her little boy, Scotty, live here with me."

"How old is Scotty?" Since I'd heard him ask for water, I assumed he was young.

"He's five going on twenty. He sure keeps his mom hopping. The truth is, he has me twisted around his little finger, and I wouldn't have it any other way."

In those few sentences, I heard more love in Lyle's voice than I'd ever heard in David's for anything or anyone. The depth of Lyle's affection touched me deeply. Had I been privy to a rare look into his intense kindness?

With the feeling of closeness, I pressed further. "What about you, Trooper Dickerson, protector of the fine citizens of the state of Georgia? Why aren't you married with a couple of little Scotty's of your own running around?"

"I was married for five years. The operative phrase here is *I was married.* She wasn't." He paused, and for an instant I thought I'd overstepped my boundary.

Quickly my doubts were relieved. He continued, sounding relaxed and calm. "I came home early one evening and caught her cleaning the plumber's pipes, if you get my drift."

An awkward pause followed.

"I'm sorry," I finally said. "It's rude of me to ask such personal questions."

"No, it isn't. It all happened a lifetime ago. You know what they say—'time heals all wounds.' They just don't say how much time it will take."

As I thought of the vicious hurt he must have felt when he found his wife with another man, my own pain filtered in. I, too, knew the misery of an unfaithful spouse and the devastating blow to your ego that came with it.

Lyle broke the heavy silence. "I haven't talked about Vanessa in years. It should've been more of a blow to my pride than anything else. I should've known her capabilities. But the fact is, I didn't. I was blinded by her . . . That's funny. I used to think of it as charisma. Now I just think of it as crap." A gentle laugh rippled through the telephone. "Anyway, I never saw it coming until she easily threw away our marriage for the tidy bowl man."

I smiled in spite of the pain his words inflicted. Strange, those were the same words I had hurled at David. How could he throw away our marriage so easily? But he did, and listening to Lyle, I took a little comfort that I wasn't alone.

"No other serious relationships since then?" *Good heavens, Evie, is it just impossible for you to mind your own business?*

"You might call them a couple of semi-serious relationships, but I'm better at figuring out criminal minds than women's," Lyle said in a matter-of-fact tone. I pictured him at the other end of the line smiling thoughtfully.

That image evoked a warm, fuzzy feeling, which I suddenly realized I needed to quell. The ink on my divorce decree had barely dried. My dear friend had just been murdered. I was a basket case emotionally, and now would not be a good time to plunge headlong into another relationship. Lyle had asked me out for dinner, and we'd enjoyed a short conversation over a telephone line. To allow my excitement to grow so quickly showed the vulnerable state I was in.

Surely being aware of it, I would be able to rein in my apparent raging libido and spend a fun evening with an attractive man without jumping his bones, ultimately embarrassing him and me. I sat up straighter and made a conscious effort to move away from personal topics to the real thing that should be on my mind.

"Has the ballistics report come back yet?" I asked.

"We're not expecting it until next week."

"If the bullet that killed Jake did come from Sheriff Beasley's gun, what will that mean for him?" And what would it mean for Hyattville if their beloved sheriff was proven capable of cold-blooded murder?

The pause that followed let me know Lyle was weighing his words. Through David, I'd learned about damage done to cases where too much information had been leaked to the public. I'd probably put Lyle in an awkward position by asking him something he wasn't at liberty to discuss.

"I'm sorry. I know you can't discuss information about an investigation." I let him off the hook.

"Actually, there are very few things about this case I can't talk about. With such a close-knit community, nothing stays secret for long. I hadn't stopped to wonder what it would mean for Johnston Beasley if the bullet came from his gun. I'm really not sure what will happen then. Maybe we can talk about it tomorrow night. You did say you'd go out with me, didn't you?"

"Yes, I did."

And I'd also promised myself I'd quit acting like a schoolgirl around Lyle Dickerson.

About five minutes later, the phone rang again. I answered it. In the background soft, classical music played, but no one said a word. I looked at the ID, and it read, *Caller Unknown*. "Hello? Hello?"

I could hear light breathing.

Suddenly, the line went dead. I immediately went to fearful mode. Was that the killer? Was he coming after me? Ultimately, I laughed at my overreaction. With my luck, it was a perverted breather.

The crash sounded in the night. The noise ripped me from my serene sleep. Wide-eyed, I listened, trying to identify the source. It definitely came from far away, but not far enough to be ignored. I had no choice but to investigate. I pulled Dad's pistol from the nightstand, where I'd tucked it for safekeeping.

From the top of the stairs, I heard scratching against the screen door. Someone or something was right outside. Through the darkness and on tiptoes, I crept down the steps. All the while I reminded myself surely if someone were trying to break in, they wouldn't be so noisy.

By the time I reached the bottom landing, my eyes adjusted to the black night. With care, I pulled back the curtain of the front window. A flower pot, which earlier rested on the railing, lay smashed on the porch.

I flipped on the outside light and there, in the corner, hunkered a black cat. His green, glowing eyes watched the window where I stood, intent on my every move. I opened the door. He hissed and scampered under the porch.

"Yeah, right. Break my flowerpot, wake me up, and then hiss at me." Although my heart pounded loudly, I breathed a big sigh of relief. I couldn't begin to imagine where the cat came from. My nearest neighbor lived four miles away. After walking this far, he would surely be hungry. I went to the kitchen and filled a saucer with milk and placed it just outside the door.

Leaning against the door casing, I waited to see if the cat would peek from under the steps. Again, the eerie feeling of being watched from somewhere out there in the darkness inched its way through my body.

I couldn't shake the creepy sensation. Not wanting to wait any longer for the cat, I slammed the door behind me. Even securely locked inside, I couldn't dispel the unsettling thought. Surely my overactive imagination would settle down in a day or two. After all, the past week had been filled with dead bodies, eerie feelings, and things that go bump in the night.

Except for glowing candlelight, darkness filled the small pizzeria where Lyle and I ate dinner. Multicolored wax cascaded down the sides of a Chianti wine bottle used as a holder. Amber fire from the candle flickered gently between us, softening Lyle's frown.

"A drunk ran a stop sign and broadsided them on 442 between Hyattville and O'Brien. Sandy's husband, Chad, died instantly." Lyle's voice trailed to a whisper, low and hoarse. "She lay in a coma for two days."

How sad. "What about Scotty?"

"The little guy escaped with only a scratch on his forehead. He stayed with a babysitter during the day, and until Sandy could leave the hospital, I took him home with me at night." Leaning back in his chair, he took a sip of wine. I sat quietly. Composure returned to his troubled face.

Slowly and carefully, he continued. "Sandy rattled around in her home in O'Brien. And I lived alone across town in the house our parents had left both of us. Scotty needed her with him, and she needed to be with Scotty." Lyle's face came alive with a smile. "And I needed someone to feed me. So, she moved in four years ago, and it's worked out great."

We'd been talking for half an hour, picking at the remains of Luigi's evening special: medium pizza, all the way, a large Italian salad, and two glasses of wine.

Lyle picked up his glass of red liquid, swirled it, and drank it to the last drop. Then he asked our waitress to bring a pitcher of Pepsi.

I debated whether to broach the subject of the murder investigation, but he had said on the phone the night before that we would talk about it over dinner. "Anything new with the investigation?" I asked.

"I'm working another case. That's why I was out of town all day, so I don't really know any more than we already knew, but I can say I don't like the way the case is headed."

I knew exactly what he meant. Since I'd been mentally stacking evidence against Sheriff Johnston Beasley, I felt sure others would be, also.

"It's all pretty much out there in everyone's face," I said. "The sheriff was very close to Jake, and we all know he would have done anything for the sheriff. And where did Jake go immediately after burying Denise? Right to Beasley."

"That's right, and I know you were there when her daughter told us Denise was pregnant. Of course, that was confirmed by the autopsy."

"Merrilee also said her mom issued an ultimatum over the phone, and later when Merrilee pushed the redial button, the sheriff's office answered," I added.

"There is any number of people she could have been talking to at the sheriff's office, but with the chips falling where they have, Johnston is the most likely suspect. I'm having a really hard time believing it would be him, though. Before his death, my dad and he were good friends. Actually, Johnston helped me get into law enforcement.

He's a deacon in the church, a loving husband and father. He's going to be a grandfather in a couple of months." Pain on Lyle's face made it obvious his heart was breaking.

"Something that has really bothered me is, when I called that night, Lonnie said Jake was just backing out of a parking slot in front of the police station. Beasley came straight to my house with the other officers. When would he have had time to kill Jake?"

Lyle's dark eyes flashed, and I shivered slightly under his gaze. Suddenly, he looked toward the front door and raised his hand in a wave. Lt. Moore pulled an empty chair from the next table and plopped into it at the end of our booth. I hadn't seen him since he'd held the press conference across the street from the Victorian Sampler, but I immediately knew who he was.

"Evening, Miss Carson." He remembered me, too. "Been looking for you, Lyle. I saw your Mustang outside. We found the Farrell woman's car this afternoon."

"Where?" Lyle leaned closer to Moore.

"At the Lockwood Motel on Simmons Road." He looked at me and explained, "Ol' man Lockwood rents efficiencies by the month. Each cabin has an enclosed garage." Looking back at Lyle, he said, "We found her car in one of them."

The waitress appeared at our table. "Can I get you anything?" She smiled at Lt. Moore.

"Black coffee, please."

"Sure thing, honey." She winked and sauntered behind the

counter. Moore watched her walk away.

"What about the car?" Lyle asked.

"The maid reported it'd been there for a couple of days, but no one had been in the room."

"So Lockwood provides maid service even if it's rented on a monthly basis?"

"Apparently she goes in once a week, cleans the room, changes linens and towels. She vacuums."

"I'm guessing she did that before you were notified about the car." Aggravation edged Lyle's voice.

"Unfortunately, that's correct."

The waitress set a cup on the table. Steam rose from it and disappeared into thin air. Lt. Moore took a long sip of coffee. "We've been there all afternoon gathering evidence."

"Anything show up?"

"Plenty." Moore ogled our passing waitress, swallowed the hot liquid too quickly, and choked back a cough. "Lockwood recognized Jake Harley's picture. He's been renting the room for a year or more. The receipts were made out to T. Sawyer, and he paid cash."

It came to me in a flash. "Tom Sawyer," I blurted out. Apologetically, I smiled at Lt. Moore. "I'm sorry. I used to swim at Folger's Lake where Jake lived. He pretended to be Tom Sawyer and made his front porch his island. Some of the younger boys would pretend they were Huck Finn, and Jake would play like a big kid." Until that moment, I hadn't realized how dear those memories were to me. Jake acting out his childlike fantasies while Denise and I swam in Folger's Lake in the hot summer sun. Major slices of my childhood had been tainted forever by tragedy. Nothing could lift the heaviness in my chest or the sadness in my heart.

"Yeah, that's what we've been told," Moore said.

Everyone in Hyattville thought of Jake as a big kid. He would do anything anyone asked of him. Anything short of murder. That, I'd never believe.

Lyle's strong voice broke my thoughts. "Did you find anything else? The weapon?"

"No, not the weapon. We're pretty sure she died in that room, though. Probably loaded her into Harley's truck there. We found a few drops of blood on the windowsill and the wall. Plus there were scratches on her back that can possibly be matched to the jagged wood of the windowsill. The coroner has photos of every mark on her. All of that will have to be processed to be positive, but with her car there, we're pretty sure it will prove she'd been in that room."

He finished his coffee. "You know, with Harley renting the room where the Farrell woman died and then burying the body, it sure would stand to reason he killed her. Except for one thing. The real murderer killed him, too."

Lyle and I nodded in agreement.

"Poor bastard." Lt. Moore stood and threw a couple of dollars on the table.

Lyle handed them back to him. "This one's on me. Thanks for

bringing me up to date. I've been in Glynn County all day."

"Well, catch the late news. The media always seems to know more than the prime investigators do. They'll fill you in on anything I've forgotten." I detected laughter in Moore's voice. "Oh, I forgot something. We found Johnston Beasley's twenty-five years service ink pen under the bed. We figured it got shoved under there by the maid when she vacuumed."

Lyle's shoulders slumped. "Damn. I have to go back to Glynn County tomorrow, but I'll check with you when I get back."

"Yeah, do that." Lt. Moore raised his hand in a slight wave in my direction and then left.

Silence blanketed our booth. I waited for Lyle to absorb the new information. The battle inside him played across his face.

"Before Lt. Moore arrived, I believe I'd hit a nerve when I asked how it would have been possible for Beasley to have killed Jake. Am I right?"

Lyle rubbed the back of his neck. "Yeah. While the crime scene was being processed, Johnston went to find Jake. We all figured since they were so close, the sheriff was the best person to find and question Jake. When he returned, Beasley said he hadn't found him, and gave orders for an APB to be issued."

"That's sad," I agreed.

My heart ached with the new developments. Visions of Denise's nude, battered body being dragged out the motel window and then being thrown into the back of a pickup splintered my thoughts. The image of Jake's large, grease-stained hands against Denise's pale skin brutally pounded my raw nerves. More profound than anything was the faceless, nameless evil presence of Denise and Jake's murderer lurking in my imagination. Trying to dispel them, I shook my head adamantly.

Lyle touched my hand. "Are you okay?"

"As okay as I can be, I guess."

He patted my hand reassuringly. He understood how I felt. Filled with gratitude, I gave him the biggest smile I could muster, yet on the inside, hopelessness tormented me. I'd made a promise to my dead friend I wouldn't let her death go unsolved. Add to that my feeling partially responsible for Jake's death. No wonder my gut twisted into knots.

Because of my ex's inflated ego, our dinner conversations nearly always revolved around how brilliantly he had used evidence to full advantage to bring the jury to his side and to ultimately find in favor of his client. Because of that, I'd been given insight into what to look for in piles of evidence gathered at a crime scene.

I would have loved a chance to look over the evidence gathered by the elite group of law enforcement officers handling Denise's and Jake's cases. Since that wasn't even a possibility, I made a plan to commit to paper everything I knew, had been told, or could find out on my own. Maybe David's ability to sort through evidence and come up with answers had rubbed off on me. I thought it was worth a shot.

When Lyle and I arrived back at my house, we found eyes glittering from a dark ball of fur lying on the front porch swing. Before I could explain that the cat didn't belong to me, Lyle sat beside him and scratched the furry fellow.

"He's black as midnight." Lyle looked up at me. "What's his name?"

I sat next to the lazy kitten. "Midnight sounds good to me. He just wandered up here last night. He's been hiding out under the porch." The cat shifted his body next to my leg, his motor purring. "I guess I'd better add cat food to my shopping list."

After unlocking the front door, I slipped into the dark living room. A scent of honeysuckle wafted to me. Quickly I flipped on the light and looked around, but saw nothing that could have been causing the lovely smell. Although it was familiar, I couldn't recall where I'd smelled it before.

Midnight strolled past me and made his resting place on the rug in front of the fireplace as if he belonged there. At least I wouldn't be alone for a change.

"I had a good time, Evie." Standing in the doorway framed by the light pecan door sills with the night behind him, Lyle's presence was striking.

Before I could say anything, the phone rang.

"Excuse me," I said to Lyle. "Hello? Hello?" I could hear someone breathing. "Who is this?" I waited. "What do you want?" I heard a *click,* followed by dead silence. The unexplained honeysuckle fragrance still lingered.

As I hung up the phone, Lyle stepped next to me and waited patiently. An uneasy feeling settled over me.

"That's the third time that's happened. This was a little different because with the other two calls I could hear classical music playing in the background. They are on the line for a short time, and then they hang up." At any other time it would have been just an annoyance, but with so many unsettling events going on around me, I couldn't stop my hands from shaking. I shoved them in my skirt pockets.

"I'll let Lt. Moore know about that." Lyle nipped his bottom lip between his teeth. "What about at your shop? Have you gotten any of those calls there?"

"No, just here. That's the third time in the last two days."

"Do you have caller ID?"

I pointed to the LCD screen. "It says *unknown.*"

The phone rang again. Lyle snatched the receiver from its cradle. "Who is this?" he demanded.

His cheeks flushed, and he spoke with authority, "Who I am isn't important. Here's Evie." He handed me the phone and then silently mouthed, *Sorry.*

I glanced at the ID screen. "David? What do you want?" I didn't even try to curb my irritation.

"Who was that?" he asked.

"That's none of your business. You have fifteen seconds to tell me what you want," I said and actually looked at my watch to start counting.

"It certainly didn't take you long to get back in the dating scene."

His egotism never ceased to amaze me. "At least I waited until I was divorced. Your time's up." I hung up.

I turned to Lyle. "I'm sorry about that."

He shook his head. "No, I'm the one who should apologize. I had no right answering your phone."

"It's fine. Don't give it another thought."

I'd earlier been concerned about my feelings for Lyle moving too quickly. With strange smells, a mysterious call from an unknown entity, topped by hearing from David again, I needn't have worried about being overrun by raging hormones. Instead of being shot by Cupid's arrow, David stabbed me in the back with it.

My front door stood open wide. Lyle made his way onto the porch. "I hope we can do this again sometime," he said.

"I had a good time." I didn't make a move to join him outside. I was a bit weary. "Thank you for everything. I hope you'll let me know if anything new develops even if you don't think Denise's family should know. I want the murderer caught. I vowed I wouldn't let it rest until someone was held responsible for Denise's and Jake's deaths."

"You let me know if you hear something we should know. Deal?" He held out his hand.

We shook. "Deal."

He held my hand only a heartbeat longer than normal and then walked down the steps. He turned slightly. "Go ahead inside and lock the door. I'll call you soon."

Inside, I locked the door and latched the safety chain. I'd had a really good time on my first date in over fifteen years. Being with a man who talked freely about himself yet also wanted to know me was a whole new experience. One I could learn to like.

I had a few things to do before I went to bed. Showering and getting into my nightgown topped the list.

Normally I used the upstairs bathroom, but for the first time since I'd returned home I decided to fill the old claw-footed tub in Dad's bathroom with bath salts and hot water. A nice long soak would really feel good. From the hall linen closet, I pulled out a couple of fluffy towels. Something fell to the floor. I picked it up and read the words on the packet. *Honeysuckle Sachet.* The lavender paper had yellowed with age, but its scent remained strong.

It was then I remembered the scent I had been confronted with when I first came into the house earlier that evening. What I had smelled at the front door was strong like the honeysuckle perfume from Denise's keepsake box. Much more powerful than the weakened fragrance of the aged sachet inside the linen closet, but the mahogany box was tucked away in the trunk of my car and had been since Merrilee had given it to me.

Could fatigue be playing tricks with my mind? Could the fragrance I'd smelled when I had entered my home earlier have been caused by the sachet being locked in the house all day? It probably had been in the air all the time, and I hadn't noticed. Sticking it back under another stack of towels, I chided myself for making so much out of every little thing that happened.

My imagination was working overtime. Did I imagine Denise's spirit floated through my house leaving a trail of honeysuckle perfume? For crying out loud, stepping into your house and finding it smelling nice was a good thing, something Martha Stewart would have approved of. I, on the other hand, had tried to make it something sinister. While lounging in the tub, maybe I needed to soak my head and relax my short-circuited brainwaves.

Almost every day, I received samples of lotions, shampoos, conditioners from distributors who wanted to fill my boutique with the latest body care products. I dumped one of the samples under the running water. The room came alive with the inviting fragrance of *Sand and Surf.* As I sank into the warm water, bubbles swirled around my naked body and eased the tension gripping tightly to every muscle.

I'm not sure how long I'd been dozing, but I knew for sure what had awakened me. My kitchen door had a distinctive squeak. I was getting out of the tub, sloshing water over the sides, and putting my robe on when I heard the even more distinctive click of the deadbolt slipping into its holder.

In my living room, the sofa faced the television. It was far enough from the wall to make a walkway from the front door directly into the kitchen. I had a loaded gun in the table behind the sofa, but that was at the front of the house. I couldn't just stand there and wait for whoever it was to come to me. I hurriedly ran down the hallway to the living room, flipping on lights and calling, "Who's there?"

No one answered. I grabbed the gun from the drawer.

"Who's there?" I yelled again. I turned on the kitchen light. No one was there. The back door was closed, the deadbolt locked.

Before I'd left to go out with Lyle, I'd checked all the doors and windows. Cautiously, I moved through the house checking them all again. They were all secured. No one was in the house. I saw no signs anyone had been.

Was I losing it? Had I dreamed that noise? Evidently, I had. I couldn't continue to be so spooked by every little thing. I would stop allowing the unknown to control my every waking moment. Apparently it was seeping into my sleep, too. I was the only one who could stop it, and I would.

Evie Carson. You stupid bitch. You're just like Denise. Damn festering thorn in my side. She tried to ruin everything for me, but I stopped her. And I'll stop you. I didn't do all this hard work and planning for you to spoil it all now. But you're pushing

me, messing with my timeline, making me do things that aren't necessary. Like killing Jake. He'd still be alive if you hadn't found Denise's body.

I was in your house tonight, bitch. Just a few feet away. God, what a rush getting out before you caught me. I even locked up for you. Saw the lights go on as I headed for the woods to my car. Bet you nearly pissed your pants knowing someone was in your house.

Maybe I'll call you again later—after I've wound down with a little Wagner or Beethoven. Maybe some Mozart. Nothing like riding around listening to Mozart. Did you know music soothes the savage beast?

Chapter 6

THAT NIGHT, MY BRAIN HEARD THE NORMAL CREAKS AND groans of the old farmhouse and magnified them into something threatening. I'd hoped my uneasiness of being in the big house alone would mellow after Denise's funeral. But with phone calls and no one on the line, plus my inability to convince myself I hadn't heard my back door closing and the deadbolt being locked, no wonder I was freaked out. Since I'd searched the house extensively and found no one hiding, it made sense that whoever closed the door had to lock it from outside.

But how could that be? To do that, the person would absolutely have had a key. Other than me, the only person who had one was Goldie Douglas, Lonnie's mother. She'd looked in on Dad during the last couple of years he was alive. She'd clean and sometimes cook for him.

Until I could decide what to do with the house, Mrs. Douglas took care of it after Dad's death. She tended Dad's roses, and before winter freezes, she had Lonnie wrap the pipes. Although I knew she'd do it without pay, I insisted she take the money I sent once a month. It was payment to ease my guilt of not being there to take care of Dad myself. At the time, David was more important.

Luckily, it'd taken me a while to decide whether or not to sell the old homestead, because it was the first place I thought of going when my divorce became inevitable. Mrs. Douglas aired and cleaned the house so it was ready for me the day I returned home.

With my divorce settlement and big hopes of having my own boutique, I sailed through the first month expecting and receiving nothing but happy, fulfilling days. Denise's and Jake's deaths changed all that, leaving me disillusioned and afraid of my own shadow.

The next morning, on my way to the boutique, I stopped at Goldie Douglas's house. The two-story Victorian stood just inside the city limits. Its yard, shaded by two hundred-year-old oaks, was surrounded by a dark green ligustrum hedge. My parents and Mr. and Mrs. Douglas had been best friends. Mrs. Douglas was the only one of the four still living.

Many Saturday nights, while they played canasta, I hung out with Lonnie, usually beating him at the board game *du jour.* Of course, I'm sure he'd say he always won. Either way, those Saturday nights were a happy part of my growing up.

As I parked in the driveway, I saw Lonnie's squad car. While I wondered if I should follow an old habit and go around the house to the back door, Lonnie came outside.

"Hey, Evie," he said, then opened the front door again. "Mom, Evie's here."

Mrs. Douglas joined us on the porch. "How are you doing?"

I'd seen her at the Farrell home at Denise's wake. Then, as now, she hugged me like I was one of her lost children. I adored her hugs. They reminded me of long-ago embraces with my mother. I needed that comfort more than I cared to admit.

"I'm tired. I haven't been resting very well, but other than that, I'm fine."

Lonnie opened the door, and his mother and I went inside. "I've got to get going. It's good to see you, Evie. Catch ya later. Bye, Mom."

He bounded down the steps. Mrs. Douglas didn't wait for him to drive away. She shut the door and led the way to her kitchen. "I'll get you a cup of coffee."

"Thanks, but I really don't have time. I'm on my way to the boutique. I need to ask you about the key to my house. Do you still have it?"

"Sure do." She opened a drawer and pulled out a key laced on a large paperclip. "Do you need it? Did you lock yourself out of your house?"

I smiled. "No. Uh . . . did you by some chance come by my house last night?" I felt as foolish as the question sounded.

She stared at me. "I'm sorry. I don't understand."

"Someone unlocked my kitchen door and then went back out and locked the deadbolt. The only way that could be done is from the outside with a key."

"It wasn't me, honey. How do you know this happened? Didn't you see who it was?"

I explained about being in Dad's tub and hearing the distinctive sounds of the door closing and locking.

"Well, my goodness," Mrs. Douglas placed her hand to her chest. "Who do you think that could have been? Does anyone else have a key?"

"No, ma'am. Just you and me." I shook my head, which hurt from lack of sleep. "Could anyone have borrowed it last night and you not know it?" I was grasping at straws.

"No, I was here alone all night long. Lonnie comes by for breakfast most mornings. But since he works evening shift, he's seldom here in the evening. I'm sorry I can't be more help, but the only time this key is out of this drawer is when I go over to your house. I haven't done that since you got home." Mrs. Douglas closed the few steps between us and handed me the key. "Here, I don't even have a need to keep it since you're back."

I took the key. "Thanks. I have to believe I was just sleeping and dreamed I heard the door being closed."

"That has to be it. I'm sure it's spooky out there all alone, especially with a murderer still on the loose. Why don't you come and stay with me for a while. I'd love the company."

The sweet sentiment touched me deeply, and I knew Mrs. Douglas meant it from the bottom of her heart. But just because my nerves were raw and my mind had taken a side trip from reality didn't mean I could run away.

"Thank you. I'll be just fine. I'm sure I'm overreacting." I glanced at my watch. "I have to run. I only have ten minutes before I should have the boutique open for business."

"Stay safe, Evie."

I left Mrs. Douglas and hurriedly drove to the alley behind my boutique. Once I'd let myself in and made my way to the front of the shop, I noticed two ladies waiting patiently outside the front door. I opened it and invited them to come in and browse while I got things set up for the day.

As the ladies looked through the clothes I'd proudly displayed, their chatter turned to Denise's murder. I tried to zone them out, but the curious side of me insisted on listening to every word.

"Didn't your son date that Farrell woman?" the older of the two asked.

"No, he wouldn't go out with trash like that," the other one replied.

Her words stung. I longed to ask her what she based her assumption on but knew I couldn't do that. In light of what had happened and with what I'd learned about Denise's behavior before her death, I couldn't be sure the woman's statement wasn't justified. And I couldn't alienate customers just because I wanted Denise to be the same sweet, kind, and reputable young lady I had known so many years ago.

Still, I wanted to busy myself with anything to keep from listening to the hurtful conversation about someone who had once meant the world to me, so I looked up the phone number of Northside Lock and Key. My heart said I didn't have any reason to think someone had been in my house last night, but my brain said it wouldn't hurt to have the old locks changed and to be in possession of the only keys.

As luck would have it, voice mail answered. I left my number and asked them to return the call. The receiver had barely hit the phone base when the bell over the door signaled another customer's entrance. I looked up in time to see Lyle and a pretty lady with long, auburn hair coming in.

Lyle's pale yellow Polo shirt, tucked into his belted waist, emphasized his broad shoulders. Denim jeans wrapped his long legs tightly. He put his hand on the lady's back and led her to the counter, where I waited with more excitement than I cared to admit. A strong family resemblance told me the woman with Lyle had to be his sister.

"Good morning," I extended my hand. "You must be Sandy."

Her warm, slender hand took mine. "I am. Lyle insisted I come in and meet you." Her smile was identical to Lyle's. "I hope we haven't caught you at a bad time."

"Oh, no. It's a little early for a big rush." I glanced at Lyle. "No uniform? Are you off duty today?"

"Yes. I had some time coming. Today is Scotty's birthday, and I not so wisely promised him a speckled pup when he turned five. He'll probably be six before Sandy forgives me." Lyle cocked an apologetic smile at his sister. "I should have asked her permission first."

"Why break tradition now?" She shot him a not-so-threatening glare and then laughed. "My son is so excited. I couldn't disappoint him. We're getting it from the pet shop next door."

On a couple of occasions, I had looked at the puppies in the window of the Give a Dog a Bone store next to my boutique and even thought about getting one myself to break some of the silence. But then Midnight had come along, from where I still didn't know. He didn't make any noise, but he'd become a welcome companion, sticking close to me when I was at home.

"Violet Thompson has really cute animals. Believe it or not, she was my home ec teacher in junior high school."

"A school teacher turned pet shop owner." Lyle shrugged. "That's different."

Remembering a conversation I'd had with Mrs. Thompson a few days after I'd opened the boutique made me a little sad. "When I asked her about why she changed occupations, she told me that when I was in school, kids wanted to learn, but things changed. A few years ago, she says, she traded animals with smart mouths for animals that don't talk at all."

Lyle chuckled.

One of the ladies who'd been slowly looking through garments for the past five minutes laid a light blue blouse on the counter. Lyle and Sandy stepped back, freeing me to take care of my customer.

"How frequently will you be getting new merchandise in?" The woman's pleasant smile alleviated some of the bad feelings I'd had earlier from her harsh remark about Denise.

"I've only been open a little over a month, but so far, I've added new things every week. I'll be going to market in Atlanta in a couple of weeks, and after that I'll bring in the new fall fashions. Stop back by anytime and check them out."

There were several other customers milling around the shop. While waiting, Sandy looked at the new line of jewelry I'd put on display last week. On my way from behind the counter, I asked a couple of women if they were finding everything okay. Assured they were, I went to Sandy, and we were joined by Lyle who'd been looking out the display window watching cars cruise up and down Burnt Magnolia Street.

"Sandy used to work for J. C. Penney in Brunswick before Scotty was born," Lyle said, putting his arm on her shoulder.

"Really? What did you do there?"

"I worked in women's clothing and accessories. After my husband died, I felt the need to stay home with my son. Lyle made that possible by sharing his home with us. I do most of the cooking and cleaning in exchange for room and board, and that's afforded me the luxury of not working outside the house. But now . . ." Her voice faltered slightly.

"But now," Lyle said, "when school starts, Scotty'll be in kindergarten. Sandy will have time on her hands."

She nodded, and I could see on her face a sadness I would never know. Having children had not been in David's plan, and believe me, how he planned things were exactly the way his life would go. I'd often wondered if he committed it to paper: *Marry Evie, have no children, work her until she is used up, and dispose of Evie for newer, more vibrant model.* Heartaches usually brought on by such thoughts had been replaced with a heartfelt chuckle. What a good feeling.

I smiled at Sandy. "I'll bet you'll miss the little fellow being around all day. Where is he now?"

"He was in a pre-K class until May. I decided to send him to a daycare during the summer so he'll be in the routine and won't have trouble adjusting when school starts again. That time is almost here."

"That sounds like a good idea."

The phone rang.

"Go catch that. We're going to run. It was a pleasure meeting you, Evie. I hope to see more of you," Sandy said and headed to the door.

"Talk to you soon." Lyle caught up with his sister.

I answered the phone to find David on the line. "Have you bothered to look for the key?" he asked.

The man had no clue who he was dealing with. I certainly wasn't the Evie who'd made a surprise visit to his office on East Wacker Drive and caught him and his paralegal in the middle of a sex act straight out of the *Kama Sutra.* Of course, then, hurt nearly brought me to my knees, but lately all I felt was loathing for him. As a matter of fact, he really irked me.

"Guess what, David. My life no longer revolves around your wants." Luckily, the phone was portable. I stepped into an empty dressing room and lowered my voice so the shoppers couldn't hear me. "I have a vengeful side. Since you don't even have the good sense to say *pretty please,* I'm not giving you the key. You work it out however you need to, but don't bother me again about it. I'd hate to have to put you under a restraining order. If you aren't sure what that is, check with your paralegal the next time the two of you are together. And I mean that in the truest sense of the word."

By the time I emerged from the dressing room, I had three customers waiting to pay for their merchandise. Despite the crappy feeling David's call had poured over me, I forced a smile and took care of my customers. After a few minutes of listening to them tell me how happy they were they had another option for buying clothes other than McGovern's Department Store, I exonerated my brain from the lousy funk David had instilled.

At the Victorian Sampler, business was amazing. During the first month, I'd far exceeded my expectations. One problem I would have to take care of very soon was hiring another clerk. I barely had time to go to the bathroom during the day. In the evening, I'd carry armloads of catalogues home with me to pore over and prepare my lists to order when I arrived at the shop the next morning.

It was a vicious cycle, and I was tired. Yes, hiring help had quickly moved to the top of my to-do lists. That and disposing of that damnable key David wanted. *I'll die before I'll give it back to him.* I instantly regretted the analogy and quickly amended my thought. *I'll bury the key in the backyard before I'll give it back to David.*

Not a moment too soon, my workday ended. Exhaustion had overtaken me a few hours before closing time. I refused to take any catalogues home with me, but I did have a book of cloth samples I wanted to look at. After locking the back door of the boutique, I opened the trunk of my Mercedes Benz. I slung the sample case onto the floorboard, and it landed on Denise's mahogany keepsake box. I'd put it there after Merrilee gave it to me and forgotten all about it.

When I got home, I took the box and samples into the house.

Even though nightfall was about an hour away, the inside of my old farmhouse was dark. I switched on the kitchen light and suddenly remembered Northside Lock and Key hadn't returned my call. As I examined the lock, anger mentally shook me. How foolish I'd been, dozing off in the tub and imagining I heard the door. That was all there was to it.

Midnight paced a figure eight around one of my legs and then the other. "Okay, buddy. Here you go." After dumping his food into his bowl, I stroked Midnight's soft, shiny fur a couple of times.

While he ate, I took Denise's box out front and sat on the wooden swing suspended from the sturdy beams of the front porch. Although different swings had come and gone over the years, they'd all hung from the hooks anchored into four-by-four supports my grandfather had used to build the Carson family homestead in the early 1920s. When I thought of the hard work that had gone into the house, I couldn't help but sit a little taller and feel a little prouder.

A warm breeze swirled around me, whipping my hair away from my face. The sweet aroma of a freshly mowed field of hay hung lightly in the air. How I'd missed the small things I associated with home.

I used the tiny key to open the lock on the wooden box. When I lifted the lid, a faint scent of honeysuckle reminded me of the smell I'd been confronted with last night when I returned home from my date with Lyle.

In Chicago, an acquaintance of mine believed strongly in *woo woo,* and she would have justified my two encounters with the pleasant but illusive scent as a possible visit from Denise's spirit. Luckily, I didn't believe in things like that.

What I did believe was that Denise's spirit would forever be in my heart. No matter what, she would always be the fun-loving, beautiful young woman in the pictures stored in the shiny mahogany box that Merrilee claimed held the best parts of her mother's life. Looking at those pictures, I could make the same claim about my own life.

Days had passed. Massive amounts of evidence had been gathered. Yet, no arrests had been made. Denise's and Jake's murderer—or murderers—were still out there breathing air they'd taken from two people in the space of less than twenty-four hours.

I kept reiterating my promise to Denise that I wouldn't let her murder go unsolved, but what had I personally done to make sure that didn't happen? A better question would be—what could I do? I had a business to run. It wasn't like I could spend my day hunting a killer. I barely kept up with the flow of traffic through the boutique and managing the inventory by myself. I needed to go to market in Atlanta to preview the fall fashions.

Unless I hired someone to run the store, I'd have to close for at least two days, losing a lot of business. I had to hire an assistant, and soon.

After I put the pictures back in the box, I picked up the watch stuffed into a corner. Although Merrilee and Mrs. Farrell had insisted they wanted me to have the contents of the box, something about the watch niggled inside me. Could someone have professed their love for Denise and even given her an engraved present without anyone in her immediate family knowing about it? Something didn't gel with that idea.

I relocked the box, but slipped the watch into my pocket. Tomorrow I'd take it by the jewelry store and see if Mr. Comstock could tell me anything about it.

The next morning, since I didn't open the Victorian Sampler

until ten, leaving earlier than usual would give me time to take care of a couple of things that had worked their way to the top of my to-do list. I kept stacking things on that mental list until everything seemed jumbled.

Before I left, I committed it all to a notepad so I could free my mind for more important things. A quick check of my pocket confirmed I had Denise's watch. I'd go by Comstock Jewelers first. The newspaper office was close by there, and I could drop off the ad for an assistant.

During the night, I'd awakened with a pang of guilt for not giving in to David and sending him his illusive key. I didn't wish him any harm, at least not on most days. I felt sure not getting into that safe-deposit box would mean something unpleasant would surely come his way. I pulled the key out of Dad's old desk drawer and put it in my other pocket. *Mail key to David* made my list of the day.

On the sheet of paper, I scribbled two items I would count as my helping to find a killer: *Go to Lockwood Motel, and make a trip to Jake's home at the lake.* Why? Not sure, but I had to start somewhere.

I parked in the alley behind my store and then walked the four blocks to Iver Street.

"Good morning, Mr. Comstock," I called to the man walking along the sidewalk just ahead of me. He turned and raised his hand to shade his eyes from the sun.

"Morning, Evie. It's good to see you, sweetie. How ya been?" Melvin Comstock gave me a fatherly hug. As one of Dad's best friends, Mr. Comstock had been very much a part of my earlier years.

"I'm doing fine. Sorry I haven't been by sooner, but I've been really busy."

"I know, dear. Sure was sorry to hear about Judy's girl."

"Yes, sir. It's tragic."

"Then Frank's boy, Jake. Who would ever want to kill some poor soul like him?"

We'd stopped in front of the jewelry store. "Is there something I can do for you, Evie?" He unlocked the door and then held it open for me.

I pulled the watch from my pocket and handed it to him. "Do you have any way of knowing where this watch was bought? Do they have serial numbers that can be traced?" I asked hopefully.

The jeweler took the watch and studied it closely. "No way to trace it, Evie. It's not worth much except possibly to the person it was given to. But see here," he said, pointing with the tip of an ink pen, "that's an engraver's mark. Very few jewelers do that anymore. Usually the older ones."

"How can I find out who engraved it?"

Mr. Comstock cocked his head and smiled. "I could tell you."

"You know?"

"It's Isaac Barack from Barack Jewelers in Atlanta. He's one of the few people still around that hand engraves. We've been friends for a hundred years."

"Of course you have, Mr. Comstock, and the way you're going you'll be friends for another hundred. Thanks. It's good to see you again."

I left the store feeling I'd made some headway. I wasn't sure what it could prove, but when I made my trip to market in Atlanta in a couple of weeks, I would stop by and see if Mr. Barack could shed any light on the engraved watch.

The Hyattville NewsLedger was also located on Iver Street just a couple of blocks from Comstock's. I gave the clerk the handwritten ad for the boutique I wanted run in the next two issues of the biweekly newspaper. The young lady assured me I was in time for the issue coming out Saturday morning.

The two errands had taken longer than I anticipated, so mailing the key to David would have to wait until later in the afternoon when I could lock up the boutique long enough to run to the bank and the post office. I headed back to the Victorian Sampler.

Sometime during the morning hours, Ben from Northside Lock and Key returned my call from the day before. He apologized but said he wouldn't be able to go to my house to change the locks until Monday. His wife had delivered their first child, and he was on his way to pick them up from the hospital. There really wasn't anyone else in town, but they did carry locks at the hardware store, and they were pretty easy to install if I couldn't wait for him to do it.

"No, Monday will be fine, but it will have to be after I close up my store at five. I can be at the house by six. Will that work for you?" I asked.

"Yes, Monday will be fine. Sorry I couldn't do it today, but you understand."

It really was okay. I had the only keys to my house in my possession and had come to realize I'd been foolish believing anyone had entered my house.

The rest of the day had been so busy I didn't have time to go to the bank. Once I'd closed up for the evening, I made a drop in the bank's night deposit. Traffic on the country road to my house was very light, and I arrived in record time.

I'd had very little for breakfast, and lunch hadn't happened at all. As soon as I could grab a bite from the fridge I planned to take a ride down to the lake. It would be the first time since I'd watched them drag Jake's truck out of the water. It was time to revisit that place and possibly face some of the ghosts lingering in the back of my mind.

Midnight waited for me on the porch swing. He ran to the door. He was hungry, too. I had my key in the lock and had just turned it when I noticed one of the panes of the twelve-light, double-hung windows had been broken. I was already in the process of swinging the door open when the realization that someone had broken into my house gripped me deep in my gut.

I looked inside and saw shattered glass on the floor. Whoever had broken the window had been able to reach in and unlock the door. Fear and anger fought a battle inside my brain. I knew I should race back to my car and use my cell phone to call the police, but I was so mad someone dared violate my home I wanted to go in, hunt them down, and beat the crap out of them.

A quick search of my shoulder bag and my pants pockets garnered me only David's stupid key, which I'd forgotten to mail. Since I had nothing to fend off a burglar or worse yet a—

I sprinted off the porch and climbed back into my car, locking the doors behind me. I flipped open my cell and dialed 9-1-1. I waited there, all the while searching the windows of the house for any movement inside. I saw nothing. Surely, the intruder was gone.

Lonnie and another deputy arrived. While they did a room-by-room search, I waited in the front yard. When it was all clear, Lonnie motioned for me to come in.

I wouldn't say the place had been ransacked, but someone had definitely been looking for something. Drawers appeared to have been opened, shuffled through, and then slammed shut with contents sticking out. Upstairs in my closet, some of the things had been knocked to the floor and two of my coats had been thrown on the bed with pockets turned inside out.

"Any idea what they were looking for?"

I jumped. I'd left Lonnie downstairs, so the unexpected sound of his voice startled me.

"Damn, Lonnie. Scare me to death, why don't you? You should wear a bell."

"You're crazy as ever, Eva Lynn."

It had been a long time since Lonnie had called me by my full name. Normally I would have been mad and slugged him, but right then it brought me comfort to know he was there to protect me.

"I don't have any idea who it could be," I said, "unless whoever killed Denise and Jake thinks I know something that might lead to their capture, which is ludicrous." I thought about telling Lonnie there was a chance someone had come into my house and left through the back door with a key, but since they'd broken a window to come in, the key theory wouldn't make any sense. I decided not to divulge that info lest it confirm my dear friend's opinion of me.

Crazy? Maybe. Shaken? Definitely.

We walked back downstairs. The deputy had finished his report and taken a couple of prints. The towels and sheets from the linen closet were on the hall floor. Nothing was really in bad shape. I could straighten it all up in short order.

"Do you want to go to Mom's for the night?" Lonnie asked.

"I'm not going to be run out of my house. Can you help me secure the broken window?"

He looked at the deputy. "You through here, Parker?"

Parker nodded.

"There's some wood in the lean-to behind the house. How about getting a piece to cover this window?"

As the man went out the front door, Lonnie bent to pick up the broken glass. I brought the trash can from the kitchen into the living room. As I passed the end of the couch, I noticed the ear portion of a pair of glasses sticking out from under the piece of furniture. I kicked it out into the center of the floor. Picking them up, I looked closely at the expensive Oakley sunglasses with an MP3 player attached. I knew instantly who they belonged to and ultimately who had broken into my house.

"That son of a bitch," I said through clenched teeth and handed the evidence to Lonnie.

Chapter 7

"I take it you know who did this?" Deputy Lonnie Douglas asked as he took the expensive sunglasses from me.

I'd spied them sticking out from under the couch and knew instantly who they belonged to.

"Oh, yeah. My ex-husband, David Holmes. He came here looking for a key I have. During our last conversation, I told him I wouldn't send it to him. I guess it's more important than I suspected."

Lonnie handed the glasses back. "What's the key to?"

"It's for a safe-deposit box at the bank. He had me secure it and never had his name added to it."

"Must be something important in there." He dumped the last of the broken glass into the trash can.

"It's a huge bundle of—" I stopped dead. Lonnie may have been a longtime, dear friend, but he was also a law enforcement officer. I decided against telling him David had hidden illegal money for one of his clients. "It's just important to him," I said and let it go at that.

Lonnie eyed me suspiciously.

"Trust me," I said, "you don't want to know."

"If you say so."

Parker returned with a piece of wood and a few nails. Lonnie affixed it to the window frame, cutting down the natural light spilling into my living room.

"What do you want me to do about your ex?" Lonnie carried the trash can back into the kitchen.

I shrugged. "I assume shooting him is out of the question."

Lonnie nodded.

"I don't guess there's anything." I pulled the key from my pocket. "He didn't get what he came after. If he comes back while I'm here, can I shoot him?"

"You wouldn't like it in jail, Evie." Lonnie smiled. "Just call if he shows up. I'll come out and take care of him."

Parker strolled across the yard to the squad car.

Lonnie lagged behind. "I'm sorry things have been so rocky for you lately. Surely they'll straighten out soon."

"I hope so. No matter how much you know it's for the best, divorce is always hard."

He shrugged. "For a while, that was something I thought very seriously about."

"Wow, I thought you and Kitty had a solid marriage."

"Ah, you know as well as I do that Kitty's dad spoiled her rotten, and I'm afraid I picked up where he left off. She is so insecure, she overcompensates by putting other people down. When I told her I couldn't put up with it anymore, she had some kind of breakdown. She agreed we should get some help, and the therapist suggested Kitty take up something that would have her thinking about the less fortunate.

"She took it very serious, and now she spends three days a week working at the soup kitchen sponsored by our church. She seems to love it. As a matter of fact, last year they gave her an award for her volunteer work for the community."

I loved Lonnie, and I wanted him to have the happiness he deserved. "That's really good to hear. I can tell you are proud of her."

"I am."

"What about kids? I figure you have a baseball team by now."

Lonnie had loved Kitty since elementary school. He would have married her even if she hadn't gotten pregnant just before we all graduated. Their wedding was one of the last events I attended before I went off to college in Chicago. That fall, Dad gave me the sad news that Kitty had delivered a premature baby girl who died the next day.

I'd called them to give my condolences. Lonnie answered, and when he heard my voice, he sobbed uncontrollably. Kitty took the phone from him, and although she sounded weak, she thanked me for taking the time to call and told me they both appreciated it. I hurt deeply for their loss because I knew what a wonderful father Lonnie would have been.

"After our baby died, Kitty couldn't get pregnant. Our therapist suggested we try to adopt, but that didn't work out."

"I'm sorry to hear that."

"Everything is fine now. Kitty is so proud of the work she does, and I like my job. We're as happy as pigs in slop." Lonnie's blue eyes twinkled.

I didn't see a need to tell him Kitty still seemed a little self-absorbed to me. It didn't matter what I thought. I didn't have to live with her.

"Lonnie," Parker hollered from the car. "Come on, they need us back at the station right away."

"Call me if something else comes up," Lonnie said and sprinted across the yard.

He'd been gone about an hour. To clear my head and to keep from calling David on his cell phone to tell him exactly what a lowlife I thought he was, I went to the rose garden and worked on ridding it of weeds. The setting sun was slowly disappearing behind the oak and pine trees, which, along with the massive azalea bushes, obscured the view of the highway.

Just as I started to climb the three steps to the porch, I remembered the key David wanted enough to drive from Atlanta and break into my home. I quickly made a side trip around the house to the tool shed out back. After getting a shovel, I dug a small hole in the corner of the backyard near Grandma Carson's camellia bushes and proudly planted David's coveted key.

You had my full attention when I saw you digging that hole like a fishwife. I would have found the whole scenario funny if you weren't so pathetic. The hole was so deep, I expected to find fish guts in there to fertilize the bushes—the very ones I was hiding in. I could have almost reached out and touched you. But I'll wait until a better time. A time when you can give me what I want with no chance of interruption. Until then, I'll play silly games with you. I'd love to be a fly on the wall when you get home from work tomorrow night.

Saturday morning came earlier than I wanted. I'd tossed and turned most of the night. So by six o'clock, I gave it up, got dressed for work, fed Midnight, and drove to the Victorian Sampler. I had plenty of paperwork to keep me busy until ten when I opened for business.

The *Hyattville NewsLedger* lay on the floor where the paper boy had shoved it through the mail slot. While the aroma of brewing coffee filled the whole boutique, I watered flowers, balanced the checkbook, and flipped through the mail. All the while, my mind played over and over the fact that David had broken into my house.

I'd been angry because I felt he was still showing his authority by ignoring my right to privacy. His power over me had been broken into a million pieces when he destroyed our wedding vows. But whether I was angry or not, David could be in a lot of trouble with corrupt and wicked people if he didn't produce that money. Another thought nagged persistently in the pit of my stomach. What if he told them I had the key?

My first thought would be that David would never put me in harm's way, but if I'd gotten nothing else from my divorce, I'd come to know the real David, and I couldn't bet my life on his protecting me. No, the most rational move for me would be to dig up the key and send it to him. Have it over and done with. Worrying about the Hyattville murders was enough on my plate without wondering when the mob would show up.

I glanced at the Georgia pine grandmother clock standing against the wall flanked on one side by expensive evening wear and on the other by a glass jewelry case. I still had an hour before I needed to unlock the front door.

After pouring a mug of coffee, I opened the newspaper. The headline was like a slap in the face: *Sheriff Arrested for Murder.* As if the words weren't enough to dishearten anyone who read them, the black-and-white photo of Johnston Beasley being led away from his home on Elm Haven Drive caused my stomach to churn. He wore everyday jeans, chambray shirt, and an Atlanta Braves baseball cap. His arms were behind his back, presumably restrained by handcuffs, but I couldn't be sure because Lonnie hid the view of the sheriff's hands.

The night before, I knew by the urgency in Deputy Parker's voice that he and Lonnie were needed somewhere fast, but I never dreamed it would be for that reason. Being there while the state police arrested their boss must have been surreal to all of Hyattville's deputies.

The one thing not hidden in the photo was the hurt and bewilderment that must have been on Clara Beasley's face as she watched from the door of her home as her husband was led to a waiting patrol car. Salty tears stung my eyes. I ached with an inner pain that couldn't be measured against what Mrs. Beasley must have felt, but it was real all the same.

Guilt caused my grief. In a brief stretch of time, many lives had been turned upside down, many souls crushed. I, in a remote way, felt responsible. I had been the first person to bring the horrific news into the public eye and had even helped gather information that would later be used against Johnston Beasley. Although I knew I had no other choices, the underlying feeling of guilt still plagued me.

The telephone rang.

"Hello, Evie." Lyle's voice was a pleasant surprise.

"Good morning."

"Have you read the paper?" he asked in a gentle tone.

"Just doing that now. It's terrible. Sheriff Beasley arrested for Jake's murder." I took a sip of coffee in hopes of clearing away the knot of sadness from my throat.

"The ballistics confirmed the bullet that killed Harley came from the sheriff's gun. The state police had no choice but to take him in." Lyle sighed, sounding as if he carried the weight of the world on his shoulders. He seemed almost defeated. "It will be a couple of days before he is arraigned. So much of the evidence is circumstantial, but there's too much of it to ignore any longer. The public, with the help of the media, is making a lot of noise saying action isn't being taken because Johnston is one of us."

"Are you part of the team working on this case?" The few times I talked to Lyle, he only knew developments because another officer had told him.

"No, thank goodness. There are things that would make it a conflict of interest for me. The sheriff was my dad's best friend. He helped me get into the police academy. His wife, Clara, was there every day for Sandy after her accident. I'm involved in the trial of the drug dealers arrested in that major bust out on Interstate 95 a few months back."

"Well, I'm glad you don't have to be part of trying to put him away. There has to be a logical explanation for all the evidence pointing to Beasley." I hoped it would surface soon, especially for Beasley's wife's sake. And Lyle's.

As if he'd read my mind, Lyle asked, "Did you see Clara's picture in the paper? I don't know why the media couldn't have left her out of it." Lyle spaced his words evenly.

"Have you talked with her? Is she doing okay?"

"Sandy called Clara late last night. She's holding up. She has a lot of faith in her husband." I heard Lyle swallow hard. "So do I."

"I understand they were waiting for a DNA report." I couldn't remember where I'd heard that—from the newspaper, the television, or possibly even Lyle.

"It's not back yet."

"If the DNA isn't tied to the sheriff, will they set him free?"

"I'm afraid not. The only thing the DNA will tell us is whether he had sex with Denise before her death. All that is known for sure is that someone did. If it was Johnston, that will be the nail in his coffin. If it isn't, then it will be suspected that Denise had sex with someone else, and there is the possibility that she was killed by a jealous boyfriend. In light of all the other evidence, that could possibly be Johnston."

The clock chimed ten. "I have to open up shop," I said. I looked up to see if anyone waited at the door and saw Lyle's sister. "Sandy is waiting for me to let her in."

"Really? If you don't mind, tell her I won't be home for dinner tonight. I would like to call you when I do get in, if it isn't too late. Is that okay with you?"

I held up one finger to acknowledge Sandy and rose from my desk. "That'll be fine. Talk to you then. Bye."

I hurried to unlock the door. Sandy held the newspaper and smiled widely.

"Come on in. I was just talking to Lyle on the phone. By the way, he said to tell you he won't be home for dinner."

"Neither will Scotty. He's staying at his Aunt Nina's. I'll have the evening alone." Sandy laughed, and I had to smile at her adorable pixie sound.

"Come in. Is there something in particular you're looking for?"

Sandy held out the newspaper she was carrying. For a short moment I thought maybe she wanted to talk to me about Beasley's arrest.

"I'd like to apply for the job you advertised in the morning paper."

With the big news happenings, I'd forgotten all about the ad. "Great! Come on back and let's talk." I led the way behind the counter and indicated for Sandy to have a seat on one of the stools.

"You said you would like to go back to work while Scotty is in school. I got the impression you were looking for a part-time job. I'm looking for a full-time employee. Would that work with Scotty's schedule?"

"I gave it some thought. He's in a daycare three days a week until school starts again. Until then, his aunt would watch him on the days he's usually home. Since you don't open until ten, I would have time to get him to school. I had planned to see about getting him into extended daycare there at the school, but my sister-in-law told me this morning she would love to pick him up at 2:30 and take him to her house to play with her twin boys. They're a year older than Scotty. That would save me money, and the three boys play well together."

"It sounds like that would work well. I close the shop at five, but the last hour and a half is always slow. You could leave at four if you needed to."

"Great." Sandy smiled, and instantly I thought of Lyle. Both their mouths curved in a distinct way, forming a contagious grin.

I was just moments away from asking Sandy when she would like to start working at the Victorian Sampler when the door burst open. The bell over the door chimed, welcoming about six well-dressed ladies. Their laughter rang loudly through the shop.

Hyattville was only a stone's throw from the beautiful tourist islands off the Georgia coast. While their husbands played golf, the women shopped. Even before I opened my doors for business, I promoted the Victorian Sampler all over the major cities and islands within a hundred-mile radius. That extra effort paid off. Many women who were vacationing in the area made their way to my store and usually left with bags full of the latest fashions.

I asked Sandy to excuse me and quickly went to greet the latest group of shoppers. The ladies properly *oooh*ed and *aaah*ed over the merchandise, and I checked the storeroom for different sizes of certain styles. While they spent thirty or so minutes browsing and trying on clothes, other patrons came in and out.

I was ringing up the third sale. Someone asked if they could try on a couple of things. I only had two dressing rooms, and they were both busy. Sandy stepped from behind the counter and took the clothes from the lady.

"Both rooms are occupied right now, but I'll hang these right here. You can browse a little more, and I'll call you as soon as one of the rooms is open." The lady returned Sandy's warm smile and went back to sifting through the racks of summer fashions.

I liked Sandy. Apparently today was a good day for her to start working with me, and I hoped she and I would be good friends, too.

When the day ended, I remembered that Sandy had no one waiting for her to feed when she got home. "Would you like to go somewhere and have dinner before we head home?"

"Yes, I would. Where shall we go?"

I pointed out the front window to a small café across Burnt Magnolia Street. Nestled between Brubaker's Hardware store and Nat Priestly's law office, A Taste of Cuba was a small establishment with wonderful Cuban food. Sandy and I crossed the street.

Joe Posadas owned the café and greeted each patron personally. His wife, Sonya, oversaw the cooking, and in most cases, did it herself. The heavy aroma of fried onions and garlic made my taste buds dance. We were seated near a front window.

"It certainly smells good," Sandy said.

"It still mystifies me that a café serving nothing but Cuban food to die-hard Southerners could be successful." I put the bright yellow napkin in my lap and looked over the menu. "But they've done something right here. This place has been serving Hyattville for over twenty years, and most people say they doubt you could get finer Cuban food even in Havana."

While Sandy and I waited for our order, I asked, "What did you think of your first day?"

"I loved it. I'm sure it will take a little while for me to get back in the swing of things. Right now, I could curl up on one of those doggie beds Violet Thompson has in her pet shop and take a long nap."

"I felt that way when I first opened, but you'll get used to it."

Just then, Lonnie and Kitty entered the café. He looked tired, washed out even. Kitty looked like . . . Kitty, smiling, offering perfunctory waves to several of the diners. I motioned for them to sit with us, and they did. Joe Posadas took their orders and brought their drinks. I introduced Sandy to them.

"Lonnie and I used to play together when we were in playpens," I explained to her. "Kitty and I were in school together from the first grade on. Her dad owns McGovern's, one of the few family-owned department stores left in the nation."

"It's very nice to meet both of you," Sandy said.

Kitty beamed from ear to ear. "You, too." She then looked at me, and I wondered what was about to come out of her mouth. "I'm surprised you didn't say what you used to about us going to school together." She was still smiling, and I took that to be a good thing.

"You mean that we went through school together, kicking and screaming all the way?"

"Yeah, that." Kitty's chuckle made me laugh, too.

"That was a long time ago," I said. "We've grown up a little since the days we were at each other's throats all the time. Don't you agree?"

Kitty gave me the biggest surprise I'd had in a long time. She laid her hand over mine and with the most serious expression said, "Most of those bad times were my fault. I'm truly sorry."

Lonnie, who was sitting next to me, placed his open hand under my chin and closed my gaping mouth.

"That's really good of you, Kitty. I was no saint either." I laid my hand on top of hers, which was still on mine. "Let's just call it a truce. How does that sound?"

"Sounds good to me. By the way, the clothes I bought the other day weren't really for my niece. They were for me."

I wasn't sure I could stand any more shocks from Kitty.

"I hope you like them."

The rest of the meal was pleasant, and I left there with a renewed spirit. My lifelong nemesis had apologized, and that felt pretty good.

After finally leaving historic downtown Hyattville, I sped along the highway to my home. For some reason, though, I really didn't want to go there, so I took a side trip through some of the country where I hadn't been in years. Housing developments stood where old friends had once lived in single-family dwellings surrounded by acres of farmland.

As I passed Hyattville's Baptist Church, I saw Reverend Stirling entering a side door. More than likely he was preparing for Sunday morning service. Seeing the tall, white steeple, I felt a twinge of regret pull heavily on my heart. I should have been attending services every week since I'd returned, giving thanks for my many blessings.

I'd gone to church for a couple of Sundays, but Reverend Stirling's lectures didn't feed my soul. That wasn't a complete cop-out. The good reverend had looked my way a couple of times when he talked about *damnation.* He made me uncomfortable, or at least that is the excuse I gave myself for not getting out of bed on Sunday morning.

Some of the back roads had changed to the point that they were unrecognizable to me. I soon found myself on a dirt road, which eventually came out at Folger's Lake very near Jake Harley's house. The lake was one place where I always found peace and tranquility. The beauty of the sunset glistening across the water took my breath away. At one time, the lake's calmness would have smoothed the fraying edges of my aching heart, but now it held questions my curiosity and I needed answered.

After parking, I got out and walked to Jake's house. As I leaned against a shaky porch post, my gaze scanned the roofs of the homes on the opposite shore. Slowly, one by one, yellow lights came on in the distant windows. Evening was closing in. People were arriving home after long hours at work. Their lives were moving on as usual. Mine, too. But Denise and Jake would never face the daily chores the rest of us did. Shivers waved over me. I tried hard to hold onto the inner peace I'd found moments before.

"I refuse to dwell on things I can't change." My whispered words drifted to the evening dusk. A bird fluttered from the eaves of Jake's porch, calling my attention to a window next to the battered front door. It appeared to be opened. A pale curtain, yellowed with age, poked through the slight opening. I walked across the creaky planks, drawn to the window by my natural curiosity.

I felt a mischievous smile pull at the corner of my lips. If Grandma Carson were with me, she would say, "A nosy nose can cause you to lose your toes." I looked down at my feet, deciding my shoes would protect me.

After raising the window and pushing the curtain aside, I stuck my head in. The sun was almost out of sight, so if I was going to go in and look around, I'd have to hurry.

I swung my leg inside, straddled the sill, and balanced on one foot until I was completely inside Jake's living room.

A mix of foul smells assaulted my nostrils. A quick glance around told me where they came from: dirty dishes stacked high in the sink, pizza shriveled and moldy on the coffee table, and a litter box near the hallway.

"Wonder what happened to the cat?" My voice echoed through the deserted house.

At the end of the hallway, I could see the last of the sunset lighting a bedroom. However, the narrow passage contained two closed doors and more darkness than I wanted to walk through. Again, my curiosity won out, and I eased my way down the hall, opening the two closed doors, allowing more light to brighten my path. Behind one door was a bedroom, probably Jake's Dad's. The other was a bathroom with only a tiny window above the shower.

The small room at the end of the hallway contained an unmade bed, its sheets dirty and smudged with several dark streaks. I wondered if it was blood, but a stack of crumpled candy wrappers on the floor led me to think the dark streaks were chocolate. Shelves flanked one of the walls, loaded with books, games, and puzzles. Joystick wires ran from an old video game station across the floor to the television. If I didn't know better, I would've sworn the room belonged to a child. But it belonged to a man. A dead man. My stomach churned, as it always did when I thought of the injustice of Jake's and Denise's deaths.

Jake probably never thought his life was pathetic. Only those outside his world would think that way. However, nothing in his life could have been as bad as his death. I'd agonized over and over again, picturing the last moments of his life. The killer had to be someone Jake knew. Someone he trusted. What would such a childish mind have thought as the barrel of a gun was placed to his head? Did he realize what was happening?

Was it truly possible that Johnston Beasley, Jake's caretaker, blew his brains all over the cab of his truck? Beasley appeared to have a stable family life. He had a job he was good at—bringing criminals to justice. And he had loved Jake like one of his own children. I couldn't fathom that same man could end Jake's life.

And what about the bullet lodged in the headliner of the truck? Beasley wasn't stupid. He would have been careful to ensure the spent shell wasn't found, not left a few feet from the body. Even the most inept investigator would have found it. Logically, I couldn't come to terms with all of it, but then again, when did murder ever make sense?

I hurriedly looked at a corkboard attached to the wall above the headboard of Jake's bed. It held a few black-and-white pictures of Jake as a child with his father. There were colored ones of Jake with various Hyattville citizens. But the one I found most interesting showed Jake holding a black cat with green eyes.

My cat. Midnight. Had the poor creature walked all those miles from Jake's house to mine? Apparently he had. At least by giving Midnight a home, I was able to do something for Jake.

The bedroom had grown dark and the hallway even darker. I scurried past the closed doors into the living room hoping no figments of my imagination would jump out at me. Suddenly, headlights from an approaching vehicle shone through the flimsy curtains, lighting the whole room. I crouched and then walked like a duck to the wall under the opened window. My lungs ached from fear.

"Come out of there!" A husky, threatening voice boomed from outside.

My heart pounded frantically. Footsteps on the porch vibrated the floor beneath me. Evidently, this was a big man. I leaned closer to the wall, wishing I could disappear into it. Someone grabbed me by my collar and hoisted me to my feet. "Don't hurt me." I twisted around to face my captor, who still had a death grip on the back of my blouse. "I was just looking around."

The beam of light from the car's headlights illuminated the outline of the man, but his face remained obscured in darkness. "Let go of me, you overgrown clod." I jerked one more time and heard material rip. He released his hold, freeing me to take a stance. I wasn't sure what I thought I could do, but I wasn't going down without a fight.

"Evie Carson." His deep voice thundered. Was I already dead and God himself was calling me into the light? Not since I'd sat perched up the oak tree had my insides shaken so violently. The man turned his head slightly, which gave me a clear view of his face. I lashed out, striking my fist hard against his shoulder.

"Lyle Dickerson." I rubbed my aching hand. "You scared me to death."

"You're lucky it was me. I could have been the maniac who's been killing people right in front of this very house." He reached through the window to the inside lock. It clicked, and he opened the door. Why hadn't I thought of that?

"Are you following me?"

"No, I finished earlier than I thought I would today. I stopped by your house. When you weren't there, I decided to ride down here. I haven't been here since the day they pulled Harley out of the lake. I saw your car but didn't see you anywhere. My headlights lit enough of the porch for me to see where you'd stepped into the dust. When you didn't answer when I called out, I wasn't sure if you were hiding or if possibly the murderer had brought you in here. I looked in the window right down on top of your head, but I couldn't see well enough to know for sure if it was you."

Lyle's words were like a bucket of cold water splashed in my face. They had arrested Beasley, but I was sure he wasn't guilty. So why had I been stupid enough to go there alone? "I'm sorry. I wasn't thinking. All I know is things are not sitting right with me. I had to take a look around."

"What did you think you would find in there?"

"Something no one else has been able to."

"Like what?"

"A clue to who killed Denise and Jake, of course. Maybe I would tune into something they hadn't."

"Think it would just be lying there waiting for you?"

"All I know is I have to do something. I feel so helpless. Denise is dead, Jake is dead, and the murderer is still walking. It's not fair."

"Sheriff Beasley is in custody for those murders."

"You and I both know he didn't kill Jake. While he's in jail, the real murderer is breathing free air. I can't stand that thought. It's tearing me apart." I shivered.

"Come on. You need to get out of this night air." Lyle put his arm around me and led me to my car. "When I was at your house, I saw the window was boarded up. What happened?"

"My ex broke in looking for a key I have of his." I'd almost forgotten about that. I shook my head. "It was so ridiculous. He really needs the key, and I told him I wouldn't send it. He drove down from Atlanta and broke in, but he didn't find it because it was in my pocket.

"At the time I was so angry, I buried it in my backyard and said to hell with him. Today I came to my senses. When I get home, I'm going to dig it up and send it to him." Quickly, I got into my car.

As I drove home, Lyle followed behind me. What a roller coaster of emotions I'd been riding during the past three hours. I couldn't believe I'd admitted how childish I'd been by burying that damn key. A sudden slip of composure caused my eyes to fill with tears and eventually stream down my face. They continued to flow for the whole drive to my house.

Once we arrived and before he could open my car door, I swiped away all the evidence of my crying. I grabbed my purse and keys and then walked to the porch. After unlocking the door, I turned on the outside light.

"Would you like to come in for coffee?" I asked.

"Yes, I'd like that." Lyle followed me into the living room.

"Have a seat." I pointed to the couch. "I'll put on some coffee."

Once in the kitchen, I flipped the switch, allowing florescent lighting to brighten the room. Lifting the carafe from the coffee-maker, I turned to the sink. Something on the dining table caught my eye. I jerked to a quick stop. The glass pot slipped from my hand and crashed to the floor.

Chapter 8

As my dumbstruck mind searched frantically for an explanation, Lyle hurried from my living room to the kitchen. "Are you okay?" he asked as he stooped to pick up the pieces of the shattered coffeepot at my feet.

His steady tone shoved aside the stark fear sweeping through me, but nothing could keep my insides from shaking.

"I buried that in the yard last night." I pointed to the mud-encrusted key lying in the middle of the table. "That's what David broke in here yesterday looking for. I buried it. Now here it is inside. How can that be?" My voice bordered on hysteria, and I couldn't rein it in. Tears were back in full force.

Lyle dumped some of the glass into the trash can and then helped me step away from the remaining shards of the carafe.

"Don't touch anything," he told me. "Let me look around to make sure they aren't still here, and see where they came in."

"No need to do that." I shook my head and pointed to the back door. "They came in that door right there, and they used a key."

"How do you know that?"

"When you left the other night, I took a tub bath right down the hall. I dozed off, but woke up to the distinct sound of that door closing and the dead bolt locking. That could only be done with a key."

"Did you report it?"

"No. There was only one person who had a key besides me. That was Lonnie's mother, and I knew she wouldn't be out here that late at night, but I went to see her the next morning. She gave me the key and said she was home alone the night before, and no one had access to the key or even knew where she kept it. So, I explained away the door closing by concluding I must have truly been asleep. I rationalized I had dreamed it. But I didn't dream that." I pointed to the safe-deposit key, which struck terror in my heart.

"Someone has easy access to my home. They saw me bury the key and dug it up. Now they're taunting me with the fact they can come in and go through my house whenever they please." A cavalcade of shivers marched up every inch of my spine. "Dear God, Lyle. They were in here the other night when you brought me home. They waited until I was in the bathroom, and then they went out." I suddenly felt violated in the worst possible way.

"We need to think about this logically. When I brought you home the other night, the phone rang and no one was there. How could they have been in here and called you on your phone?"

"They had to be on a cell phone. They have to be watching me. That would account for the fact that the other calls had classical music playing in the background, but that night there was no music. Remember? I mentioned that at the time."

He nodded. "I guess we can eliminate your ex since he had to break a window to get in here. I'm going to take a look through the rest of the house." Lyle walked down the hallway to Dad's old bedroom and bath. I followed closely behind. In front of the linen closet, he stopped. "Where is that sweet smell coming from?"

"That's honeysuckle or jasmine. There's a sachet in here." As I spoke, I opened the door to show him the source of the fragrance. Towels and sheets, which I had carefully folded after David's invasion, tumbled at me. I screeched and jumped back. "Someone was looking for something in here." Finally, anger kicked in, and I wanted to lash out at anything or anyone near. But Lyle was the only person there, and he certainly wasn't the cause of my world being turned upside down.

"We know it wasn't your ex-husband. What could someone have been looking for in these sweet-smelling towels?" He cocked a half grin.

Was Lyle trying to ease my fear by being funny? If so, it wasn't working. Anger, almost to the point of rage, wouldn't allow me to find humor in any of the strange things going on in and around my house. Whoever this intruder was had to be stopped. I couldn't stand by as a helpless victim.

"I have no idea what they are looking for, but since this all started after Denise died, I have to assume it has something to do with the murders. It certainly can't be Sheriff Beasley since we all know right where he is tonight. I guess I'd better call Lonnie. He's on duty right now." While I went to the phone, Lyle searched the downstairs bedroom and bath and then went upstairs. With Lonnie on his way, I joined Lyle.

There were a few things out of place on the second floor. The contents of the drawers from my nightstand had been dumped onto the floor except for the handgun I kept there. It was lying on my pillow.

"Let's not touch anything. Douglas will need to check for fingerprints," Lyle said.

"This has really unnerved me. What's going on, Lyle?"

He pulled me into his arms and for a short moment I wanted to melt against him and never leave his warmth, but that was more than wishful thinking on my part. I had to face what was going on and be prepared for any repercussions.

"Someone is watching me. They have to be, or they wouldn't have known about the key being buried out there." I shivered. "It makes my skin crawl."

Lyle rubbed my back, and with his lips next to my hair, he whispered. "I won't let anything happen to you. We'll find out who is doing this."

"It has to be connected to the murders. Neither of us believes Sheriff Beasley killed Jake or Denise. Whoever did it is terrorizing me. But why? Other than witnessing Jake burying Denise, what do

I have to do with any of this?"

"I think it's time you have another talk with Lt. Moore. There's too much happening for it to be a coincidence. He strongly believes Johnston Beasley is guilty, so he may not be receptive to the theory that the murderer is still out there and is focused on you. I agree that they're watching you." Lyle pulled back to look at me. "If they were going to harm you, they could have done that while you were bathing or burying the key. You have no alarm system. If they have access to your house and can come and go as you suspect, they could have killed you anytime they wanted. Considering the way the house was searched, I'd say they were looking for something important, and they need you alive to be able to find it."

At first his words sliced through me, causing me to tremble with fear. The fact that someone thought I had something they wanted, which was the only thing keeping them from killing me, would make anyone shudder. But the fear was quickly replaced with anger and determination to reclaim my life with no interruptions from the evil apparently lurking around me.

Headlights streaked across my bedroom wall. "Lonnie's here," I said and reluctantly moved out of Lyle's embrace.

As I went to answer the door to Lonnie and his partner, Lyle called Lt. Moore. I filled Lonnie in on all the details, and surprisingly, he didn't act like he thought I was losing my mind. He and his partner went about their business of gathering evidence.

Twenty minutes later, Lt. Moore arrived. Lonnie told him they'd only been able to lift a couple of fingerprints. He took imprints of my fingers for later comparison, but he had a strong feeling whoever had come in had used gloves and evidently had a key since there was no forced entry. Even the piece of wood he'd put over the window the day before had not been moved.

When the activities buzzing around my house wound down and everyone except Lyle and Lonnie had left, we stood on the porch in the humid night air.

"Either come home with me or go stay with my mom," Lonnie demanded. "You can't stay out here alone until we find out what's going on."

"I refuse to be run out of my house. Dad's guns are here, and you know he made sure I knew how to use them."

"Evie, most people killed in their homes are shot with their own guns. I'll feel better if you aren't here alone, at least until you can get the locks changed. I think you need to get an alarm system, too."

"I'll stay with her," Lyle said.

Lonnie and I stared at him in surprise.

"Good idea." Lonnie gave Lyle a good-ol'-boy back slap.

"Absolutely not. This is my home, and I have to protect it myself. Leaving or having someone stay here is not an option." As I spoke, I wondered how crazy I truly was to think I should stay alone. Something was wrong, and finding out what could garner deadly consequences.

"Then you're coming home with me if I have to handcuff you

and drag you." Lonnie glared at me in that defiant way he'd used many years ago. Things were going to be his way or else.

"Lonnie's right. You can't stay here alone. And you're right. Leaving your home unprotected is not smart either. I'll sleep here on the couch. I have a gun, too, and a permit to use it."

I knew Lyle was trying to lighten the mood, but the uncertainty of what was happening shook every fiber of my being. I hated feeling dependent on someone else for my safety. I'd gone from the protective shield of my father to that of David, however tarnished his was. But somehow, no matter how much I wanted to be independent, being alive was more important.

After scanning the stern faces of both of my hero lawmen, I gave in. "Okay, Lyle can sleep on the couch for tonight, but tomorrow I'm going to Walmart to get locks." I looked at Lyle. "If you have time, you can help me change them. If not, I'm sure I can do it myself." That one last stab of self-reliance felt good, but not as good as knowing Lyle would be sleeping very close to the back door should anyone decide to come through it.

On Sunday, after a trip to Walmart, Lyle changed the locks on my front and back doors. He made sure the patch job on the front window was secured, and then insisted I prove to him I knew how to safely handle the pistol tucked in my nightstand. Once satisfied, Lyle left, and I was alone to defend my castle. Why and from whom, I had no earthly idea.

First thing Monday morning, I glanced at the calendar and realized my upcoming trip to market in Atlanta was creeping up at the speed of light. I needed to start getting my plans in order. Sandy had a good head for the fashion business and a gift of gab where the patrons were concerned.

"I plan to go to market in Atlanta next week. I'll leave on Thursday and come back on Sunday. I know you've just started, but do you think you could run this place without me during that time?"

"I think so. I'd love to give it a try."

"Denise's aunt worked at McGovern's Department Store for years. I'm going to ask her to help out while I'm gone, especially during the busiest part of the day. You're doing a great job. You're a natural at it. By next week, it will be old hat."

"I love the job so far."

With that settled, I made a run to the bank and to the post office to mail David his now infamous key. I was convinced my selfish act of not sending it had caused my karma to be out of kilter, so I decided to right that wrong and send the key to David, possibly keeping him from sleeping with the fishes.

Also, there was another reason to send the key. What if David told his client where it was, and that client came after me? I definitely didn't need something like that to up my chances of being killed by a deranged person. I had enough of that going on.

After Sandy left, I straightened my desk and came across Denise's watch, which I'd stuck in the top drawer after I'd talked to Mr. Comstock. I would be sure to take it to Atlanta with me and then visit Mr. Barack's store in hopes of finding out who'd bought it. It was a slim chance, one I was sure the authorities would have checked out while they were in possession of the watch. But it was something I needed to do. For Denise and for me.

Something else I felt drawn to was driving to Simmons Road to the very old Lockwood Motel. A need to see the exact place where Denise died seemed to be shoving me in that direction. Slipping into the gravel parking area in front of the cabin-like rooms, I wondered which one of the small structures with an enclosed garage attached was the place where Denise sucked in her last breath of air.

What was her last conscious thought? Did she know she'd never see Merrilee again? Did she think of the baby she carried, a baby she barely had time to feel inside of her? Weighted with so many sad thoughts, I wondered if my heart would ever beat at a normal rate again.

I turned off the Benz's engine. The cool car air quickly began to match the outside temperature–stifling. At that very moment, a tap sounded on my driver's door window, startling me. For an instant, I wondered if my heart would ever beat at *any* rate again.

With his nose literally pressed to the glass, Artimus Lockwood, the legally blind owner of the motel, stared at me through bottle-thick eyeglasses. Rolling down the window, I hoped my voice would not fail me.

"Good afternoon." Trying to smile actually hurt my face.

"What'dya want?" Mr. Lockwood blasted me with stale coffee and cigarette breath.

"Well." *Where to from here?* "I'm here in a legal capacity. I need to look at the room where the Farrell lady was murdered." I nearly choked on the words, but I hoped it did the trick. Quickly flipping through my secondhand law knowledge, I tried to remember the punishment for impersonating an officer. Mr. Lockwood squinted even more, if that was possible.

"I'm with the sheriff's office." My voice squeaked.

"No, you're not. You're Harry Carson's daughter who moved back and opened that store in town selling citified clothes."

"Well, I'm that, too." I made a mental note: *Being legally blind does not mean you're dumb.* "I just wanted to see where Denise died."

"Why didn't you say so?" He started walking across the parking lot in the direction of a middle cabin. I assumed I was to follow, so I did. He pulled a huge ring of thirty or so keys from his pants pocket. I figured this would take a while. To my surprise, the first key he tried opened the door of cabin number six.

"Police finished up a couple of days ago. Said I should call a professional service to come in and clean up." Shoving the door open, Mr. Lockwood stepped aside and motioned me to enter. "It's a mess in there, but go ahead."

I hesitated. By *mess* I imagined he meant blood all over the place. Then I remembered Denise had been struck in the throat. Except for a small amount of blood that oozed from her mouth, her bleeding had all been internal.

"You going in or not?"

"Yes, sir." I started in, but the hot, stale air stopped me. A faint odor, too sickeningly sweet to be fresh, gagged me.

I turned back to Mr. Lockwood, but he was gone. Gold, foam-backed curtains framed each of the two small windows in the room—one window on the front wall and the other directly across from the entrance. Filling the major part of the right side of the room were a door, apparently leading to the enclosed garage, and a king-sized bed. The bedding had been removed. Probably taken into evidence along with a square of carpet missing in front of the back window. Just past a worn chest of drawers, which stood against the left wall, a door opened into the bathroom.

Fingerprint dust covered almost everything, and my mind felt as black and smudged as the room. What happened in that very space that brought about the end of Denise's life? Did the father of her unborn baby fear for his reputation enough to kill them both? How could that be?

Heartsick and nauseated, I leaned out the back window and breathed in the warm, fresh air. Across the alley that ran behind the motel was a solid, wooden privacy fence. A beat-up dumpster filled to overflowing was backed against the fence a little ways from room number six.

I wondered what business was on the other side of the

whitewashed barrier, but it was at least eight feet high and I couldn't see over it. Whatever it was had to have been built during the last twenty years because it wasn't there when I grew up. Long ago, the property was nothing but woods. In my mind's eye I saw Walmart in that general direction, but I couldn't figure out what the fence could be protecting.

Once I turned back to the room, I suddenly recognized that sweet smell hanging repulsively in the air. It was the same honeysuckle scent from the perfume bottle in Denise's keepsake box. A confirmation she had been there and, by all accounts, had died there.

I wasn't sure what I'd thought would come of a visit to the motel, but I left room number six with a crushed spirit and an overwhelming need to vomit. I raced around the cabin to the alley, where I emptied the contents of my stomach.

When normalcy returned, I noticed a tall bucket sitting upside down next to the dumpster. A perfect step to climb and get a look over the privacy fence. Once I'd braved the filth and stench of rotting garbage, I managed to climb on top of the container. From up there, I could see into a storage yard for electrical supplies—light poles, massive wheels of wire, streetlights, and electrical service panels. The equipment stretched out over what I would guesstimate to be about fifteen acres. A long metal building situated at the front part of the fenced area I surmised would be offices and inside storage. I had an end view of a huge sign in front of the building, but the angle kept me from being able to read it.

I assumed the words written on the yard's inventory would tell me the name of the business, but it was too far away. Looking down next to the fence, I spotted a large cardboard box. I could slip over the fence, lower myself to the box, get down, find out the name of the business, then reverse the process and come back to the alley.

With relative ease, I made it over and when my feet made contact with the cardboard, I let go. The box gave way under my feet. There was nothing I could do to stop from crashing through the cardboard and landing squarely on my butt in the dirt.

"Evie, you idiot," I said to myself. "You could have driven a couple of streets over until you found the front of the property." But that would have been too easy.

Quickly, I scrambled to my feet and looked around to see if anyone had seen me. Once I was sure no one had caught my fall, I rubbed my backside, which would surely be bruised by bedtime. The writing on the equipment was inventory numbers, and nothing had the name of the company whose land I was trespassing on.

Finally, deciding it would be safer to drive up the next street until I found that property, I tried to climb back over the fence, but it quickly became apparent that wasn't going to happen. The cardboard box was destroyed with no hope of being used for a boost up and over. Nightfall was coming fast, and being stuck in that storage yard after dark was not an option. I would have to walk to the front of the property and admit I'd broken into their yard. If I wasn't arrested, I'd have to walk all the way around the road and back to my car, which I would estimate to be about a four-mile walk.

"Damn," I said, crossing my arms and leaning my back against the fence. Without warning, the bottom of a section of the fence swung out and with the grace of a lummox I again landed on my ass. Slowly I rose, and on closer examination discovered a piano hinge attached to a four-foot section of the fence, allowing the bottom to swing out into the alley. Unless you knew it was there, it was undetectable when closed. From the alley side, I was able to grab a piece of wood and pull the swinging gate to me and easily walk inside the yard.

I found the whole idea of a secret passage into the alley mystifying. Could someone from that place of business have used it to come to the motel, make his way to room six, and meet a lover? I couldn't wrap my head around all that. Denise supposedly issued an ultimatum to someone at the sheriff's office. I'd have to find out exactly what that place was before I could decide if there could be a connection between the electrical place and the sheriff's office.

Looking at the gate that swung open from the top reminded me of a children's story. Could this little rabbit hole have led someone to the wonderland of the Lockwood Motel? And who could that be?

I ran to my car and drove down Simmons Road to Cassatt Avenue. After turning right, I followed the highway until I came to what had to be the front of the fenced property. From that angle I could plainly read the sign advertising *Neal Lancaster, Electrical Contractor.*

Neal Lancaster had been a year ahead of us in school. His father was an electrician. Apparently, Neal followed in the family business.

By the size of the place, I surmised he was doing well. Did Neal use the hidden opening through his back fence to go to and from the motel room just across the alley? Surely, I wasn't the only person who knew about that hole.

Just to be sure, and while I was still parked in Neal's driveway, I called Lonnie at the sheriff's office. The deputy who answered the phone put me on hold. It was after seven o'clock, and dusk shadowed everything in its path. A light came on from an office inside the large metal building. Through the window I could see a man dressed in a white shirt and khaki slacks. He had a phone to his ear. His back was to me, but I assumed it was Neal. Suddenly he turned and looked out the window directly at me. He continued to talk on the phone, nodding his head.

My cell phone crackled. "Deputy Douglas." Lonnie came on the line.

"Hi, this is Evie. Uh, I was looking around behind Lockwood's Motel. I discovered a hidden gate at the back of Neal Lancaster's place. I'm sure you all know about it, but I thought I'd mention it just in case no one had pursued the possibility of someone going to the motel room through that gate. It would give you something to think about, wouldn't it?" I rambled on with no response from Lonnie.

"Hang on, Evie," he said and clicked me into a dead line.

The man inside the electrical office hung up the phone and raised his hand to wave at me. It was Neal. I offered a slight wave, but because darkness had closed in, I wasn't sure he could see me.

"Evie." Lonnie returned. "Just before you called, I was on the phone with Neal. He has closed-circuit cameras that keep an eye on his inventory in the back storage yard. He called to tell me some woman was snooping around back there and fell over the fence." Lonnie couldn't hide his amusement. "While he was talking to me, you pulled up in his driveway. Since not a lot of people around here drive a silver Mercedes, I asked him to see if it looked like you behind the wheel." Lonnie Douglas busted out laughing.

"Knock it off, Lonnie. I was just trying to help." I meant to sound threatening, but the image of me falling over, and then through, the fence kept me from seriously concentrating on giving the deputy a piece of my mind.

Neal had turned off the light in his office. I assumed he'd be coming outside at any moment. I didn't want to talk to him. I wanted to talk to Lonnie and see what they knew about Neal's easy access to the alley. I started the car before Neal came outside, and I pulled onto the highway.

"Okay, so you knew about the gate. Does that mean you questioned Neal and eliminated him as a suspect?"

"Evie, the investigation was taken away from Hyattville Sheriff's Office when Johnston Beasley was only a suspect. We have no say in any of it now that he's been arrested, but I do have the right to tell you to keep your nose out of the investigation. Let the state boys do their job. You will either screw up evidence or end up getting killed, and I don't want either of those things to happen."

"You don't believe Beasley is guilty either, do you?"

"Not for a moment. Evie, you can rest assured, I'm checking out every lead in an unofficial capacity. I want Johnston released and back on the job helping to find the real killer as soon as possible."

"Can you tell me what you found that eliminates Neal as a suspect?"

"That opening has been there for years. His heavy electrical supplies are delivered back there. The gate swings out and up because it's attached by a piano hinge. It's high enough for the truck to back up to the hole in the fence, and the gate then rests on top of the truck. Neal's people use a forklift to unload the supplies, but when it's closed no one else knows it's there. Especially mischievous kids who think it's fun to get into places like that and vandalize anything in their wake."

"And you didn't find any evidence that placed Neal in that room, like fingerprints?"

"His fingerprints are in that room and every other room at the motel because he rewired the whole place less than a year ago. I don't need to tell you Lockwood isn't the cleanest guy in town, so those rooms probably haven't had a good cleaning in a while. Vacuuming and hopefully changing the sheets are the best we can hope for if you rent a room there. Any cleaning heavy enough to wipe away fingerprints is totally out of the question. Come to think of it, you'd be hard pressed to find a place in town that didn't have Neal's fingerprints in it. He's a busy contractor."

"Did he have an alibi for the time of the murder?"

"A good one. The medical examiner determined Denise was

killed between two and four in the afternoon. Neal was doing some electrical work at the courthouse. Everyone has to sign in to get past the front desk. He'd gone to lunch early, but was back at work around 12:15.

"I'm not usually here during the day, but a couple of the guys had to testify in court so I pulled a double shift that day to pick up the slack. I know for a fact that Neal was here because he was on a deadline to finish the job, so he worked alongside his men all afternoon. As a matter of fact, he hadn't been gone very long when you called to report the murder."

"You might want to suggest to Neal that he move the dumpster away from his fence. If I can get in back there, kids would have no problem." I started to hang up but quickly added, "I better not see that video of me falling over that fence splashed on YouTube, or you'll have another murder to handle." I flipped the phone shut so I wouldn't have to hear Lonnie heehawing like a jackass, and I broke the speed limit all the way home.

That evening, when I got home, I did laundry, cleaned out the refrigerator, and vacuumed the whole upstairs. While dusting the living room furniture, I noticed my telephone message light was blinking. I checked the caller ID to see who had called. It was from David's home number. As much as I didn't want to talk to him, I was curious what he wanted. I debated with myself for several minutes, but in the end, I decided to listen to it. Dropping into the black leather desk chair, I pushed the *play* button.

You can imagine my surprise when I heard a woman's voice on the other end of the line instead of the husky, haughty voice of my ex-husband.

"Evie, this is Katy Beard. I need to know if David is there with you. Please give me a call back. I'm at David's apartment. Please call your old number."

Sounded like there was trouble in David's paradise. Sadly, I didn't want to know anything about it. I opted not to return the call and went to bed. For the first time in a long time, I slept soundly.

The next morning, after I'd eaten my peanut butter toast and enjoyed a cup of coffee, I carried the trash to the can outside the back door. Midnight followed me out and, after squeezing through the partially opened gate, made a mad dash across the meadow. Shading my eyes against the bright sunlight, I watched him dart into the trees where Denise had been buried.

"Midnight," I called, but he'd disappeared.

Since the night he'd shown up on my porch, he'd stuck very close to the house. During the past week, he even looked too comfortable in front of the fireplace for me to put him outside while I was at work. So, after I put a litter box in the laundry room, I started leaving him inside.

Glancing at my watch, I realized it was only a few minutes before I'd have to leave for work. Suddenly, late or not, I felt the need to protect the cat, to make him come back. Somehow he'd made the trip from Jake's house to mine. I didn't want him to go back to his old home, because I knew no one waited there for him. On the other side of that thought came the awareness that I'd be losing another friend.

"Here, kitty, kitty, kitty," I called as I walked to the gate and started following a path of trampled grass that led across the meadow. I'd made the first swath through there the day I'd walked from my house to the old tree house.

The day Denise died.

For several days after that, the authorities made the pathway more prominent. Since Midnight was forcing me to chase him, I was glad the trail was still there. At the edge of the stand of trees, I stopped, allowing the crushing sadness to level out to a bearable state.

"Midnight?" I stepped into the shade of the stand of trees and saw the cat coming out of a thicket. For a second, he looked surprised to see me. Then he sat and licked his front paw.

"Did you find something to eat in there, you silly boy?" I moved in his direction.

Slowly he edged his way to the path that led through the woods to Miner's Road. I followed like an obedient cat owner. He stopped and looked into the underbrush to his left. I took advantage of the lull in movement to make a quick lunge at him.

But then my feet became tangled in a stray grapevine sending me headfirst into God only knew what. Snakes, spiders, varmints quickly sprang to mind. Sharp palmettos sliced my cheek; briars jabbed my hands. Midnight, who had preceded me into the shrubbery, made a quick getaway, pouncing on my back as he made his escape. The cat left me sprawled in barbed bushes and gagging from the most horrible stench I'd ever smelled. Evidently, one of the aforementioned critters had crawled into the area and died. I could only hope that wasn't what Midnight had been feasting on. I had to get out of there before I puked.

With absolutely no grace whatsoever, I managed to get to my feet. A quick touch of my left cheek proved what I'd feared—my face was bleeding. Looking around for the best route of retreat, I stepped over a palmetto bush onto a narrow strip of open, level land. Releasing a string of blue words into the hot morning air, I plainly described my feelings for the stupid cat and for the bad karma that section of my land seemed to evoke.

I'd taken only two steps when my knees went to jelly. The threat of vomiting became imminent. Protruding from beneath a low scrub oak lay the body of a man. Flies buzzed the corpse in a hum that painfully pierced my ears. Suddenly, the truth of what I was looking at hit me with a staggering force.

Horrified by the unfathomable sight, I gaped into the filmy, dead eyes of David.

CHAPTER 9

I VIVIDLY REMEMBERED SCREAMING AND SCREAMING AND SCREAMING, but other than that my next rational thought came when I woke up in a bed in a strange room. Kitty Douglas stood over me, and Lonnie's mom was next to her.

"How are you feeling, sweetheart?" Mrs. Douglas asked.

"Like I've been hit by a—" I tried to sit up, but my body wasn't cooperating. "What happened to me?"

Kitty pulled a chair beside the bed and then sat. "Do you remember anything?"

About what? I almost asked, but the fog in my brain cleared, and the unthinkable memories flooded in with the force of water through a broken dam.

"David?" His name barely escaped from my parched throat.

The despair on Kitty's face told me all I needed to know. She pulled me into her arms and held me tightly while Mrs. Douglas sat on the bed and held us both.

"He's dead, Evie," she whispered in a tone obviously intensified by sadness and concern.

There in the two women's arms, I tried to cry, but no tears would come. My eyes hurt. When I blinked it felt like they were full of dry, hot sand. I pulled free and touched my left cheek. Covered by some sort of bandage, my flesh hurt.

"Please. What happened?" I'd finally realized I was in Goldie Douglas's upstairs guest room. "How did I get here?" I pleaded.

Mrs. Douglas kissed my forehead. "I'll go make tea. Kitty, tell Evie all you can."

I needed to know, but with the way my head hurt, I couldn't concentrate. Inside it, things were fuzzy except for the clear image of David lying on the hard ground, eyes open, mouth looking ready to speak. Someone who didn't know him would have missed the terror etched on his face, but I didn't. As I remembered that look, my heart threatened to crumble.

Kitty took my hands. "After you found your ex in the woods, you ran back to your house and called Lonnie. When he arrived, he found you pacing the yard. You were screaming hysterically." She rubbed her thumb over my skin. "The paramedics had been dispatched at the same time as Lonnie. From what he said, you were really out of it."

I stared at her lips, watching them move, listening to her words, but none of it made any sense. David was dead. Murdered.

"Don't feel bad," Kitty said, giving my hands a squeeze. "I would have been out of it, too. Finding a dead body on my property, not to mention my ex-husband's. Anyway, you flipped out and had to be sedated."

As the horrifying image of David lying on his back with a hole in his chest continued to burn into my mind, I couldn't keep the tears from blurring my vision, nor could I keep the mournful whimper from escaping my throat.

Kitty moved next to me on the bed and put her arms around me. "You're going to be just fine, Evie."

While she held me, I cried like a baby. It was then that I understood why my eyes felt like sandpaper. Evidently, even though I'd been drugged, it hadn't kept me from shedding tears. By the feel of my face and eyes, I knew I'd cried a lot.

"How did I get here?" I asked.

"Lonnie called me, and by the time I got there, you were asleep. We decided to bring you here until the medicine wore off. Mama Douglas and I have been by your side ever since."

"Thank you, Kitty." At one time in my life, I would never have believed I'd be happy to wake up to find Kitty taking care of me. "How long have I been here?"

"It's 2:15 right now, and you've been here since about nine o' clock yesterday morning. About thirty hours."

My heart sank even further. I'd missed a whole day. What about the boutique? "Do you know anything about the Victorian

Sampler? Did Sandy open it?"

"Sure, Trooper Dickerson called her, and she met him at your house. You gave her the key and told her the alarm code to get into the shop."

"Lyle was there?" I couldn't remember any of that. Being sedated by the EMTs. Lyle and Sandy being there. None of it came back to me. Only the picture of David, dead and decaying, filled my mind's eye. My stomach churned.

"Sure. Trooper Dickerson helped us get you here. He's been by several times since then. He's quite a hunk." Kitty left the room and quickly returned with a damp cloth.

Mrs. Douglas brought a tray with tea and an egg sandwich. "Here you go. You need to eat to keep up your strength." She set the tray in my lap.

Surprisingly, I was hungry. While I ate, Kitty called Lonnie to let him know I was awake.

"Lt. Moore from the state police will be here shortly to ask you some questions," Kitty said. "Do you have any idea who would have killed your ex-husband or what he was doing here in Hyattville? Doesn't he live in Chicago?"

"Yes, he does . . . did." Sadness constricted my throat, and I had to swallow hard to force down the food I'd been chewing. "And I know why he was here, and I also know who could have killed him."

Kitty rushed to my side. "Who?"

No way was I going to tell Kitty what I suspected had happened to David. That would be like taking an ad out in the newspaper. I would tell it all to Lt. Moore, and he could decide what everyone else should know. "I'd better wait until the police get here." I took another bite of my sandwich. Kitty let the subject drop.

The news that I'd awakened must have been announced as an APB. Officers from several branches of law enforcement converged on Goldie Douglas's house. Lonnie from the Hyattville Sheriff's Office, Lt. Moore from the state police, and a new face from the Georgia Bureau of Investigation.

Lonnie and Lt. Moore were concerned about my physical and mental state. Cabler from the GBI, however, was interested in "just the facts." Had it not been such a dire situation, I would have found his no-nonsense stance amusing. Instead, I found it frightening.

"I have a few questions for Mrs. Holmes," Cabler said to Kitty and Lonnie's mom.

"I no longer use Holmes. My name is Evie Carson," I corrected.

"Duly noted." While he scribbled on a yellow legal pad, everyone except he and Lt. Moore left the room. "I know you've had quite a shock, but I need to ask you a few questions." Cabler paused, and I wasn't sure what he wanted me to say. "Will that be okay with you?"

I had the strong feeling that if I said no he'd take me to the police station and make me answer anyway. "Ask me anything you'd like." Since I'd basically blacked out after finding David dead in the bushes, I couldn't imagine what Agent Cabler thought I could tell him.

"That must have been quite a shock when you found Mr. Holmes."

I nodded.

"Do you usually go for an early morning walk?" Cabler's gaze never left me.

The question struck me so oddly that I couldn't form an answer. I never took a morning walk. Time didn't permit it. I stared at the GBI agent until I was sure he thought I was a nutcase. "I don't understand," I admitted.

"I'm sure you're still a little groggy from the sedative. Why were you in the woods early yesterday morning? Is that a better way to word it?"

"When I took the trash out, my cat, actually it's Jake's cat, no, I guess it's my cat now." I was rambling, and I knew it. Too much haze inside my brain.

"Who the cat belongs to—is that pertinent as to why you were in the woods?"

"No, it isn't. Midnight sprinted across the pasture, and I didn't want to leave him out there. I followed him into the clearing where my friend had been buried. When I tried to catch the cat, I fell into the thicket, and that's where I saw David." A wave of nausea pounded inside my stomach. "I guess I immediately went into shock, because I don't remember anything until I woke up here a short time ago."

"I can understand that. Of course, you had recently divorced Mr. Holmes. Can you tell me exactly why your marriage ended?"

"Infidelity." My answer was quick and to the point.

"On his part?"

"Yes."

"That's too bad. I'm sure you must have had a lot of hatred for him."

"No. Disappointment, disillusionment, maybe even apathy, but never hatred."

"Not even a little?"

"Please don't try to put words in my mouth." I glanced at the wedding band on his finger. "How would you feel if you discovered your wife has been unfaithful?"

"I'd be mad as hell."

"Oh, I was mad for a while, but let me ask you, would that be a reason to lure your cheating wife over a thousand miles, and then kill her and stick her in your backyard?" The sharp tone of my voice didn't seem to faze him in the least.

Agent Cabler remained stoic. "Ms. Carson, I have a job to do. I need to ask the right questions and keep asking them until I find out what happened to Mr. Holmes. At this point, I'm only interviewing you."

"Do I need an attorney?" As the words left my mouth, a sharp jab of loss assaulted my heart. My attorney was dead. My ex-husband, the man I'd lived with and loved for fifteen years, was dead. I wouldn't even know who to turn to for legal help in Hyattville.

"You tell me." Cabler's sharp tone sent a chill down my spine.

Lt. Moore stepped closer. "Evie, there are questions we need answers to. I can't advise you whether you need an attorney or not. So you decide, but we need your help, and we need it as quickly as possible."

"I understand."

Lt. Moore's low, gentle voice eased my raised hackles.

I looked back at Cabler. "Ask me whatever you want to."

And ask he did. I thought he'd never run out of questions. My brain was still foggy, and I'm sure he asked the same question three different ways.

"I read the police report from last Friday. You say your ex-husband broke into your house looking for a key."

I nodded.

"Did he find it?"

"No, I had it with me."

"I also understand you buried the key only to have it show up on your kitchen table."

He had all the information. Why was he belaboring it?

"That's correct, and yesterday I put it in an envelope and mailed it to David's office in Chicago."

At long last he got around to the question I would have asked first.

"Who do you think killed your ex?" By this time, the agent had taken a seat on a nearby chair. Since he no longer towered over me, he'd lost some of his intimidating power. My thoughts took more sensible paths.

"I think it was the mob." Okay, it may not have made sense to others, but it did to me.

My answer propelled Agent Cabler to his feet. "Is that a feeble attempt at humor, or has your sedation not completely worn off?"

"No to both questions. David had a client who had mob

connections. When the client was sent to prison for a few years, he gave David a large sum of money to keep until he was released. The con is either due to be released or is already out, and I had the only key to the safe deposit box where the money is stashed." That made enough sense to me that I could even speculate about how the scenario may have played out. "Evidently, they followed David to my house thinking that was where the money was. When he couldn't tell him where it was, they forced him to go out into the woods with them, and then they shot him."

"Do you really believe an organization like the mob would come to a backwoods town to kill Holmes because he had a few thousand dollars of theirs?"

"That makes more sense than my killing him because he did me wrong. We were separated for almost a year. Our divorce has been final for months. Too much water under that dam for me to even wish David any harm."

"During our search of your home, we found a gun with the same caliber as the one used to kill Holmes."

"All the guns there belonged to my dad. Which one was it?"

"The .38 in a nightstand next to your bed."

"I haven't even touched it since Trooper Dickerson and I had target practice on Sunday afternoon. He wanted to be sure I could use it to defend myself if the need arose."

"So you recently used the pistol?"

"Yes. Lyle was with me when I did."

Cabler scribbled notes onto his pad. For a while, I wondered if he was writing a book. Finally, he stopped and looked at me. "I guess that's all I have for now. Where will I be able to find you if I need to ask more questions?"

"I'll let you know where she'll be once that's decided." Lyle's sharp voice caught us all off guard.

He rushed to my bedside. "Are you feeling better?"

Now that he had arrived, I felt much better. "I'm fine. I'd really like to get up from here."

Lyle glanced in Agent Cabler's direction.

"I just told her I was through for now."

"Good. Lt. Moore will know how to get a hold of me. I'll know where Ms. Carson is. Until we catch the maniac who's killing off people around here, Evie needs to be kept in a place where we're sure she's safe."

"By the way, Ms. Carson," Agent Cabler put his pen into his breast pocket. "I'll take your theory about the mob under advisement, but I doubt seriously they would be involved."

I started to ask why, but he proceeded rapidly into his professional summation, leaving me to stare at him bewildered.

"The mob would not go to such lengths to take out an arrogant attorney for a small amount of change. If, however, it turned out to be more money than you know about and they did follow Holmes from Chicago, they would have laid him facedown on the ground and shot him in the back of the head. One nice, clean shot. They wouldn't have shot him while he stared them in the face. Only a heartless person who didn't care how they killed him would do that. It would have been someone who just wanted him dead.

"Also, the mob wouldn't have killed him without getting their money. Nor would they have taken him into the woods. Had they caught up with him after he broke into your house, they would have whacked him right there with no regard to blood splattering on your beautiful hardwood floor and furniture." As he left the room, he called over his shoulder, "I'll be in touch."

The entire next week felt like an out-of-body experience. Lyle insisted I couldn't go home until the person responsible for the murders had been captured. He didn't have to persuade me. I was scared beyond anything I'd ever known. Since Mrs. Douglas's house was only a few blocks from the Victorian Sampler, and even closer to the police station, everyone agreed that would be the best place for me to stay for a while.

My stay with Mrs. Douglas brought warm reminders of my parents. They and Lonnie's parents were very close.

"You know, Evie," Goldie Douglas said, pouring a mug full of hot coffee and handing it to me, "I have a large collection of pictures in the attic of your mom and dad and all of us on the summer vacations we took together each summer for about ten years. Do you remember them?"

"Very much so." The memories warmed me even more than the hot coffee I sipped.

"Bring your cup with you." She motioned for me to come with her. With great anticipation, I followed her to the end of the upstairs hallway, where she opened a desk drawer and removed a sawed-off broom with a cup hook screwed in the end. Reaching to the ceiling, she used the stick to latch onto an opening to the attic. She pulled it down and unfolded a ladder.

"Lonnie and I used to sneak up there while the adults were playing canasta." I giggled like a child. That was another happy memory.

Mrs. Douglas laughed, too. "I remember. Watch your step." She led the way up the ladder.

Heat boiled from the unfinished rafters. Dust covered everything. Through openings between the slats in the vent windows at each end of the attic, dust particles danced in the sunlight. Baby furniture sat abandoned against a wall.

"That was for Lonnie and Kitty's baby who died at birth. It's never been used."

"That was so sad." I had called when it happened and vividly heard the devastation in Lonnie's voice. My heart had broken for my friend, who would have made a great father. "When I called them," I said to Mrs. Douglas, "I talked to Lonnie for a few minutes, but he broke down, and then Kitty took the phone. I didn't really know what to say to either of them."

"That kind of hurt can't be helped. I'm sure they were both glad you called. They both handled their grief in different ways. Lonnie was a mess for a long time after that. I don't remember ever seeing Kitty cry. I think she was afraid if she fell apart, it would be the end of Lonnie for sure." Mrs. Douglas opened the lid to one of several steamer trunks. She lifted an album from the top of the pile, dusted it with a piece of material also stacked in the trunk. "Here." She handed the album to me. "This one is full of pictures of your parents. I'd like you to have it."

I took it and opened to a random page. Sure enough, there were pictures of all six of us—Lonnie, me, Mom, Dad, and Mr. and Mrs. Douglas. What fond memories each of the photos evoked. Memories I needed more than I realized. A lone tear dropped onto the album.

Mrs. Douglas touched my arm. "Come on, honey. It's too hot up here."

I climbed back down the ladder, all the while clutching the special photo collection to my heart.

Eight days after I'd found David dead, the authorities released his body and he was sent home to his parents, who'd been waiting to lay their only son to rest. On Thursday, Lyle and I flew to Chicago to attend David's funeral. Needlessly, I'd worried about how I would be received. His family graciously welcomed me and Lyle. The one who appeared to be uncomfortable was Katy Beard, David's lover.

She attended the service but didn't go to the gravesite. Nor did she go the Holmes's house afterwards. There, Matthew Holmes asked Lyle if they had any leads on his son's killer. Lyle answered him honestly. David's dad tried to hold back a sob but failed. My heart broke into a million pieces for the man who had worshiped his son. He must have realized what I was thinking. He smiled and put his arms around me.

"I love you, Evie," he whispered. "I thank you for the happiness you brought my son, and I'm so sorry for the way he hurt you."

I couldn't answer. I held the elderly man tightly. At that tender moment, we were joined by David's mother. Even though she didn't say it, I knew she felt the same way. I truly wanted to tell them how much I cherished them, but right then, the words wouldn't come.

During the short day and a half we were in Chicago, everyone around us assumed Lyle was an officer of the law sent to keep me safe. That wasn't entirely true. I wanted him at my side. He comforted me. So when he'd volunteered to go with me, I'd jumped at the chance.

Once Lyle and I returned to Hyattville, I threw myself into my work, catching up on bookkeeping, paying bills, ordering new inventory, and getting ready for my trip to market. Neither Lyle nor Lonnie thought it a good idea for me to make the trip to Atlanta alone.

For the two weeks following David's death, someone had been at my side almost every minute. The authorities didn't take seriously my theory that he was killed by the mob, yet they couldn't exactly lump his demise in with that of Denise and Jake, because the investigators were convinced Sheriff Beasley was responsible for their murders. Since the sheriff was being closely monitored during the time of David's death, any hope of connecting the three murders to one killer was splintered into a thousand pieces.

Yet, who could have done it became the hot topic. Every conversation I had with anyone centered on the murders. Debates were heard all over town: Was Beasley innocent or guilty, and what did that big-time lawyer's death have to do with the other two murders?

By the time I was ready to leave for Atlanta, I craved solitude. Just to be alone and to never have to talk about, think about, or see another dead body for as long as I lived would be wonderful. But I knew that wasn't going to happen. All three of the deaths were too close to me. How could I not think about them? Somehow I managed to put my life back on track and got back to the things that were important to me—the Victorian Sampler and my promise to my deceased friend, Denise, that I would do whatever I could to help put her murderer away.

Two items I'd found in the mahogany box continued to weigh heavily on my mind. Once I got to Atlanta, besides going to market, I would do my own investigation into the roots of those two items. One thing I would do was go to Barack Jewelers to see if by some remote chance Mr. Barack knew who had purchased the watch found in Denise's keepsake box. Also, I would go to Garnet's

Emporium to smell firsthand the honeysuckle perfume. I had no real expectations of what that visit would do, but doing anything was better than doing nothing.

The night before my long-awaited trip, I insisted on going home so I could pack and be ready to leave as soon as the sun came up. Lyle insisted on staying with me. Admittedly, I was nervous about being in my house for the first time in over two weeks and since a third murder had been committed. So it was agreed that Lyle would sleep on my sofa, and I would finally get to sleep in my own bed again.

I finished packing my things and gathered blankets and pillows and stacked them on the sofa for Lyle.

I told him, "Good night," and was about to climb the stairs when he stopped me and pulled me into his arms.

As his lips lightly touched my ear, he whispered, "I'd give anything to be able to take away all the sadness you've been suffering through since Denise died."

He pulled back just enough to look at me. As his gaze searched my face, his eyes sparked in the same way they did when he looked at the people he loved. Sandy. Scotty. Could he possibly love me, too? Was that something I wanted? My emotions were too raw to even think like that, but as my pulse quickened I wasn't sure I could do much about it.

"I don't know what I'd do if anything happened to you." His words seemed to catch in his throat, but I felt them deep inside.

"You are so caring. I feel safe and very lucky to have you here with me."

He kissed me slowly and held me for just another instant, and then he whispered, "Good night, sweetheart."

"Good night." I had already started climbing the stairs before I took a deep breath. There wasn't a doubt in my mind that I loved Lyle Dickerson. I felt he loved me, too.

Despite the excitement of discovering Lyle's feelings for me, sheer exhaustion made falling asleep easy. Staying that way took more effort. I was slammed hard by a horrible nightmare. It started with Denise begging me to find her killer. Then Jake innocently smiling while he sat in the front seat of his truck. Then David's terror-glazed eyes looking into mine. I awoke paralyzed with fear. I thought I'd heard someone calling my name.

I whispered into the blackness of my bedroom, "Daddy? Grandma Carson?" Of course, neither answered, but how I wished they could. I turned on the lamp, and although I was absolutely alone, one of my grandmother's wise sayings came to me. *Drink warm milk when sleep won't come. Say "pretty please," and I'll make you some.*

I scrambled free from the twisted covers and placed my bare feet on the cold floor. Some warm milk might steady my shaking hands and help alleviate some of the frightening images fogging my brain. Still barefooted and with my gown clinging to my sweat-soaked body, I crept down the stairs.

Moonlight, streaking through cracks in the curtains, lit my familiar path from the stairs to the kitchen. Leaving the refrigerator door open to cast enough light for me to see, I poured milk into a small pan and then set it on the stove.

Lyle's breathing, tranquil and balanced, floated to me from the next room but did nothing to calm me. My lips still burned from his good night kiss. Was I allowing that kiss to mean more than it really did? Lyle was there in my home, sleeping on my sofa, for one reason—to keep me from harm. He hadn't said he loved me, yet I'd allowed myself to believe I'd seen it in his gaze. How crazy was that? My heart waged a battle against my brain. I was caught in a tug of war of he-loves-me, he-loves-me-not.

I stepped to the doorway and studied him closely. The dim light behind me cast seductive shadows in all the right, or wrong, places across Lyle's bare chest. With his arm flung over his eyes, little of his face could be seen. My gaze halted on his lips, slightly parted and inviting. A white sheet, draped low across his hips, covered the lower portion of his body. My heart lurched. The milk boiled over. Loud sizzling and the smell of burnt milk brought me back from a place I shouldn't have ventured.

My distant punishment for watching Lyle as he slept would be having to clean the burnt milk from under the burner in the morning. My immediate punishment would be trying to go back to sleep with images of Lyle's perfect body engraved in my mind.

I poured the remaining hot milk into a mug, closed the refrigerator door, and tiptoed into the living room.

"Can't sleep?" Lyle's husky whisper penetrated the darkness.

I jumped guiltily. "I slept a little. I didn't mean to wake you."

"I'm glad you did."

I heard rustling in the dark, and then Lyle switched on the lamp next to the sofa. Soft light bathed the room. The sheet slipped away revealing bare feet and unsnapped jeans. From a sitting position, Lyle looked me over from the hem of my long, cotton nightgown upward, stopping only a second at my breasts and then continuing until our gazes locked. My cheeks warmed, not from uneasiness, but from desire.

I wanted Lyle, and if the invitation in his eyes meant anything, I would no longer need the warm milk.

With only one thought on my mind, I joined him on the sofa. Immediately I sank against him. His arm came around me and pulled me close, and I enjoyed the most natural feeling of being where I belonged. Nestled against him, I pressed my lips to the pulsing hollow of his neck. I felt, more than heard, the muted rumble of his groan. He gently pulled back to face me. First he kissed the tip of my nose, then my eyes, and finally my lips. As shock waves exploded through my body, my lips demanded the strong hardness of his.

We separated slightly. He whispered, "You taste so sweet and warm." His voice, strong and smooth like polished oak, heightened my already swirling senses.

He traced the outline of my jaw with his fingertip. I relished his touch. So light, so feathery, so . . . tender. Had I imagined it? Opening my eyes, I gazed into his, which glistened with a look I couldn't identify. Lust? Desire? Love? I hoped for all three.

Being with Lyle gave me a tremendous rush of passionate energy that I'd never felt with David. With that thought, I pulled away from Lyle's embrace. He slid his hands along both of my arms, around my back, and along my spine. His touch, almost unbearable in its tenderness, melted all doubts.

My fingers trailed over his hard stomach to the opening of his jeans already unsnapped, and then along the bulge pressing willfully against the restraint of the zipper. I shook with urgency.

Lyle rose from the sofa, pulling me with him. He grasped the hem of my nightgown, and in one swift movement, he pulled it over my head and tossed it aside. In a flash, he lifted me into the cradle of his arms and climbed the stairs.

The light beside my bed shone dimly. Lyle placed my nude body where I had earlier lain fighting fitful sleep and horrendous nightmares. Those harsh feelings were gone, replaced with sensuality and the security of Lyle's embrace. He slipped from his jeans and joined me under the covers.

We began to explore each other's body. His touch burned the flesh of my breast, tender with desire. Gently rolling my nipple between his thumb and forefinger, his mouth alternated between nibbles and feather kisses along the side of my neck. I sucked in a sharp breath and held it.

"Breathe," Lyle urged.

"I'm afraid that if I do, I'll wake up and you'll be gone."

"I'm not going anywhere. This is where I want to be forever."

"Me, too." Everything felt so right. So perfect.

I wanted to feel the moist heat of his skin, to taste the delicious sweetness. I rained light kisses across his shoulders and started down his chest. "Stop," he groaned. Grabbing my wrist, he pulled me to him until we were face-to-face. "Slow. I want this night to last." His soft breath brushed my cheek. As he caressed every inch of my body, I wilted under the movement of his hands. Low groans floated from my lips, carrying his name.

"Lyle."

When his whisper touch became demanding, I met his fervor with equal enthusiasm. I pulled him to me with an aching need for another deep kiss. Willingly, his lips covered mine, his tongue caressed my mouth.

The love I already felt for him intensified. I couldn't get enough of him. I wanted to possess him—his heart, his mind, his body, and his soul.

"I need you," I cried, nudging him to move closer. He rose above me.

"I love you, Evie," he whispered.

My heart jolted. His hands slid under my hips, urging me to lift to him. I yielded totally and completely. As Lyle lowered himself to me, our bodies instinctively became one. We matched each other's movement, breath for breath, passion for passion.

"I love you, Lyle." The words came easily and honestly. The warm wetness of a tear rolled across my cheek and into my hair. To this day, I don't know if it was mine or his.

CHAPTER 10

LUNCHTIME IN THE BUSINESS DISTRICT OF ATLANTA FOUND me making my way along a very busy street. After driving around for about ten minutes, I finally found an empty space four blocks away and across a heavily traveled street from my destination. I got out of the car and joined the masses of people hurrying past me, jostling me as if I were a rag doll. I probably could have found a better time to visit Garnet's Emporium, but once I'd left the hotel, I wasn't about to turn back.

Delivery trucks inched into alleys, blocking crosswalks, adding exhaust fumes to the already sweltering air. All in all, a definite contrast to the laid-back snail's pace of Hyattville.

With the thought of my hometown, Lyle also came to mind. Just before sunup that morning, I'd awakened in his warm and protective arms. Heat radiated through my body. Not from the glowing sun and scorching sidewalks, but from the sudden urge to be with

Lyle. Unfortunately, that would have to wait. I would be home the next afternoon. Until then, I'd take care of business for the boutique and for Denise.

Door chimes announced my arrival at Garnet's. The mix of many fragrances and burning incense attacked my nostrils and burned my eyes. Maybe I'd have to rethink the idea of selling several perfumes in my shop if they were this strong and overwhelming.

It quickly became apparent that the unusual store sold more than perfume. A small, round table layered with multicolored scarves filled a corner. In the center of the table sat a crystal ball. I thought that was something they only used in movies.

Through long, hanging, red beads, a woman entered from a back room. She smiled widely, her lips red with bright lipstick. She pushed her raspberry red hair back from her face, every finger glorified with showy garnet or ruby rings. As she stepped closer, I could see her eyelids heavily striped with several shades of blue and green eye shadow. The woman's earlobes sported two different kinds of earrings—one large, dangling hoop and one ruby stud.

That was enough to keep me from ordering more than one fragrance to carry in the Victorian Sampler. Evidently, the heady scents seeped into the brain and kept those affected from seeing into a mirror.

Once she was behind the counter, she extended her hand. "I'm Garnet Windsor. I own this shop. May I help you?"

I took her hand. "My name is Evie Carson. I own a boutique in Hyattville. I may be interested in carrying some of your special perfumes." I reached into my purse, pulled out the bottle I'd found in Denise's keepsake box, and held it out to the lady. "Do you sell this perfume here?"

She took it and studied it. "Yes, that's a potion I make myself. Would you like me to mix some for you?"

"No." I'm sure I said that a little too quickly. "I'm curious about this particular bottle. Do you have lot numbers that might tell you when this batch was made or for whom?"

"Sometimes I mix up a brew for a certain customer, but then I fill several bottles and sell it through the shop. I won't be able to tell you for sure who bought it, but I can tell you when the batch was mixed."

The woman disappeared through the beads, but was gone only a few minutes before she returned waving a 3x5 card. "I found it." She appeared proud of the fact. "I'm really bad about not putting these back where they belong." She smiled, and for the first time, I noticed a small red stone in the middle of one of her front teeth. I ran my tongue over my own teeth and wondered if that hurt.

"Let's see. I call it *Ray de Miel*, A Touch of Honey. There is a funny story about this particular cologne." Garnet looked at me for a sign I was interested in hearing the story. If she only knew how badly I wanted to know everything about the fragrance.

"I'd love to hear it—if you have time, that is."

A smile graced her lips, and I knew she was more than excited to tell me. "About a year ago, a man and woman came in because the woman wanted me to read tarot cards for her. While we were doing that, her husband looked over a brochure that explained my perfumery mixology, and he decided he wanted me to mix a special fragrance just for his wife. Honeysuckle was her favorite scent. I mixed some samples. She picked the one she liked, and then they went shopping while I mixed a batch for them."

By that time her grin was so wide, her bright red lips hid a large portion of her face. And for some strange reason, I was smiling along with her even though I hadn't found anything funny about her story so far.

"About an hour later, the man returned to pick up his specially made bottle of *Ray de Miel.* When he saw I had made two extra bottles, he said he wanted those, too. I was a little disappointed because I thought it was one of my best concoctions in a long time, and I hoped to have some left to use as a sample.

"You'll never guess why he wanted so much." As she talked, she toyed with a rhinestone choker surrounding her ample neck. Red rhinestones, of course.

"Okay, I'm in for a penny. Why?" My gaze darted from her hair, to her neck, to her teeth, and then gave a quick once-over of her tropical parrot muumuu. She was so colorful, she hurt my eyes.

"It seems Mr. Casanova wanted extra perfume so he could give them to his girlfriends, and I emphasize *girlfriends*, as in more than one." She winked knowingly. "That way they could wear the same fragrance as his wife, and she wouldn't be able to detect he'd been with another woman." Garnet burst into a full belly laugh.

"Do you think he was joking?"

"No. I just think he was a jerk. Is that man a dirty, low-down snake or what?"

I didn't know whether to laugh or cry. My mind whirled with the meaning of it all. Since Denise had never remarried, she would have been the girlfriend who was ultimately a recipient of perfume made to fool the wife of a cheating husband.

"Do you know who the man was?"

"No, I never saw him again. My card does have a date on it. May 23 of last year, but unless I shipped some, I wouldn't have a name. Is that important?"

It could have been very important, but I didn't want to get into that with Garnet. "No, it isn't." Sticking my hand in my skirt pocket, I touched the watch and remembered I still had that errand to run. "I thank you for your time." I extended my hand. When she took it, static electricity buzzed up my arm. I started to pull away, but she clutched my hand with both of hers. Her deep, penetrating stare set off alarm bells in my head.

Her behavior changed so drastically I thought maybe she was upset because I hadn't placed an order for my boutique, but at the moment, I was too uncomfortable with her actions to make a decision.

"Is something wrong?" I asked, my throat parched from the dry, nauseating air in the small store.

"Do you believe in psychics?" Her grip tightened.

No one had ever asked me that question before. Certainly not the crowd David hung around with. Remembering he'd been murdered chilled me. I visibly shivered.

"It's okay if you don't. Not everyone does, but I am a psychic. Your life has been upside down lately. I hate to tell you this, but I feel I must. You're walking a dangerous path. You are delving into things that should be left for the authorities. Each step you take puts you deeper in harm's way."

I pulled free from Garnet's painful grasp. Disturbed by her haunting predictions, I had to ask, "Where is the danger coming from? Who is responsible for it?"

"I don't know. That's all I can tell you, but I feel it to the depth of my soul . . . and yours. You must be careful and always look over your shoulder everywhere you go." She spoke slowly, her speech carrying waves of tremors.

"You are very kind to be concerned for me. I'll be careful. Thank you." As fast as possible, I got out of there and never looked back.

Weary from Garnet's disturbing performance, along with the stifling heat, I debated whether or not to walk the few blocks to Barack Jewelers. I touched the watch again. The metal burned my fingers. Surely the heat of the day caused the warmth, yet a quiver in the pit of my stomach compelled me to move toward the jewelry store on Cone Street.

After being greeted by an elderly lady behind the sparkling glass counter, I asked to see the engraver.

"Certainly. I'll get him for you." The woman's words swished from her lips like air through a straw.

Shuffling her feet, she dawdled her way down a small hallway. I searched the glass case stretching the full length of the store, looking for the same type of watch as the one in my pocket. I saw several.

The shuffling feet were returning. Fully expecting to see the little lady, I turned to find a tall, lanky, elderly man instead.

"I'm Isaac Barack. How may I help you?"

I handed him Denise's watch. "Do you remember engraving this?"

He took it, eyeing me suspiciously for a moment before studying the watch. Sounding miffed, he asked, "What's wrong with it now?"

"Nothing," I stammered. "I mean . . . you obviously remember the watch. Do you remember who bought it?"

Was I on the verge of learning who gave Denise the watch and possibly who had killed her? My heartbeat thundered in my ears. Would Mr. Barack say the man's name? Would I be able to hear it?

"I don't remember much about the man who bought the watch, but I certainly remember the woman he bought it for." His tone told me it wasn't a fond memory.

"Why is that?"

His eyebrows furrowed into one long one. He wiggled his fingers in front of him and said, "These may not work as well as they used to." He tapped his index finger against his temple. "But what's up here is better than ever."

The lady beside him sweetly touched his hand. "Of course it is, Isaac. Now tell the lady what she wants to know and get back to your nap. You know what the doctor said."

"Yeah, he said I should go home and sit down and die. And if you don't mind, I don't want to do that." Isaac smiled at the gray-haired lady and then at me. "The man. Seems to me he was from the southern part of Georgia." He paused a moment, scratched his head and then continued. "Damnedest thing I ever saw. He came in one morning, oh, I guess about a year ago. Picked out this watch and said he'd be back that afternoon before I closed to pick it up. He wanted me to engrave it. I did. He did. Come back, that is. Had the queen of Sheba with him."

"Who?"

"Well, that's who she thought she was." Shaking his head, he continued. "Pitched a fit. Didn't want a plain watch. She wanted one with emeralds and diamonds. Her husband tried to explain it had already been engraved and he couldn't afford one with emeralds and diamonds."

"An ungrateful lady, huh?" I tried to keep him talking, hoping to hear anything he could remember. "Do you recall their names? Would you have it on file somewhere?"

"No. My memory is good, but not that good. She came back though."

"Really. When?"

"The next day. Wanted me to remove some of the links from the band. She had a small wrist and needed it adjusted. Immediately. I did it as quick as possible just to get her out of here."

"Do you remember what she looked like?"

"No. I just remember she was a real—"

"Isaac." The lady spoke loudly through her teeth.

"Yes, dear." He shook his head and moved his lips, mocking her.

I bit back a smile. "Did he say she was his wife, or could she have been a friend?"

"That I don't know, but surely she was his wife. Why would he put up with someone like that if he didn't have a ball and chain attached somewhere?"

Mr. Barack's wit warmed my heart. "Thank you. Sorry to have interrupted your nap."

He turned and shuffled down the hallway.

I left with not much more than I'd gone in with. A man from south Georgia bought the watch for a not-so-nice woman. Sarah had said Denise had changed. How could she have changed that much? At least that adventure had not been as intimidating as my trip to the perfumery. The eerie feeling flooded back.

For the remainder of the day, Garnet's unsettling predictions, as well as the perfumery scents, blanketed me. To divert my attention from the staggering feeling, I returned to my hotel, back to the reason I'd come to Atlanta. The hotel ballroom held booths set up by various vendors and many displays of merchandise. By late afternoon, I'd finished placing orders for the boutique.

Tired and longing to sleep in my own bed, I wished I could pack up and head back to Hyattville, but it would be well after midnight by the time I got home. Besides, if I weren't apprehensive about going alone to my house where evil had been breeding lately, Lonnie and Lyle both would have a fit when they found out I'd gone home alone.

Instead, I pulled a notepad from my briefcase to jot down things I'd learned during my investigation in Atlanta. The perfume bottle with the sweet smell of honeysuckle was especially developed for a man for his wife, and he bought two extra bottles to give to his girlfriends so his wife would not detect another woman's fragrance on him. As far as Garnet could remember, it was approximately a year ago.

Mr. Barack didn't remember the man who bought the watch, but remembered the ill-tempered woman for whom he bought it. He, too, recalled it was about a year ago.

Could it have been the same man? The woman described by Mr. Barack didn't sound like Denise, but everyone said she'd changed. Could she have changed that much? Could they have gone from the jeweler to the perfumery and Garnet mixed a concoction for Denise and her lover? Could both merchants have assumed the woman was their patron's wife? Pondering the confounding questions gave me a headache.

Exhausted by all the possibilities, I put everything back in my briefcase and turned out the light. I tried counting sheep, but they soon turned into cats jumping over my pasture fence. A vivid reminder that David was dead.

I tried self-hypnosis by imagining I was floating in a body of water. That vision turned into a floating dead body in a lake.

Even pretending I was lying on the ground in my front yard

picking out shapes in the white puffy clouds, inhaling the fresh grass smell, didn't help. Instead, the shade of oak trees covered me and yanked me from any form of tranquility.

The last time I remembered looking at the bright numbers on the digital clock, the time was 2:30. I turned away from its mocking red glare and hugged a pillow to my chest. With a warm thought of Lyle, sleep finally came.

Sunday morning, as I drove across the Hyattville County line, my cell jarred me from my thoughts of getting home and, hopefully, having my life return to normal.

A glance at the caller ID told me it was Sarah Dupree. Happy for the opportunity to talk to her, yet fearful of something else being wrong, I answered the phone. "Good morning. Please tell me everything is okay," I begged.

"Everything is fine, honey. I have a favor to ask, and please feel free to say no if you can't help me."

"Sure, what is it?"

"I'm here at Judy's, and I'm packing up Denise's bedroom. Would you be willing and able to come and help me? Judy and Merrilee are at church, and then they're going to the minister's house for lunch. I'd like to have it all done and out of here before they get home."

I was so happy it wasn't bad news, I answered quickly. "Of

course I will. I'm about four miles from you. I'll be there in a minute." Helping to pack away my friend's things wasn't what I would have chosen to do on a beautiful Sunday morning, but I'd do anything to make Denise's family's tasks easier, even invading Denise's private belongings—clothing, jewelry, possible secrets.

As I got out of my car and made my way to Mrs. Farrell's front door, a strange thought gave me pause. If I died, I wondered what I had in my possessions I wouldn't want anyone to find. What did it say about me that I couldn't think of one interesting thing I had hidden? Before I could answer my own question, Sarah opened the door.

Her red eyes told me she had been crying. "Are you okay?"

She wiped at her nose with a wadded tissue. "Now that you're here, I'll be fine. It's the first time I've been alone in this house since . . . It's so quiet here."

As I watched Sarah study the tissue she twisted between her fingers, I felt the same deep-down heartache. Try as I might, I couldn't find comforting words for her or for me. Standing in Denise's house, which I remembered being filled with love, laughter, and happiness, I felt the dead silence hit me hard and roil through my insides.

I shook off the feeling. "Come on," I urged. "We'll both feel better when this job is done."

In silence, we climbed the stairs. Denise's bedroom looked exactly as it had the day of her funeral. Sunshine streamed through the bay window, spilling light onto the upholstered seat where I had found Merrilee crying. We had just buried her mother, and the wretchedness of the day had overwhelmed her.

I looked around the room and realized I was there to help Sarah erase visible signs of Denise. Yet, the room *was* Denise. The bright white curtains, printed with flowers reminiscent of her favorite violets, were light and airy.

A Raggedy Ann doll slumped against several pillows on the neatly made bed. As teenagers, we spent every one of our weekends at one or the other's house. I'd watched Denise hundreds of times go through her morning ritual, which included making the bed instantly when she got out of it. I was pretty certain no one had slept in the bed since my friend's death. The last time it had been made would have been by Denise.

I touched the spread, which matched the curtains, and whispered a prayer that she was once again in a happy place. Framed pictures lined the walls. All smiling faces of people Denise loved. What must they have meant to my lost friend, and could one of them have ended her life? Sadly, I realized those questions could go unanswered forever.

Next to Denise's graduation picture hung a print of her and me holding a banner that read *Friends Forever.* I had a copy of that same picture, but I had no idea where or even when I'd last seen it. Guilt and regret filled my heart and left me more determined than ever that Denise's killer had to be found.

"Evie, look at this." Sarah pulled a large painting of roses from the closet. In the picture, some of the flowers were opened, some still buds, and a few petals were scattered around a vase.

"Very pretty. Who did it?"

"Merrilee." Auntie Sarah's pride beamed across her face.

"She's very talented." I took the stretched canvas to have a closer look. "Acrylics?"

"Yeah. She does oils, too, but acrylics are her favorites. Did you notice the picture over the sofa downstairs? The one of the blue heron landing in a clearing in the marsh? She gave that to her grandmother for Christmas last year. She's won several awards." Sarah lifted a blue ribbon attached to a frame surrounding a picture of Denise cuddling a baby.

Holding it out for me to see, Sarah read, "First prize in state competition. Merrilee loves painting."

A bright idea came to me. "You know something?" Excitement filled me. "I've had the idea of getting someone to paint a flower on the bags and boxes I use to package my customers' purchases. Sort of a logo." I looked closer at the picture. "This rosebud would be perfect." I glanced at Sarah, who appeared to be trying to figure out what my point was. "Do you think Merrilee would be willing to paint a simple rosebud like this on the bags and boxes we use at the Victorian Sampler? I'd pay her, of course. I could set her up a place in the storeroom. She could come by for a couple of hours after school each day."

That would be a real asset to the boutique. Handpainted bags. Done by a local artist. People would make purchases just for the packaging. "What do you think?" I looked at Sarah, almost pleading for her to say she thought it was a good idea.

"I think she'd love to do it. She's getting her driver's license this week. Judy is giving her Denise's car. So, she'd have her own transportation."

"Great. Have her come by to talk with me."

"Sure. Merrilee will be thrilled."

Sarah hauled two empty boxes onto the bed and began pulling armloads of clothes from the closet.

"I'll pack these. You start with the drawers over there." She was already folding pieces of Denise's clothes and stuffing them into boxes. Sarah was anxious to have the chore behind her. "Merrilee asked for a few of her mom's things. I packed them in that box over there."

"I was just wondering if there was anything here she might want."

The first two drawers I packed held Denise's lingerie, socks, and nightgowns. The last drawer contained several sweatshirts and sweaters. Tucked beneath the assortment of clothing was a picture. Locked in an ornate silver frame, a man and a woman posed in an embrace in front of a pickup with a ladder hanging from supports on the back. The photographer's image reflected in the windshield, but his face was hidden behind the camera.

The male in the picture wore a baseball cap pulled low and sunglasses, which totally obscured his face. The woman was unmistakable.

Denise.

Although twenty years older than when I'd last seen her alive, her radiant smile beamed from the photo.

I turned to Sarah. "Who is this with Denise?" I thrust the cold frame into her hands.

She examined it closely. "I'm not sure. He favors Neal Lancaster, but I can't see enough of his face to be sure."

"Neal is married. Remember that Merrilee said she believed her mom was seeing a married man."

Sarah shrugged. "Who knows? I'd believe anything at this point."

I took a closer look. "Do you believe it could be Neal?"

"Probably not. I was under the impression that she couldn't stand Neal. She drove me to my doctor's office a few weeks before . . . before this mess started." She paused to clear her throat. "We ran into him at the drug store. When he spoke to her, she rudely ignored him. I asked why. She just said he was a real jerk."

I felt the corners of my mouth pull to a frown. "That doesn't sound like Denise."

"That was *exactly* like Denise." Sarah slammed a full box onto the floor and shoved it into the hallway with her foot. She folded her arms across her chest. "You wouldn't have known her anymore."

I was beginning to believe she was right. My old friend was sweet and kind. Not the person her aunt and the watch engraver described. A sudden wave of grief engulfed me, and with it came a flood of sadness. Not for Denise's death, but for her life.

As we continued to pack, Sarah asked, "You never met Kevin Trammell, her husband, did you?"

"As a matter of fact, I did. I talked to him a few minutes after the funeral. That was the only time, but when they were married, Denise and I were writing back and forth all the time. In one of her letters she told me she'd met the most wonderful man. Now that I think about it, I didn't get many more letters after that."

Sarah gave her head a shake as if to dislodge unpleasant thoughts. "She loved that man. God, how she loved him." Moving to the window seat, she stared out into the beautiful sunlight. "Kevin worked on the railroad. Denise met him at the café. She dragged him home like a lost puppy. They were married real quick. I guess about three weeks after they met. They stayed here with Judy. Kevin quit the railroad to work with Carl McGee doing plumbing. Denise continued to work at the diner, of course. They were as happy as pigs in slop."

Sarah walked across the room, removed pictures from the wall, and began packing them in another box. "We'll put these in the attic. The clothes are going to the Salvation Army."

Looking into the hallway, I saw the stacks of boxes loaded with my friend's clothes, packed and ready to be given to strangers. Not because they were old, not because they didn't fit anymore, but because she was dead. The weight of the many things I didn't understand tore at my insides.

"What happened to their marriage?"

Sarah shrugged. "We don't know for sure. One evening Kevin came home. Judy said he went upstairs where Denise was. About fifteen minutes later, he came down with a suitcase and a gym bag and walked straight out the door. Judy never laid eyes on him again until the funeral."

I stopped dead in my tracks. "What did Denise do?"

"Judy waited about thirty minutes to see if Denise was coming downstairs. When she didn't, Judy went up." Sarah pointed to the window seat. "Denise was sitting right there staring out into the darkness. Judy said she asked where Kevin was going. Denise said he'd left her and wouldn't be back.

"When we tried to find out what happened, she said he didn't love her anymore and he'd left with another woman. She refused to speak another word about it. If we tried, she'd leave the room or the house."

I found Denise's reaction to her husband's infidelity and desertion so different from mine. "When I found out David was having an affair with his paralegal," I confided in Sarah, "my first reaction was to drive to downtown Chicago, climb to the top of the Sears Tower, and yell to the world, 'Let me tell you what a bastard my husband is.' I can't imagine Denise not having any reaction at all."

"She dealt with it by pulling within herself and becoming a different person than we all knew and loved. Totally withdrawn, she was hardened, and in some ways, even heartless. Shortly after Kevin left, she found out she was pregnant."

Suddenly, Sarah had my full attention. Since the day Kevin had told me he wasn't Merrilee's father, I hadn't found the right time or, perhaps the courage to ask who her father was. Hopefully, Sarah was about to tell me without my having to ask. Did she even know Kevin Trammell wasn't Merrilee's father?

She continued laying out the facts of Denise's sad times, but she never mentioned who Merrilee's father was.

"When she went to stay with Aunt Carrie in Atlanta to have the baby, it just about killed Judy. It was as if Denise didn't want any of us to have anything to do with Merrilee. After Aunt Carrie died, Denise had no choice but to come home. By then, Merrilee was four, and Judy's health was too bad for her to work the diner." So Denise went back to work there, and Judy stayed home with Merrilee. Judy was happy with the situation, but Denise never seemed connected to anyone but her daughter. Everything went okay, until about a year ago. Not great, but okay."

Sarah returned to the window. "Denise started acting strange again. Disappearing for days, not telling Judy where she was going. Denise had taken the diner over completely, so she didn't waitress anymore. When Denise wasn't there, her assistant manager handled everything. So it didn't matter if she didn't show up for a couple days at work, but it mattered a lot here at home."

Sarah crossed her arms. Even though sunlight streamed through the window, she rubbed her upper arms as if warding off a chill. She turned toward me. "Judy was frantic all the time. I'd get hysterical calls from her because she hadn't heard from Denise in a couple of days."

As Sarah started packing again, her demeanor grew progressively agitated.

"It turned my stomach the way Denise hurt her mother." Sarah stared at me, the intensity of her gaze sending chills through me.

"Judy had such high hopes for Denise, especially after you went off to college. She wanted so much for her daughter to go, too. She wanted Denise to get an education, meet a great guy, and live happily ever after. Denise wanted that, too. That's all she talked about, but the finances weren't there and then Judy's health started to slide. She needed Denise's help at the diner."

Sarah pressed the heels of her hands to her eyes and then formed two fists.

"We were all sorry Denise didn't have the chance to do the things she wanted, but she acted like Judy deliberately kept her from having those things. She also blamed Judy for getting sick." She picked up the last picture, the one of Denise and the unidentified man in front of a truck with ladders. As she glared at the picture, I saw rage flash in her steel gray eyes.

Surely I was mistaken. Sarah loved Denise.

Sarah squeezed the framed picture with such force, her hands began to shake.

"Sometimes I hated Denise for the way she treated her mother."

I quaked at her words, cold and hard, spoken with a strained voice. Without warning, the distraught woman slammed the picture against the door frame. Simultaneously with the crash of glass, a mournful cry ripped from Sarah's throat.

"Oh, my God. I'm so sorry." She collapsed to her knees and picked up the broken picture frame. Her shoulders shook while sobs shuddered through her body.

I was too stunned to move. I felt the blood drain from my face. It must have been as white as the background of the curtains framing Denise's bedroom window. I couldn't speak. Finally, I knelt to help pick up shards of glass.

While I stared in disbelief at the exact spot where the frame collided with the wooden casing, Sarah went into the bathroom. I sorted through conflicting emotions dancing in my brain. Disappointment at the twists and turns Denise's life had taken, sadness for her resentment toward her mother who loved her daughter dearly, and unmitigated shock at Sarah's display of animosity.

She came back into the room, wiping her face with a damp washcloth. Her saddened gaze swept from my face to the damaged door casing and then back to me.

"I'm so sorry, Evie. That was a horrible thing to say. You know I loved Denise very much." Sarah's shoulders drooped in resignation. Tears pooled in her gray eyes and streamed down her face. "I feel so helpless. I did everything I could to ease Judy's suffering." With the washcloth, she wiped away her tears. Quickly, she began packing away the last of Denise's possessions.

Helpless. That covered my feelings, too.

"I understand. I even feel partially to blame. My head tells me it's silly, but in my heart I feel responsible because I found her. Sometimes I think I caused all this heartache. I have night terrors over it all."

"You're right. That's very silly." Sarah locked her hands on my upper arms. "Sweetie, those shoulders aren't broad enough for all that burden."

I returned the cheerful smile she flashed. With that motion, a familiar Sarah Dupree, Denise's unfaltering aunt, replaced the tormented and angry woman from a few minutes before. She removed the last picture from the wall. The one of Denise and me as *Friends Forever.*

"Would you like to have this?" She held it out. I took it and clearly recalled the day we took it—the last day of school our sophomore year. A lifetime ago. Denise's lifetime.

Picking up the other picture of her and the anonymous man, I asked, "I'd like to take this one, too. I'll replace the glass and bring it back."

"Thanks. That's kind of you."

Kindness was not my motive. I wanted to investigate the man behind the sunglasses. Surely someone would know who he was.

"By the way, Evie, did you ever make it to the top of the Sears Tower?"

"Naw. I handled the situation a little differently. I went to David's girlfriend and told her to hang onto what he had in his pants because that was all he would have left when I got through with him. I immediately divorced him and took him for a bundle and his Mercedes."

"Whoa. Little Evie Carson has a vicious side. Who would have thought?" Sarah erupted into laughter.

I welcomed it as a much needed relief from so many sad thoughts. "I promise you David never thought it."

Sarah busied herself with packing. "Oh my goodness!" Sarah's excited shriek charged the air. "Look what I found!" As she moved in my direction, she rapidly unfolded a piece of paper, an official document of some kind.

"Merrilee was looking for this a few days ago. It's her birth certificate. She needs it to get her driver's license. She'll be beside herself. We thought we'd have to go through a lot of red tape to get a copy of it since she's under age, and Judy hasn't felt well enough to go to the courthouse." As she unfolded the document, her eyes scanned the paper. "I can't wait to show it to her. She'll be . . . ."

Sarah hastily refolded it, almost crumbling it.

"What is it? What's the matter?"

"Uh . . . nothing. Just need to finish before Judy and Merrilee get back."

I knew what she had seen. "Sarah." I stopped her hands from tucking the paper in her shirt pocket. "You didn't know Kevin wasn't Merrilee's father, did you?"

"No, I didn't, but how did you know?"

"I talked to Kevin at the grave after the funeral. He told me all about it."

"And it didn't make any difference to you?"

"How could things that happened so long ago make a difference to me?"

My heart pounded wildly. I felt I'd reached the summit of a mountain. I was so excited to know who Merrilee's father was.

Sarah handed me the birth certificate. "I'm sure you're right about it not making a difference, Evie. You're taking it really well. Personally, I'm in shock."

"For heaven's sake, what are you talking about?" As I read the name, my heart and soul plunged off the top of the mountain and plummeted to the valley below. There it was in black and white.

Father: Lyle Dickerson.

CHAPTER 11

WITH THE PAPER CLUTCHED TIGHT IN MY TREMBLING HANDS, I forced myself to read again the disturbing information boldly written on Merrilee's birth certificate—*Mother: Denise Ann Farrell. Occupation: Waitress.* That was fine. Nothing wrong with that, but it was the next part that grabbed me by the throat and made the air in Denise's bedroom grow thick. *Father: Lyle Dickerson. Occupation: Law enforcement.*

"I'm sorry, Evie," Sarah said. "Until I looked at Merrilee's birth certificate, I had no idea Lyle was her father. But by the way you were talking, I thought you knew it. I'm truly sorry."

Nothing Sarah could say would change the raw hurt raging through me.

The nightmarish events continued to sucker punch me at every turn. "You have nothing to be sorry for, Sarah. It's just such a shock. Lyle never mentioned knowing Denise, let alone having a baby with her."

"You are as pale as a ghost." Sarah put her arm around my shoulder.

"Can I get you something?"

I couldn't think of anything that would help the situation. "No, let's finish up. I need to get home." I wanted to be alone to sort through the shattered pieces of my life. And somewhere along the line, I'd have to face Lyle and let him know I'd learned his sordid secret.

When I left Mrs. Farrell's house that day, I took three things with me. I took the picture of me and Denise with our *Friends Forever* banner, the photo of her and the mysterious man, and a broken heart the size of Texas.

On the way home, I rolled down the windows of my Benz and let the wind and the cadence of the road sing their sad song: "Evie Carson is a fool. Evie Carson is a fool." I certainly couldn't argue with that. I'd allowed my loneliness to shove common sense aside, and now there would be a price to pay.

Filled with anger, I pulled into my front yard yet determined to overcome my newest setback. Lyle Dickerson wasn't the man I'd thought he was, but it wasn't the first time that had happened to me. Even though I spent fifteen years with David, I really never knew him. But I managed to pull my life back together. And now, since I only knew Lyle for a short time, I'd get over him even quicker.

It was a rock solid proclamation, but with the level of feelings I'd developed for Lyle, I feared it would take a while to not think of him every minute of the day.

After I'd carried my luggage into the house and put everything away, I decided it was not a good day to see Lyle. I tried his cell phone to tell him not to come over as we had planned before I left. It went straight to voice mail.

"Hi, Lyle. I'm not feeling well." It took major effort to keep my voice steady. "I'm going to bed early. I'll talk to you tomorrow." As I hung up, I knew my voice had betrayed me.

Out on the porch on the swing, I needed to fill my mind with anything other than Lyle, Denise, and Lyle and Denise together. I went through the notes I'd made the night before about the watch and the perfume. Trying to read my disjointed thoughts scribbled across the notepad, I still didn't have any answers. The man and woman who had entered the perfumery and the jewelers—were they one and the same? Were they husband and wife or man and mistress? What part did Lyle play in all this? He wasn't married, but then again, it was only assumed Denise was dating a married man. When she issued the ultimatum that the man on the phone had to tell "her" or Denise would, she never said it was his wife. Did Lyle have someone he wouldn't have wanted to know about Denise? A girlfriend? His sister, Sandy?

Merrilee said when she redialed the number, the sheriff's office answered. But she didn't know for sure if it was the Hyattville Sheriff's Office. Could it have been the state police office and she confused the two?

And what about the inscription on the back of the watch? "All my love, L." Could the *L* stand for Lyle? Could that be why he hadn't taken it into evidence when he went through Denise's keepsake box? Was it because he'd given it to her, so he just gave it back to the family and pretended it had no significance?

The information pounded hard against my conscience. I had to talk to Lt. Moore and let him know the things I'd discovered. Sheriff Beasley was still a prime suspect, and it was possible I had the evidence that could exonerate him.

After looking up the number, I called the state police. Since it was late Sunday afternoon, Lt. Moore wasn't there, but the dispatcher forwarded my call to his cell phone. When he answered, I almost hung up, but I finally found my voice and told him I needed to talk to him. About forty-five minutes later, he was sitting on my front porch.

"I've discovered a few things I think you need to know. I'll just lay the facts out, and you decide what to do with them." I swallowed hard. "Lyle Dickerson had a relationship with Denise Farrell."

Moore nodded, and I assumed he was letting me know he heard me and I should go on. I held out the watch. He took it. "I think he may have given her this about a year ago. When he was involved in the initial investigation, he found this watch in Denise's belongings, yet he didn't enter it into evidence. He put it back in the box and gave it back to her family. There are several other things that make me question him."

Lt. Moore tipped back his black cowboy hat so the shadows

didn't hide his face. "When this all started, Lyle came to me and told me he'd had a thing with the dead woman. He assured me he hadn't seen or talked to her in over sixteen years. As for the watch, he and I went through the box you referred to together. He had never seen it before, and we found no reason to think it would be tied to the murderer. Even though he'd had no recent connection to the woman, I thought it best to remove him from the investigation. I put him on a couple of other cases that could use his expertise. So you see, he is not a suspect in the murder in any way."

As Lt. Moore rose from the swing, Lyle pulled into the yard. He and the lieutenant spoke briefly, and Moore left. As Lyle walked across the yard, my heart ached with more love than I'd ever felt. But hadn't I learned anything from my fifteen years with David? Just because I loved did not mean I'd be loved, or that I loved wisely.

An unexpected smile pulled at the corners of my mouth. Grandma Carson used to say if I didn't tie my shoe strings together, I could walk out of any situation. That was exactly what I would have to do—walk out.

Lyle thought my smile was meant for him and quickened his stride. He climbed the steps and tried to pull me into his arms. I stiffened.

"What's wrong?" he asked, his voice edged with steel. "I asked Lt. Moore why he was here, and he said you would tell me. What is it?"

With my hand on his chest, holding him at bay, I closed my eyes and inhaled the scent of his fresh, crisp cologne. Pain seeped into my heart and held it like a vise. I would miss him.

"I just have one thing to ask, and then I want you to go." I spaced my words evenly, controlled. His expression hardened. He released me and then stepped back and waited for me to continue.

"Were you ever going to tell me about you and Denise?" My voice shook.

Lyle dropped his hands to his side. His hard facial expression softened.

"Yes. Believe it or not, I was going to tell you today."

"Don't you think before we slept together would have been a better time? Don't you think I would have been slightly disturbed at the news?"

He slowly moved to the porch railing and rested his hip on the wooden plank. His shoulders slumped. "At first, I didn't think it was something I needed to tell you, and then things started happening so quickly. When we made love the other night, I decided you had to know, but certainly you wouldn't have wanted me to say, 'Oh, by the way, years ago I slept with Denise.' I decided I would tell you when you got back from Atlanta, when you'd had time to get over some of the stressful situations you've had lately. That's why I waited."

I turned my back to him. I didn't want him to see the next notch of grief I was sure shadowed my face. Nothing else had waited. Divorce, invasion of my home, murders, and especially my runaway heart. Why had Lyle?

"To make matters worse, when I called Lt. Moore about it—"

"Is that why he was here?" Lyle walked up behind me and turned me to face him. He gripped my shoulders. "Why would you do that without talking to me first?" Betrayal showed in his eyes. His gaze burned through me.

"I thought I should tell the authorities." I wasn't completely sure I should have told Moore, but hurt and anger prevented me from admitting that to Lyle.

Muscles quivered along his jaw line. "Are you suggesting I killed Denise? Is that what you think?"

"I don't know what to think. When I found out, I remembered Denise had called someone with an ultimatum. Merrilee said when she redailed the number, it was the sheriff's office, but what if she was confused, and it was really the state police office?"

Hurt registered plainly on his face. I couldn't meet his gaze. Quickly, I continued, not allowing him to interrupt me.

"Then there's this." I handed him the watch inscribed with the letter *L*. He studied the front, but never turned it over. What should that tell me? Did he already know what it said? Or did he not even know it was there? "Did you give that to Denise?"

"I haven't seen Denise alive in over sixteen years. Why would you think I gave it to her?" He held the watch in his outstretched hand.

I flipped it over. "Because of this. And . . . you had to have seen the watch when you went through Denise's keepsake box, yet you never took it in as evidence with the hope of finding out who gave it to her and possibly killed her. Why?"

"I checked it out with two jewelry stores in O'Brien. I learned enough to know there was no way to trace it. It's a fairly inexpensive watch sold by jewelry stores everywhere."

I started to tell him I had found someone who knew about engraver's marks, but my thoughts were too broken to know if he would be the best person to tell. He'd had his chance but blown it. I snatched the watch from Lyle's hand.

"I think you'd better go." I turned to make my escape into my house.

"Evie?" The sound of my name crossing his lips stopped me dead in my tracks. I wanted to keep walking, but something held me back. I stopped, but didn't turn to look at him. My heart told me if I did, I'd be lost.

"Do you believe I killed Denise?"

My heart twisted in my chest. What could I say? I went for the best thing I could without saying I suspected him. "I believe Lt. Moore when he says he found no reason to suspect you. At this juncture, that's all I can depend on."

"But you really thought me capable of murder, didn't you? Is that why you didn't trust me enough to talk to me first?"

"Trust?" I spun to face him and pinned him with my most condemning glare. "I trusted you completely, but how much did you trust me? None." He gently placed his hands on my arms. Warmth seeped into my bones like hot lava. Before his presence could inch further into my concentration, I stepped beyond his reach.

"You didn't trust me enough to tell me you'd had an affair with a friend of mine who recently turned up dead. It certainly had to be in the forefront of your thoughts. So don't talk to me about trust."

Lyle exhaled loudly. "I love you, Evie. You have to know that. You felt it when we made love, and I know you love me, too. Can you deny it?"

"I don't know what I feel anymore. Hurt and confusion don't leave much room for rational thinking. Right now I can't even think about love. I just know I did what I thought best by calling Lt. Moore, but it wasn't necessary after all. He already knew. Who else, Lyle? He and who else knew you and Denise were lovers?"

"Lovers? For God's sake, Evie, it wasn't anything like that. Where did you hear that?"

"Does it matter? Would it change anything?"

"No, but until she turned up dead, I hadn't told another soul. Then I told Moore, but I can't believe he ran through the streets telling it. It isn't something I'm proud of. Who told you?"

I remembered the cold hard fact written in black and white on Merrilee's birth certificate. Spoken words could not have cut me as deeply. "No one told me."

"You certainly didn't pull that out of thin air."

"Of course not. How I found out is irrelevant. The fact remains, I didn't hear it from you." I forced a hard edge to my voice, but my words trembled through the air.

"Well, you've heard it now. I can't believe it should make a difference in our lives. Until I saw Denise lying in that grave, I'd only seen her one time. One time. Do you understand what I am saying?"

"I'm not sure I can wrap my head around any of this. I'm not at all sure I even want to."

Lyle hooked his fingers under my chin and lifted my face to lock my gaze. "Please look at me, Evie. I've never loved anyone like I love you. I don't intend to lose you because of something that happened sixteen years ago."

I moved from his touch, but he forced me to look at him again. "Denise was a one-time thing. A mistake. We were both just trying to deal with the hurt."

"What hurt?"

Lyle moved to the railing. I sat on the swing, swaying slightly. "Remember I told you about finding my wife in bed with another man?" Pain etched his voice.

I wanted to touch him, to console him, but my own pain wouldn't let me. "Yes, I remember."

"That man was Denise's husband."

His words delivered another sharp blow. Did I even want to hear the gut-wrenching details of Lyle and Denise's entanglement?

Before I could protest, he continued, "I have no idea how long they'd been seeing each other, but it must have been quite a while because when I caught them together, they declared their love for each other, and within an hour, they rode off into the sunset."

Lyle ran his hand through his dark hair, and then rubbed the back of his neck. "A few months later Vanessa decided she'd made a mistake and wanted to come home. By then, the initial numbness had worn off, and I didn't want to crawl back into that mess again.

Her dad had given her everything she'd ever wanted. I'd been working two jobs, and I still couldn't compete with her dad's wallet. I never made her happy. I told her to go home to Daddy. She said she was going to send her dad to talk to me and make me take her back." Lyle chuckled. "I told her to do that because I'd love a chance to tell him about his perfect daughter. That was the last time I saw her."

"What about Denise?" It was a hard question for me to ask, but by then I had to know the rest of the story.

Lyle took a seat next to me on the swing and appeared to relax. "Vanessa had been gone from the house about three hours. I was sitting in the den staring into the fireplace, wondering what the hell had just happened and what I was going to do with the secondhand Cadillac I just brought home to surprise Vanessa. There was a slight knock on the door. So quiet, I wasn't sure I'd really heard it. A woman stood on the front porch. She said she was Denise Trammell. Her eyes were swollen from crying. I remember they were so blue."

Had Lyle loved Denise's blue eyes? The thought shook me. She did have beautiful, periwinkle blue eyes, I remembered with a stab of grief.

"I had no idea who she was, but I knew she was in some kind of trouble. I asked if I could help her. I remember her voice was so raspy she could barely talk. She said she shouldn't have come, and turned to leave." He pinched the bridge of his nose and squeezed his eyes shut. "I thought she must be a homeless person. Maybe one of my neighbors had sent her to me because I was a police officer. I didn't want to be bothered with anyone else or their problems. I had enough of my own. But I had a duty to find out who she was, and what was wrong. I stopped her from leaving and invited her in."

My heart teetered between wanting and not wanting to hear the details of his and Denise's involvement. My friend and the man I loved. Did I even have a right to know? Regardless of how long ago, an old girlfriend was one thing, but having a child with my best friend was another. Jealousy burned inside me, demanding to know.

"She looked so lost. I asked again what I could do for her, and she said, 'Tell me where my husband is.' She then explained it was her husband, Kevin Trammell, who had left with Vanessa."

I rose from the swing. Lyle took my hand, urging me to sit back down. I shook free, and took my uncomfortable seat at the railing.

"Go on," I told him.

"I guess neither of us wanted to be alone. We talked for hours, drank wine, and tried to convince each other it wasn't our fault our spouses had flown the coop. The longer we talked, the closer we became until . . ."

"Until you ended up making a baby?"

"What? No, nothing that dramatic."

Why was he so flip about his own flesh and blood? "I'd say Merrilee is pretty dramatic."

"Merrilee? What are you talking about?"

The confusion on Lyle's face made me wonder, for an instant—did he not know? "Are you trying to tell me you don't know Merrilee is your daughter?" Was that my voice shrilling through the air?

"Of course she isn't. When I woke up the next morning, I knew immediately I'd made a terrible mistake by allowing things to go as far as they had. I regretted it and knew I'd have to make sure it didn't happen again.

"But I didn't have to worry about that. Denise was already gone. That was the last time I saw her."

Was it possible Denise went to her grave never telling anyone Lyle was Merrilee's father?

"Why do you insist she's my child?" he demanded, his voice laced with irritation.

"Why are you denying it? Sarah and I found Merrilee's birth certificate today. I saw it in black and white."

"That's ridiculous." He rose from the swing, and in two long strides, crossed the squeaking porch toward me. The hot summer air surrounded us, yet his stare chilled me to the bone. "She had a husband, Evie. Why would she assume I'm the one? None of this makes any sense." Lyle returned to the swing. He leaned back and closed his eyes.

All these years, Lyle really didn't know he had a daughter. My heart had found a new ache. This time *for* Lyle, not *because* of him.

"I saw Kevin the day of Denise's funeral. I asked why he'd never come back to see his daughter. He explained he'd had a vasectomy before they were married. Merrilee wasn't his daughter."

Silence plagued us for several minutes. Even if I knew the words to say, I couldn't find the strength to say them.

"Is it possible I've had a daughter for sixteen years and never known it?" Amazement and disbelief intertwined in his voice.

"It must be true. I can't imagine Denise would put that on the birth certificate if it wasn't. You said she never contacted you again. I can't image she had some ulterior motive. Can you?"

Lyle stared at the horizon. Evening dusk cast lonely shadows everywhere. A perfect backdrop for the darkness in my heart, and certainly in Lyle's, too.

"Good Lord, if you're right, I have a daughter."

I clamped my bottom lip between my teeth and bit back a sob of disappointment. I'd give anything to be able to say those words. *I have a daughter.* But I never would. I cleared my throat. "You have a beautiful, talented daughter, Lyle."

"I watched her at the gravesite and thought something looked familiar about her. I thought maybe I was remembering Denise. Now I realize she favors my sister. She has Sandy's mouth."

"No, Lyle. She has your mouth. Your smile."

His own smile trembled and then immediately turned to a frown. He looked at me with pleading eyes. "What do I do now? Does Merrilee know? What about her family? How do they feel about this?"

"Merrilee doesn't know. Her family only found out earlier today at the same time I did. We were packing up Denise's things and found the birth certificate hidden away. It'll be up to Mrs. Farrell to make the decision about if and when to tell Merrilee."

His already stern expression deepened along his brow. Acceptance brought him to his feet. "Damn. I have a daughter, and I don't know anything about her. Does she have a middle name? When is her birthday? What's her favorite ice cream? That's a lot to digest at one time."

I was a little less disappointed in Lyle now, seeing his obvious surprise at the news he had a daughter. At least he hadn't intentionally ignored her since her birth. Still, his eagerness to know her now didn't change my feeling he'd deceived me. Child or no child, he should have told me about his relationship with Denise. To me, not telling something that surely must have been at the forefront of his mind was a lie of omission, but a lie nonetheless.

Exhaustion or acceptance had returned my emotions to more level ground. My heart beat slower, more normally. My tired body needed a place to sit, but I couldn't chance throwing my emotions out of kilter again by being close to Lyle.

"It's a lot for all of us to accept." I took a seat on the top porch step. "Denise's family didn't know Kevin wasn't Merrilee's father until today. So we've all had a jolt of reality. I have no idea how Merrilee will handle this information."

Lyle leaned forward and rested his arms on his legs. Somewhere in the distance a whippoorwill called. I hadn't noticed the darkness closing in on us. Shivering slightly in the cool evening breeze, I rose and walked to the door to turn on the porch light. I returned to my seat and leaned against the newel.

A frog hopped halfway across the path leading to the porch and then turned around and went back the way he'd come. That's what I had to do. Go back where I'd started the day I returned to Hyattville, armed with goals and wishes. None of which included another man in my life. It would be a little harder now, but I could do it.

Lyle finally spoke. "I want to be there when Merrilee is told. She needs to know I didn't desert her and that I'm here for her now."

"I don't know." I shook my head. "Her aunt and grandmother will have to decide what's best for her. They know how much she can handle."

"Maybe. I'm not thinking clearly enough to know what's right. A daughter. I had no idea one night of seeking comfort could be so life-altering."

"You obviously didn't have Violet Thompson for home economics-slash-health class. That possibility ranked number one on things she thought we should know for better health." As usual, I tried to make light of a serious situation, but my heartache didn't lighten at all.

Lyle recognized my failed attempt. "Does that sweet smile mean you'll forgive me for not telling you about Denise?" His eyes looked hopeful.

"It just means I'm tired of frowning."

"What about forgiving me?"

"I'm sure I'll forgive you, but I can't go back to the way things were. I have no business being in a relationship right now. Or maybe ever. I've fallen in love with two men in my life, and both turned out to have secrets. I guess you could say I'm easily blinded by love."

I rose and brushed the dust from the back of my slacks. The porch needed to be swept. As I glanced at the window, I noticed it needed to be washed. Thankfully, those things would keep my mind busy so I wouldn't have time to miss Lyle.

"I have to go in." I started across the porch. He jumped to his feet and wedged his muscular body between me and the door.

"Evie, don't. Don't send me away like this." His crushed spirit nearly toppled my resistance, but ultimately I had to stand by my decision.

"I have no choice, Lyle."

"Every time I looked at another woman, I wondered—could I trust her, or were all women like Vanessa? The chance of being betrayed again was too great." Lyle pulled me into the circle of his arms. "Except you," he whispered, his breath hot against my ear. "I saw it in your eyes, Evie. I saw and felt I could trust you. After that, love came naturally. I do love you."

I wrapped my arms around his waist and rested my head against his chest. I held him tightly for only a second, then pulled away. Once inside the door, I turned to face him. "I'm sorry," I managed to say. "It has to end here."

With the closing of the door came the breezy scent of Lyle's cologne and the heartbreaking sound of him whispering my name.

Chapter 12

On my morning ride to Burnt Magnolia Street, while the wipers beat a steady cadence, heavy rains hammered the windshield. I felt cocooned inside my car, alone and saddened by the events of the day before. Lyle's quick entrance into my life had taken me by storm, and the dreary, gray skies were like remnants he'd left behind.

As I raced from my car to the rear entrance of the boutique, Grandma Carson again invaded my thoughts. *Run between the raindrops so you don't get wet.* I smiled, but only for a second. I was a little apprehensive about seeing Sandy that morning. How would she feel about my telling Lyle he had a daughter? And then there was the little matter of telling him I didn't want to see him anymore. What would she think of me for doing that?

My fears were relieved quickly. Sandy waited for me in the storeroom with a cup of hot coffee, which I gladly traded for my wet umbrella.

"Thanks," I said, and wondered how I should broach the subject.

"Did you have as rough a night as Lyle did?" Sandy held the umbrella out the back door and shook the excess water off of it. After closing the door, she leaned the umbrella against the corner.

I wasn't exactly sure how to answer her question. It hadn't been a good night for me, but did Sandy know what had caused her brother and me not to sleep? As I took a long sip of coffee, I watched her intently over the top of my cup.

"Lyle told me about Merrilee. He also told me you broke off your relationship with him. Let me just say upfront, I hope none of that will affect our relationship."

"I'm so glad to hear you say that. I was afraid you wouldn't even show up for work today. Thanks for being understanding. Now, if I can just understand a tiny bit of the earthquake that has rocked the world around us, that will help, too."

"Life has been strange for you lately, hasn't it?"

"I'm not vain enough to think it is just my world affected. I know there are many people suffering right now, but the crazy part is all the people are tied to me in one way or another. That's the baffling part."

"I'm not sure if it will help you to hear this, but I know for a fact Lyle loves you. I might have even known it before he did. And I also know it's been a long time . . . as a matter of fact, not since Vanessa, that my brother has given his love so wholeheartedly to anyone." She sat on a stool next to the counter in the storeroom. "He didn't know about Merrilee. If he had, I would have known, too."

I knew Sandy was right about that. She and Lyle were very close. Sometimes I envied what they had. As an only child, I'd never been close to anyone except Denise. She had been the sister I'd never had. Recently, I'd started feeling that same way about Sandy, but I couldn't be sure that would hold up, especially with the last evening's turn of events.

"I believed him when he said he didn't know, but this jolt in our relationship has made me take a look at where I am in my life and what I really want. The conclusion I've arrived at is that until the Hyattville murders are solved, I can't make sound decisions concerning love. My heart is so overwhelmed with the sadness of the three murders, I grasp onto anything that could or should bring me happiness. Whether they are good decisions or not, I'm incapable of judging. I'm not able to sort the good from the bad. Until the murderer is caught, my thoughts and actions will be on the investigation."

"I understand, but you certainly don't plan on becoming a homicide investigator, do you?" Sandy laughed.

I smiled, too. "I have the career I've always wanted right here in this boutique, but that doesn't mean I can't check out some of the questions I have. Of course, your brother and Lonnie Douglas have both warned me about sticking my nose into the investigation. They're afraid I will screw up evidence or wander into something that gets me killed."

"Do you believe your ex-husband's murder is connected to the other two?" Sandy and I had moved from the back room into the boutique, and she unlocked the front door.

"At first, I thought he might have been done in by the mob, but the state officers convinced me he was too small of a catch for the mob to venture this far to get him." I hesitated a moment to allow the knot in my throat to go away. "They told me the mob would have . . . killed him right there in my living room and not lured him across the meadow." I closed my eyes for a brief second, but had to shake my head to chase away the horrific image of David's dead body.

"Now, what I think happened to David was that he came here to look for the key I'd refused to send him and possibly saw something or someone he shouldn't have."

The phone rang.

Two ladies came in.

Just like that, it was business as usual. As a matter of fact, we were so busy for the rest of the day, I barely had time to think about Lyle. It wasn't until we'd closed up shop and we were ready to go home that his name came up again.

"Would you let Merrilee's family know that Lyle is interested in being part of her life?"

I could tell Sandy was being cautious with her question. "I already did. I called her Aunt Sarah and told her everything Lyle told me. I figured that was best, and from there she and Mrs. Farrell, that's Merrilee's grandmother, could decide what was best for her. I gave Sarah Lyle's phone number so she could talk directly to him and not through me. I hope that was okay."

"Definitely. We want to be part of her life."

I gave Sandy a quick hug, and we went our separate ways. I wasn't sure where she was going, but my destination was Hyattville's Sheriff's Office. Lonnie would be on duty, and I needed to have a face-to-face talk with him.

I found Lonnie along with another deputy behind a long counter, and about four people waiting in line for their turns. Lonnie acknowledged me and pointed to a chair along the wall. I sat quietly while Deputy Douglas finished taking a report from a woman who'd just had her purse snatched out of her buggy at the Piggly Wiggly.

When Lonnie was finished, he whispered something to the other deputy and then motioned for me to follow him a short distance down a hallway. He stopped at a door with a frosted window in the top half with the words *Johnston Beasley, Sheriff* etched in the glass.

Lonnie swung the door open. He stepped aside for me to go in. Bright fluorescent lightning drenched the cumbersome furnishings of the room. An impressive oak desk filled a large part of the floor space. Behind the desk sat a leather chair and a veneer credenza nestled under a large window. The inexpensive finish of the plain cabinet contrasted sharply with the fine wood of the desk.

A moose head, with crossed eyes and patches of fur missing, hung low on the cracked white wall next to the window. A sign hanging around the poor animal's neck read, "Have brakes checked in the morning."

A black hat and an empty holster hung from the twisted antlers. I knew the holster was empty because the sheriff's gun had been taken into evidence in Jake's murder case. Picture frames on the credenza held photos of Sheriff Beasley's wife and kids.

Suddenly I felt I was in a private sanctum where no one should be. "Are you allowed in here?" I asked.

"Yeah, with Johnston on administrative leave, I'm next in command." Lonnie folded his hands over his belly and leaned back in the sheriff's chair.

"How is he doing?" I couldn't imagine what it would be like waiting to hear if I was going to be tried for a murder I hadn't committed.

Lonnie shrugged. "About as well as can be expected. The state boys didn't have substantial evidence to hold him any longer without an arraignment. He's at home but still under suspicion. This has set the whole department on its ear."

"I hadn't heard he was free."

"Of course not. The state isn't admitting they made a mistake. So you don't hear that on the news or splashed across the front page of the newspaper."

"That's disturbing." At least he was at home, even if he wasn't sure of his fate.

"Okay, Evie, are you here to talk about Sheriff Beasley, or do you want to talk about your boyfriend's involvement with Denise?"

Gossip traveled through Hyattville like water through a fire hose. That was nothing new, but this disturbed me. What if Merrilee heard it before Mrs. Farrell had a chance to tell her?

"Where did you hear that?" I almost screamed the words.

Lonnie gave me his impish smile, and I knew wherever he'd heard it, it would be okay.

"I had lunch with Lyle today. He told me."

Okay, that wasn't exactly what I was expecting. "Why would he run to you with news like that?"

"He wanted to be sure I knew you were refusing to see him."

"Did he think you could make me? You may have a gun on your hip, but you wouldn't shoot me."

"His motives were not that sinister. He wants me to keep an eye on you. You see, Lyle, along with me, you, and most of the town of Hyattville do not believe our good sheriff had anything to do with the murders. Lyle is afraid something will happen to you, too. So he wanted me to be aware he wasn't going to be around to protect you."

"I'm a big girl. I can take care of myself."

"Denise was a big girl. Jake was a big boy. And your ex, well, I'm not sure what he was, but they are all dead. Until we find out who is behind their murders, you're my ward. Get used to it, Eva Lynn, because that is what is going to happen."

"How do you plan to take care of that, *Lonald*? You can't attach yourself to my hip and be with me every second. I'm not going to be run out of my house for another minute. I have new locks, an alarm system, and a gun." I had to pull back that statement. "At least I had a gun until the police took it away. Did you know they took Dad's .38?"

"Yes, but you have others. Keep them close at hand. Now, what did you come here to talk to me about?" Lonnie leaned forward and rested his arms on the sheriff's desk.

"The other day you said you were performing an unofficial investigation. I want in on it."

"Are you crazy? I'm not supposed to be doing it. I'm certainly not going to get you involved."

I was about to tell him about the watch and the perfume, hoping we could put our heads together and find out if they could possibly be connected to Denise's murder, but I was interrupted by the door opening. Kitty walked in.

"That's right where he belongs." She pointed at Lonnie. "Doesn't he look great behind the sheriff's desk?" she asked, but she didn't wait for an answer. She barreled on through. "How are you doing, Evie? Did you get a lot of the new fall fashions while you were in Atlanta?"

"Yes, I did. They had beautiful things. I'm excited about getting my first shipment."

Apparently, it finally dawned on Kitty that Lonnie and I might have been conducting important business. "Am I interrupting something?"

I stood. "Not at all. I was just checking with Lonnie to see if there was any new information about the murders."

She looked at her husband. "Is there?"

Lonnie shook his head and rose.

"That's too bad." Kitty went to him and kissed him on the cheek. "I brought your dinner. I left it at the front desk with Simpson."

"I'm glad you're here. I have something I need to talk to you about anyway." Lonnie said to her, then glanced at me. "Leave the legal work to the people who know how to handle it. Okay?"

"Sure." *Maybe in my next lifetime, Deputy Douglas.* "See you later." I acknowledged him and then Kitty. Soon I was on my way home, where hopefully I could sit down and prop my feet up. I needed solitude or a stiff drink, whichever came first.

When I got home I changed into jeans, a pink T-shirt, and comfortable flip-flops. My favorite kind of clothes. Casual. David had always insisted I dress in a manner expected of a corporate wife. That, in his opinion, meant no jeans and definitely no T-shirts. Until our marriage ended, I never realized how much of myself I'd given up for him. But I do know I tried everything in my power to make him happy.

I was sad he was gone, but even to the end, I'm not sure David knew what it would have taken to bring him happiness.

After I finished dressing, I went outside and swept the steps and walkway. I even managed to find the energy to wash the two windows looking out onto the porch. All the while, Midnight frolicked in the yard, chasing butterflies. When the sun sank out of sight, the cat and I went inside.

Once I was sure I was in for the rest of the night, I punched in my alarm code, which monitored all my windows and doors. I still had to look up the number in the booklet Lonnie had given me. He'd had the alarm installed while I was recuperating at his mom's house.

The night before, after Lyle and I parted ways and he left, I went straight to bed and never gave a thought to setting the alarm. I set it before I left for work the next morning, and I decided I'd better get used to using it all the time if I intended to protect myself.

Now, satisfied that I was securely locked in, I went to Dad's bedroom and retrieved another one of his handguns from the locked closet where he'd always kept them. I checked the gun, made sure it was loaded, and then placed it in the top drawer of my nightstand. I started to go back downstairs, but went back to the drawer, pulled out the pistol and took it downstairs with me. What good would it do me if I was downstairs and it was upstairs? What good would it do me at all? Oh, sure I talked a big game, but in the back of my mind, I had a niggling doubt as to whether I'd be able to actually use it.

I fed Midnight, and then fixed a bologna sandwich and a glass of wine for me. I'd just snuggled under Grandma Carson's crocheted afghan and turned on the television when car lights shone through the curtains at the front porch window.

"Who could that be at this time of night?" I asked Midnight as if I thought, first, he would know and, second, he would answer me.

I flipped on the porch light and looked out the window. The last person in the world I expected to see at my door was Kitty Douglas, but there she was. As I opened the door, my newly installed alarm system got its first workout. The siren blared in ear-splitting volume.

"Turn it off," Kitty yelled over the high-pitched noise.

I punched in a couple of numbers, but I was too flustered to remember the code. I snatched the booklet from the sofa table, flipped it open, and then successfully pushed in the right numbers. The wailing stopped, and I released a deep sigh of relief.

I looked at Kitty. "What are you—" The telephone rang. "Come in," I told her and then answered the phone.

"This is Guardian Alarm System," a female voice announced. "Is everything okay there?"

"Yes, it is. I'm terribly sorry. I opened the door without turning off the alarm."

"May I have your password, please?"

"Password?" I vaguely remembered Lonnie mentioning that I had one of those.

"Punkinhead," Kitty said.

I'm sure I must have had a puzzled look. She nodded and said it again.

"Punkinhead," I repeated for the alarm company's dispatcher.

I hung up the phone and asked Kitty the most obvious question. "How did you know my password?"

She chuckled. "I was here with Lonnie the day they put it in. He needed to give them a password, and I told him to use the name of our old cat—Punkinhead."

Lonnie had told me to call the company and change the password to something I would remember. I made a mental note to do that first thing in the morning.

"Thanks. Is there something I can do for you, Kitty?"

"Actually, I've been sent here to do something for you."

This can't be good. "And what would that be, deary?"

"Lonnie sent me to spend the night with you. He'll be at work until early in the morning. He said he promised Lyle he'd look after you."

"So where does your spending the night with me play into Lonnie's cockeyed promise?"

"He said he'd feel better if you weren't out here alone at least until he can figure out what else to do with you."

"I appreciate it, Kitty, but I'm fine.

"Lonnie said not to take no for an answer, so get used to it. I'm here for the long haul." She looked at my glass of wine sitting on the coffee table next to my sandwich. "Got anymore of that wine? I could use a glass."

I pointed to a green canvas bag she was carrying. "What's that?"

"It's my jammies. I usually sleep in the nude, but I didn't think you were going to allow that to happen." She was laughing herself silly.

Kitty pointed to the gun lying on the sofa table. "I don't like guns. Put that away."

"Oh, for crying out loud." I shoved it into a drawer. "You're married to a policeman. Looks like you'd be used to having weapons around."

"I make Lonnie keep his locked up at home. How about that wine?"

I poured her a glass and made her a bologna sandwich. We'd left the front door open, and a cool breeze brushed against my skin, which was perspiring from all the excitement.

"The night air feels good. Let's sit on the porch." I led the way.

We both sat on the swing, sandwich in one hand and wine in the other. For at least the next thirty minutes, Kitty and I swayed and talked. We knew so many of the same people. Kitty was a fountain of gossip and didn't mind telling it. As much as I hated to admit it, I was actually enjoying our conversation.

The night air had turned cool and the marlin sky held the promise of rain. Suddenly, lightning veined through the darkness, illuminating the whole area.

Kitty screamed and raced into the house. I hurried to the door, but instead of going in, I looked as far into the darkness as I could. I didn't see anything that should have caused her reaction.

"I know you've always been afraid of your shadow, Kitty, but to be that terrified of a little lightning is ridiculous." I'd just gotten the words out of my mouth when Kitty latched onto my arm, pulled me inside the house, and locked the door.

"What is going on?"

She was already dialing the phone. "Didn't you see that man standing over there across the meadow?"

"I didn't see anything. It's pitch black out there."

"When the lightning lit up the sky, I saw him across the meadow standing at the edge of the woods. I couldn't see who it was, but it was definitely a man."

"Where's Lonnie?" Kitty was practically screaming into the phone. "I don't care if he is talking to God himself, get him to the phone."

Ah, now that was the Kitty we all knew and loved. While she waited for Lonnie to come to the phone, I went to the window that looked across the meadow, but I couldn't see anything.

On the other side of the room, Kitty was chewing on Lonnie's ear. "What do you mean?" Pause. "GBI agent?" Pause. "Stakeout?"

I couldn't take it any longer. I took the receiver away from her. "Kitty sounds like she's trying to figure out a riddle. Tell me what is going on."

"I was just on the phone with Cabler from the GBI. He has your house under surveillance. He just got a call from his man saying he'd been spotted, and the two women in the house were screaming and carrying on."

"Make that *one* woman in the house. The one you sent to protect me lost her cool when lightning lit up the world and she saw a man under the infamous oak tree. For heaven's sake, Lonnie, why are they watching my house?"

"Evie, they don't tell us peons what they are up to."

"Do they think the murderer may come after me?"

After a pregnant pause, I heard Lonnie expel a pent-up breath.

"Do they think I killed David? Is that why they're watching me?"

"At this point, I'd only be guessing what their intentions are."

"Do me a favor and give me your best educated guess at what they're up to."

"All I know is that Cabler figured you'd be calling 9-1-1 to let us know there was a man lurking on your property. He called to assure me you are in no danger. Other than that, I know nothing. If it makes you feel any better, Cabler isn't pulling his man. That tells me he has taken your reports seriously that someone has been messing around your house. So don't spread it around, and let's see what turns up."

"Since the big guns are out here, should I send Kitty home to protect you?"

"Very funny. No, I don't want her driving that dark road this late at night. Let her stay with you tonight."

"Okay, I guess it isn't a really terrible idea. Night."

Kitty had poured more wine, and she handed me a glass. "I guess we are having a sleepover."

I took the offering and drank half of it in one gulp. "Looks that way."

Kitty plopped onto the sofa and propped her feet on the coffee table. I lacked the energy to tell her to get them off there. Instead, I sat in the overstuffed chair, which matched the sofa. Strange, I couldn't remember sitting in that chair not even one time since I'd come home from Chicago.

While Kitty watched Jay Leno, I alternately swirled and sipped my wine. I kept going over and over in my mind the newest level of weirdness I had sunken to. An agent from the Georgia Bureau of Investigation was staking out my house waiting to see either if a murderer happened by, or if I would do something to prove *I* was the murderer.

The strangeness didn't stop there. Kitty Douglas, the longtime, royal pain in my backside, sat sprawled on my sofa with her feet propped on Grandma Carson's antique coffee table, and the unbelievable part was I was glad she was there.

By my third glass of wine, I had mellowed quite a bit. For about ten straight minutes, I'd been studying the bottom of Kitty's shoe. It was sort of a leather sneaker, with mock laces, which she just slipped her foot into. On the sole, in the center of the heel was an imprint of a star.

"Cute shoes," I said.

"Thanks. I ordered them online from a company in Italy—J. Carmelito's. You know, you should think about carrying shoes in your boutique. I'll be sure to give you the Web site."

"Maybe. I'll think about that tomorrow, but for tonight, I've had it. I'm going to bed. You can sleep in Dad's room. Down the hall on the right." I gave her a quick rundown of where she could find towels and extra blankets, and then I went to my room and barely got into my nightgown before I passed out on the bed.

Sometime during the night, I vaguely remembered waking up and wondering if I'd set that damn alarm.

Hyattville has hit the big time, hasn't it, Evie. It only took three murders to get the feds here, but they finally made it. They think they are so clever, but I knew they were there hoping to catch me sneaking around your house.

I'm here, and they don't even know it. While they're watching you, I'm watching them. They won't stay long, and then it will be just me and you again.

I love the games we play. I hide, but you can't find me. You seek, but you don't see me. I tag you, but you can't catch me. The games will go on until I'm tired of playing.

The next morning came way too early. I dragged my body out of bed and wondered if anyone got the license number of the truck that must have run me over. But then I remembered nothing had hit me. I had drunk too much wine with my new best friend, Kitty Douglas.

I showered, dressed, and then shuffled down the stairs expecting to have to wake her. To my surprise, she was gone and had left me a note saying she enjoyed our evening together, but she had things to do. She signed it with a *K*.

"Cute, Kitty." Midnight thought I was talking to him. He meowed and rubbed against my leg. "Yeah, you're cute, too."

I opened the curtains in the living room so the cat could laze in its favorite place on the front windowsill and soak up the warmth of the sun. After setting the alarm, I made my way to the car. Once I was behind the wheel, I dared to look to my left, across the meadow, to see if anyone was watching me. I didn't see anyone, but when I looked back at my house, the upper windows, with shades half drawn, resembled eyes—mysterious eyes, looking down at me like the house knew secrets. A slight chill slowly made its way through me, assuring me I didn't want to know what my old home knew.

I hurriedly backed my car around. As I drove down the lane, I glanced in my rearview mirror and took one more look at the house. Midnight sat in the window staring at me as if I'd lost my mind. At that stage of the game, I wasn't sure he was far from wrong.

At the Victorian Sampler, Sandy told me Lyle hadn't heard anything from Merrilee's family.

"I didn't get a chance to talk to Sarah or Mrs. Farrell last night, but I'm sure that, when the time is right, they'll let him know." They were probably allowing themselves time to adjust to the news, and then they'd be in a better position to help Merrilee accept the fact that she was no longer an orphan, but in fact, had a father in the next town.

"I'm sure you're right." Sandy went to help a customer. I began mulling over unpaid invoices. Since bookkeeping wasn't my strong suit, it took every bit of my concentration to get through them.

The shop had seen a steady flow of customers all through the morning hours. Lunchtime proved to be even busier. The three o'clock sun peeked from behind the courthouse and shone through the front windows of the boutique. The door opened, and a burst of warm air swooshed in.

"Hi, Evie."

I looked away from the checkbook and found Merrilee smiling widely. *Lyle's smile.* My composure wavered slightly, and I had to struggle to get it under control.

"Merrilee. How did you get here?" I hurried from behind the counter and then hugged the teenager. She squeezed me tightly.

"I'm so excited." Her voice floated through the air.

Excited? My mind spun with the possibilities. Was she excited about Lyle?

Just then, Sarah entered the boutique.

"Child, couldn't you wait on your dear, old aunt?" Sarah pretended to be out of breath. Merrilee and I looked at her and burst out laughing. As Sarah joined in, I waited to see what this jovial invasion was all about.

"Aunt Sarah said you liked my painting and might have a job for me." Merrilee's blue eyes danced.

Of course! The rosebuds on the bags and boxes. That was why she was there. With everything going on, I'd forgotten all about that. Apparently, Sarah hadn't told her about Lyle. I hurriedly explained what I'd like her to do, trying all the while to keep from mentally dissecting Merrilee's features to see how much she resembled her father.

"I'd like to have a hand-painted rosebud on each bag and box we use to package purchases. I think that would be a unique touch. You could put your initials on it. It would be a work of art by a local artist. Does it take a lot of time to do one?"

"Naw. A couple of minutes each."

"You can use the counter in the storeroom. I thought you could come over after school and work until five, when we close. How does that sound?"

"Great. I can start day after tomorrow if that's okay. Grandma is giving me Mom's car."

Denise's car. Would my heart always hurt when I thought of her?

"Tomorrow I'm going to get my driver's license. I wanted to go when we left here," Merrilee said, tilting her head toward Sarah, "but Mata Hari here is on some grand mission and says I can't go today because she wants to have a talk with me first." She laughed.

I don't think she noticed Sarah and I hadn't joined her. We'd only exchanged knowing glances.

That night, Sarah would tell Merrilee that Lyle Dickerson was her father.

Merrilee whispered loudly to me, "I think she's going to give me a big lecture about responsibility on the highway."

Sarah smiled at her great-niece and lovingly pushed a strand of hair away from Merrilee's face. A lady came in the door, and Sarah stepped aside to let her enter.

"Well, we'll let you get back to work. Merrilee will be here Thursday afternoon."

"I'll look forward to it." I closed the door behind them.

Sarah looked over her shoulder just long enough to mouth the words *I'll call you.*

I hurried back behind the counter. Sandy had discreetly disappeared into the storeroom during Sarah and Merrilee's visit. She returned when the bell on the door rang and assisted the customer who came in.

The pretty brunette wore black slacks, a red blouse, and a black-and-white polka-dotted scarf draped around her neck. I didn't know who she was, but she was a classy dresser, and I'd kill to be able to wear my hair in a straight short bob like hers.

Sandy brought the woman's selections to the cash register and started ringing up the purchases. As the customer approached the counter, I caught a whiff of her perfume. My nostrils burned, but the blood coursing through my veins had turned to ice water.

The attractive woman with the impeccable clothing taste reeked of Garnet's *Ray de Miel.*

Chapter 13

My first impulse was to gag from the smell of the honeysuckle perfume my unidentified customer wore, but I had to stay calm and do everything I could to determine if this woman was the wife of a cheating husband, or one of the mistresses he cheated with.

Being on the edge of discovering one of the missing pieces surrounding Denise's murder made my mind swirl. I wasn't sure I could form an intelligent sentence, let alone determine the right questions to ask to find out how the woman came to be wearing Garnet's *Ray de Miel.*

While Sandy rang up the woman's purchases, I pulled myself together. Finally, I found my voice. "It certainly is a beautiful day out. I hope you found everything you were looking for. It looks like you've made some nice selections." *Shut up, Evie. Give the woman time to talk.*

Sandy gave me an odd look, and then said, "This is Evie Carson. She owns this boutique."

"I'm Patsy Lancaster," the customer announced.

"Are you any relation to Neal Lancaster?" I'd regained my composure, and thankfully Patsy had given me a nugget to find out more about her.

"He's my husband. Do you know him?"

"He was a couple of years ahead of me in school, but yeah, I know him." I helped Sandy fold the blouses and slacks Patsy had bought. "That's very interesting perfume you're wearing."

"Thank you. Neal had it made especially for me at a perfumery in Atlanta. Jared's, I believe was the name of the place."

Without thinking, I corrected her. "Garnet's."

"Yeah, that's it. How did you know that?"

"I've been to her shop, and that's really the only perfumery I've heard of where they mix the concoctions on site." So Neal Lancaster was the man who had this fragrance made, which he gave to his wife and mistresses so his wife couldn't tell he'd been with another woman.

Neal had given Garnet the impression he had two girlfriends. Denise would be one, but who was the second? I certainly couldn't find out that information from his wife. For now, I'd have to settle for the facts I had—Neal gave Denise the bottle of *Ray de Miel*, and now I knew for sure the man behind the sunglasses in the picture with Denise was Neal Lancaster.

I'd been swallowed up by deductive reasoning. Suddenly I realized Sandy and Neal's wife were both staring at me. I apologized for my momentary lapse.

"No problem," Patsy said, "I was just saying Hyattville has needed upscale boutiques. Hopefully, you'll be around for a long time."

"Thank you so much." We shook hands, and I noticed her wedding ring was about a four-carat diamond that would have set Neal back a small fortune. If he were caught in an affair, Neal would have to kiss a lot of his fortune good-bye.

My stomached roiled. My mouth had gone so dry I could barely talk, but somehow I managed to ask Patsy to say hello to Neal for me. She left. I collapsed onto the stool.

"Are you okay?" Sandy laid her hand on my shoulder. "You look like you've seen a ghost."

I felt like I had. I started to tell her what had transpired in my short conversation with Patsy Lancaster, but suddenly I decided to keep that to myself for the time being. After all, Lonnie said Neal had been questioned, and the authorities had found no reason to suspect him as the murderer. Who was I to override that?

If I passed news like that on to Sandy she would feel duty bound to tell Lyle, and I could understand that. So far, the authorities claimed to know everything I did. I needed to wait until I had more substantial evidence before I passed it on. For the time being, I'd keep it to myself.

"I'm fine. I may be coming down with a touch of the flu. Do you think you could handle the shop by yourself until closing time?"

"Of course, and I'll lock up, too. You go on home and rest."

I made a rapid departure out the back door, jumped into my car, and made a beeline to see Neal Lancaster, electrical contractor.

Three white pickup trucks, complete with racks and ladders, lined the parking spaces outside Neal's place of business. Seeing the trucks reminded me that I had the picture of Denise and who I was now sure was Neal. I took the picture out of my trunk and tucked it in my purse.

I walked across the parking lot and saw Neal with a clipboard tucked under his arm coming out of the building. He removed his sunglasses and flashed his infamous smile that had stopped many hearts in our high school.

"Evie, it's good to see you," he called. His long legs closed the distance between us; gravel crunched under his dusty cowboy boots. He removed his baseball cap, embroidered with a gold lightning bolt and red letters spelling out *Lancaster*. "What can I do for you? Need some electrical work done in your shop?" His green eyes danced.

Over Neal's shoulder I saw a woman straightening a lighting display in a large picture window. She watched us with more attention than she gave to the display.

"Not exactly."

He stood so close I had to look up into his face, but I didn't move. I stared willfully into his eyes and dug deep inside me for the intestinal fortitude to bluff my way through the confrontation. "I want to know about your relationship with Denise and why no one seems to know you were the father of her baby."

The spark in his eyes died. He appeared to have been struck mute. Neal's rough hand seized my elbow. Before I could object, he pulled me into the building, through the waiting room, and then into his office. I knew it was his office because his name plate and a picture of his wife, Patsy, and two boys filled a corner of his desk. He slammed the door and again placed himself in front of me.

"I think you better be careful about spreading lies like that. I'd hate to have to sue you for slander." Neal spewed his words through clenched teeth.

I stood defiantly. "So you deny being the man who got Denise pregnant?"

"Are you asking for trouble, or are you just plain crazy? I hope you have a good lawyer. Oh, that's right—yours is dead, isn't he?"

For a brief moment, Neal had knocked the wind out of my sails, but I stepped back and prepared for the biggest bluff of my life. "I won't need a lawyer. I can prove every word I say." I took the picture from my purse and held it out. "I found this in Denise's personal belongings, along with other things that tie you to her. Now, let's talk." I bit my bottom lip to keep it from quivering.

Neal turned away and placed both of his hands on the desk with his fingers curled around the edge. He tightened his grip. His knuckles whitened.

"What do you want from me, Evie?" His voice shook.

"I want you to admit you were the father of Denise's baby."

With the swiftness of a rattlesnake, Neal backhanded several items from the top of his desk, including the picture of Patsy. I took a quick step back, out of his immediate reach. As I looked at the shattered glass covering the picture of his wife, I realized Patsy had just become another victim of the awful events continuing to plague Hyattville.

Overwhelmed with the injustice of it all, I lashed out at Neal. "That's quite a temper. Is that what happened to Denise? Did she say something you didn't like? Perhaps she told you she was going to tell your wife." Hopeful that Neal's nosy secretary was just outside the door, in case I needed rescued, I pushed him further. "Did that make you angry or scared enough to lash out at her like that? Angry enough to kill her?"

In a flash he grabbed my arms, almost lifting me from the floor. I sucked in a sharp breath and prepared to scream for help. Just as quickly, he released me. His shoulders drooped. I backed closer to the door.

"Denise called me with an ultimatum, but I could never hurt her." He stared directly at me, his eyes brimming. "I loved her, Evie. I still love her. Every day. I met her that day at the motel room where she died. I told her I would tell Patsy that night, and then I'd marry her. She was alive when I left. You have to believe me."

"I want to." I glanced at the rubble on the floor. "I'm not sure what to believe."

"She always left the motel first, but that day I had to get back to the courthouse because one of my guys hadn't shown up, and I was on a deadline to finish running the electrical wiring for the new air conditioner for the courthouse and the sheriff's office. I was back there before noon. She was alive, Evie. I swear." Neal paced. His boots slapped loudly against the beige tile floor.

"She said she was going to nap and then take a shower. I couldn't wait for her. So I left. I had no idea she was in danger. Who could have wanted her dead, Evie? She didn't have any enemies."

"She was dating a married man, Neal. Your wife had reason to be Denise's enemy. Don't you agree?"

His gaze snapped to me. "Not Patsy. She could never do anything like that. Besides, she's never suspected me of cheating."

"The police need to make that decision. You've got to tell them everything you know," I pleaded.

"I can't." Neal pounded his fist into the palm of his hand. "It will kill Patsy."

"You just said you were going to tell her about Denise before she died. Did you think it would be easier on Patsy then?" Disgusted with the whole conversation and anxious to get it over with, I blurted everything I knew about Neal. "Denise was not the only extramarital affair you were having. You bought *Ray de Miel* perfume for both your girlfriends, for cripes sake. So please don't try to convince me of your concern for Patsy. It gets lost in translation."

"There was someone else. I admit it, but how do you know about her?" Neal slumped into his chair. "I can't believe she just volunteered the information."

I was at a lost about which path to take from there. Other than Garnet saying he'd bought two bottles for girlfriends, I had nothing, but bluffing had worked so far. So it might be worth a try.

"No, she didn't volunteer, but once confronted with the facts, she couldn't deny it." My voice shook.

"I assume you haven't told Lonnie any of this, or he would have already been here."

"I've talked to him about your involvement, but he said you'd been checked out and you weren't a suspect. Did he not ask the right questions? Is that why you aren't under suspicion?" I tried to recall my conversation with Lonnie about Neal. Since we were talking on the phone at the time, some of what Lonnie said was lost because my concentration was splintered by the humiliation of my falling over Neal's fence. I couldn't remember much except that Lonnie had said Neal had a solid alibi for the time of Denise's death because he was working at the courthouse then.

"The courthouse," I said aloud. Neal looked at me like I'd really lost it. "You were working at the courthouse."

"That's right. I just told you that."

"The sheriff's office is on the first floor of the courthouse."

"What's your point?"

My point was that Denise's last call was to the sheriff's office. It had been one of the pieces of circumstantial evidence lodged against Sheriff Beasley.

"Did Denise call you while you were working at the courthouse, and did the call come in through the sheriff's office?"

"I just told you that. She called the non-emergency number, and the guy at the duty desk called me to the phone."

"That's where you were when she issued the ultimatum?"

"Yes, so I told her I'd meet her at the motel so we could talk about it."

"You went there, and then you told her you'd tell Patsy that night you were leaving her. What happened to that plan?"

"I tried to tell Patsy, but Jason, my sixteen year old, had won a trophy at his swim meet that afternoon. We were celebrating. I couldn't find the words to tell Patsy." Neal's voice cracked. "I don't know how I'll ever get over any of this."

Plant lies—grow misery. Grandma Carson's words seemed appropriate. "You could start by going to the police. Make sure they have every bit of information about your involvement with Denise. It's vital that they know."

Neal rubbed his temple. "I know you're right. It's just going to be so hard."

"Except for the person who killed her, you were the last person to see Denise alive. You're admission will give them other people to look at." I stood and slipped my purse strap over my shoulder.

He looked at me, his eyes full of questions. "Like who?"

"Your wife, for one."

Neal rose and moved to the window with his back to me. "She's not a consideration at all. She could never hurt anyone. Even if she knew I'd been sleeping around, which she doesn't. Yet."

"Then there's the little matter of your other girlfriend. I would think she'd definitely be a suspect."

Abruptly, Neal spun to face me. "You don't know who she is, do you? You lied to me."

"No, I didn't. Just because I knew you had another mistress didn't mean I knew who it was. You assumed I knew her name. What I do know is that the police need to know who she is." I crossed my arms over my chest and moved closer to Neal.

"You say you love Denise. Think about her family. You have a solid alibi, so you've been ruled out, but you may hold the key to finding her murderer. Denise's mom and daughter need answers. They need to know who and why." And I wanted to know who killed David.

Neal took a seat in his chair and buried his face in his hands. His body shook with sobs. My first instinct was to run my hand along his shaking shoulders as a simple gesture of comfort, but I couldn't get past the fact that he had so much information that could possibly lead to the murderer, and he'd been a jerk not to tell the authorities. "The police have to know, Neal. I'll have to tell them. Of course, it would be better coming from you."

He looked up at me and swiped away his tears. "I'll go to the police, but I need to wait until Thursday. Tomorrow is Patsy's birthday. Waiting another day shouldn't make that much of a difference."

I didn't know what to say, but then I thought about the fact that every bit of information I'd come up with and tried to tell the people in charge of the investigation had been shot down. I rationalized that my newest bits of what I considered vital evidence would be better served if they came from Neal. My only fear was the uncertainty of what might happen in the next forty-eight hours. I hated to think someone else could die while I had information that might have stopped the murderer.

One look at Neal, and I saw the desperation etched on his face. Desperation to give those last few hours of happiness to his wife before he delivered the emotional blows that would tear his family apart.

"Okay, I'll give you until Thursday morning, but if you don't go to Lonnie by then, I will." I left Neal's office. My body and soul were shaken and disheartened at the new turn of events. Hyattville's victim pile grew higher.

I pulled my car to a slow stop in the front yard and deliberately stared at the house. Under the new position of the sun, the windows looked like eyes closed in deep sleep or in death. I allowed my own to close against the haunting memories forever etched in my mind. Images of dead bodies, of facing Neal and knowing he may be connected to the murders, and the smell of honeysuckle.

Dark clouds hung in the sky, promising more rain. They continued to grow darker with each passing minute. I opened the door and climbed out of the car. A crisp breeze greeted me. I wrapped my arms tightly across my chest against the coolness, or was it against the loneliness?

I was acutely aware of a need inside me. I wanted to be locked in sheltering arms, protected from the bizarre activities which seemed to escalate with each passing day. I wanted those arms to be Lyle's. I missed him, his laughter, his tenderness.

Trying to leave those thoughts behind, I raced up the porch, unlocked the door, and disarmed the alarm. Midnight met me at the door. I let him out, and then watched him disappear around the house.

As I walked by the telephone, it rang.

"Hi," Sarah said. "Well, we told Merrilee about her dad."

"How is she taking it?" I kicked off my shoes and wiggled my toes.

"Right now she's in her room, crying her heart out. Judy and I thought we'd leave her alone for a while and let her get it out of her system."

"Did you call Lyle?"

"Not yet. I want more time to talk to Merrilee and see how she feels about actually meeting him."

My head ached. The day had filled it with too much information. I either couldn't or didn't want to think about any of it any longer. It would all have to wait until morning.

"By the way," Sarah added, "before we had our talk she told me she didn't want to wait until Thursday to start working with you. She had decided to go to your store tomorrow, but now I guess we'll have to see how she feels about that."

"Give Merrilee a hug for me. Tell her she and I can talk tomorrow, if she is up to coming to work, that is. Thanks for calling, Sarah. Good night."

Midnight scratched on the door. I let him in, set the alarm, and although it was still partial daylight outside, went to bed.

Around three-thirty in the morning, I woke up with the unsettling feeling I wasn't alone. I scrambled for the light and looked around my nightstand and in the drawer for my gun. It wasn't there.

"Damn." I had put it in the drawer downstairs the night Kitty had spent with me. Panicked, I tiptoed out of my room and down the stairs. With my heart racing, I turned on the lamp on the table that ran the length of the back of the sofa. Nothing was out of place. I didn't hear any unusual noises, yet I would have bet my life someone had been in the house and their presence had awakened me.

Was I losing my mind? Surely not. Anyone in my situation would be spooked at the slightest noise. At least I had to believe that. I curled up in the overstuffed chair, covered up with Grandma's afghan, and pulled Midnight into my lap. I placed my gun close at hand on the end table.

The morning light found me in that same place. Slowly, I uncurled from my cramped position and stood on legs that ached from needles and pins stabbing up and down them. It took only a second for my muscles to wake up. I went to the window, pulled back the curtain, and looked across the meadow to see if the GBI was visible. I didn't even know if they were still watching me or my place, or both. Hell, I could fill a coffin with things I didn't know.

That wasn't quite true. I was beginning to think I knew too much. There was a lot of information in my brain that I didn't know whom to tell. Yet, I wasn't sure how much trouble I would be in for not telling someone about it.

What if Neal decided to run away instead of going to the police with the vital information he had? Why hadn't the authorities found the same information I had? Sure, the Hyattville murders had divided the investigating team several times since the day I watched Denise being buried. Each was a bigger power than the last. Local, state, GBI. Each approached matters in a different way.

Local had no idea who had murdered Denise. After Jake was found, the state came in and pointed the accusing finger at Sheriff Beasley, therefore shoving local deputies and their investigation aside. After David's murder, GBI agents came in, and apparently I became the point of their focus.

Through the power struggle, it appeared vital information was being lost or overlooked or not found at all. Yet, every time I found something I thought they should know, I was told they already knew about it and it wasn't important.

However, the newest bit of information about Neal was something I felt sure no one knew. If I had my way, I'd call Lonnie and tell him, but I'd promised Neal I'd wait until Thursday morning, and I would do just that.

Bright and early the next morning, there were plenty of people meandering up and down Burnt Magnolia Street. Some stopped and tried to open the door, so I opted to unlock it about thirty minutes earlier than usual. A few ladies wandered in and even made purchases.

Until well after lunchtime, Sandy and I were slammed with customers. In the early afternoon, a lady came in, and I stepped up to help her. Her red hair, frizzy and stacked high on top of her head, made her look taller than she actually was. While she'd overdone her jewelry, her tan slacks and white cotton blouse leaned more to the conservative side. If asked, I would say she was pretty in a rough gem sort of way. Nice to look at, but not quite polished.

I was just about to ask the woman if I could be of assistance when Kitty swept through the door. She handed me a sheet of paper. "Here's the Web site for those Italian shoes I was telling you about."

"Uh, okay. Thanks." I folded it and tucked it away in the pocket of my navy slacks.

Before I could get back to the redheaded lady waiting patiently, Kitty piped up again. "Did your new shipment from Atlanta come in yet?"

"Not yet, but please come in and look around. You may have

missed something the other day."

Kitty scooted off, and I turned back to the woman. "Are you looking for something special today?"

"You do have a lovely shop here, but actually I came to talk to you." The woman smiled widely, flashing a red gem imbedded in her front tooth. It was then that I recognized Garnet from the perfumery in Atlanta.

"Me?" Instantly, I was filled with the uneasy feeling she was going to lay more of her *insightful* advice on me. "What do you want to see me about?" My head throbbed and not from drinking too much wine the night before but from the anticipation of what Garnet had to tell me.

"Is there some place we could talk? I know you're busy, but I promise not to take too much of your time."

I escorted her to the storeroom, but the eerie vibes I was getting from the woman rattled me to the point that I was leery of being alone with her. I left the door of the back room open. As Garnet looked at me with a half smile, she reached into her pocket and pulled out a business card.

"Here." She slapped it into my hand. "I want you to call the number on the back of this card. I know I freaked you out the other day, and I felt really bad about that. When the psychic waves buzz through my mind's eye, I'm compelled to act on them."

"I'll admit you did catch me off guard when, out of the blue, you told me I was in danger. But whose number is this, and why would

I want to call it?"

"That's Detective John Archer with the Atlanta Police. I've worked with him on a few missing person cases. My hope is that if he vouches for me, you'll listen to what I have to say."

"Garnet, I appreciate your concern. Honest, I do, but Hyattville has had several murders lately, and all of it has been in the newspapers, on television. Everyone has heard about the troubles here. With no rhyme or reason for the murders, any one of our citizens could be in danger. I'm not ignoring you and your powers. It's just that . . ."

"It's not just anyone who is in danger. It's you. Sometimes I see after the crime has been committed, but sometimes I've been blessed with the power to see a crime before it happens.

"I've had the same dream nightly since you were in my shop last week. Since it persists, I have to believe I'm supposed to make you aware of a situation that may mean the end of your life. Do you understand?"

I didn't want to hurt Garnet's feelings. After all, she had come a long way, but I was too terrified by her words to think clearly. She was scaring the life right out of me. If someone didn't hurt me, as she predicted, I thought I might have a heart attack because of her. But it was obvious she wasn't going to go away.

"Have a seat." I climbed onto one of the stools next to the telephone. Once Garnet had joined me at the counter, I dialed the number on the back of the business card she'd given me.

"I'd like to speak to Detective Archer, please." I probably had a little more disgust in my voice than I meant to, but I had enough to sort through to pick out the good from the bad, the right from the wrong, without adding another rock to that pile.

"Archer," the male voice on the other end of the line said.

I told him who I was and that Garnet Windsor was at my shop. "She suggested I call you."

"Miss Windsor has worked with me on several missing persons cases over the last four years. Out of six cases, she helped us find the abductors in two cases; once she led us to the body of a missing college girl; and two more times she didn't lead us to the killer or the body, but when they were found, Garnet Windsor's visions of the perpetrator and what the crime scene looked like were dead-on. I believe she has a gift for that sort of stuff."

Stiffness from the busy workday settled across my shoulders. As I listened to Archer, I twisted from side to side hoping to ease some of the aching.

"A few days ago, she came to see me with a list of things she had seen about the Hyattville murders."

"Detective Archer, there has been so much in the news, anyone could tell you about it."

"I agree, but I called Lt. Moore with the state police and read him the list. He verified for me that her facts were correct. Some had been in the news, but there were some things the investigation team had kept quiet. She was right about them, too."

"How does that connect her to me? She's scaring the bejesus out of me."

"Apparently, Lt. Moore doesn't believe in psychics. Garnet tried to convince him you needed twenty-four-hour protection. That you are in real danger, but Moore said he wasn't going to unnecessarily upset you with voodoo stuff."

"They must have put some stock into what Garnet said because the GBI has my house under surveillance."

"Not anymore," Garnet and Archer said in unison.

"They removed them yesterday morning," Archer clarified their statement. "You may be a nonbeliever like Moore, but please just listen to Garnet and heed her warning. It may save your life. She cares enough to have closed her shop and driven all the way from Atlanta to talk to you."

I thanked the detective for his time, and then I hung up the phone. Archer was right. The least I could do was hear her out. "Okay, Garnet, tell me what you've seen that makes you think I'm in danger."

She looked as if a load had been lifted from her shoulders. "Every night I've seen you in a white, two-story, old farmhouse with black trim."

That was my house, but she could have driven by it at any time.

"There's a cat as black as midnight."

It was in the newspaper that I'd followed my cat into the woods and stumbled over David. That still didn't convince me that Garnet could foresee the future. Granted, the hair stood up on the back of my neck and I shivered slightly, but that still didn't convince me.

"The empty bottle of perfume you brought to me belonged to a dead woman. I knew that the day I held it."

Now she had my complete attention.

"In my dreams you are always holding the bottle and a watch."

Tingles racing up and down my arms forced me to my feet.

"The bottle is not tied to the murderer, but the watch is. That's what is putting you in harm's way. You must get rid of it." Her powerful words passed over me like I'd walked through a huge spider web. They were fairly soft, yet you knew somewhere in there lurked a spider and the threat of danger.

"Two different police officers had the watch, but could not tie it into Denise's murder. They didn't find it important enough to put into evidence. It wasn't found at the murder scene or in Denise's car. It was just part of things Denise had kept for years. Originally, the police looked through her personal things with the hope of finding out who she'd been seeing since no one in her family knew who it was or who could have been the father of her baby."

Garnet tapped her hard, red nails on the counter top. The *rat-a-tat* drummed against my tender nerves. "I didn't know about a baby."

I gave her a quizzical look.

"I don't know everything, but I do know that watch is important. I told Moore that, and he said he'd investigated the watch and found nothing of interest to the case. He might have taken my facts seriously if he'd opened his mind to the way I knew about it."

"Well, what should I do with the watch?" I'd tried everything I knew with no success.

"You must give it to someone who will take my words seriously. Someone who will dig into finding how the dead woman came to have the watch. When they find that out, they will find the killer."

My heart raced. Garnet had seen so much. Surely she could tell us who the murderer was. '"Have you seen him in your dreams?"

CHAPTER 14

GARNET WINDSOR GLANCED AT THE OPEN DOOR OF THE storeroom. Something had drawn her attention that way. Thinking she might be more comfortable answering my burning question if she was sure no one could hear, I gently eased the door shut.

"Have you seen the killer in your dreams? Can you tell me who it is or what he looks like?"

"Unfortunately, no. I just know he comes to your house looking for the watch, and I feel it is important to him because if anyone learns where it came from, they will know the killer's name."

"Okay, I have someone I can take it to." I instantly thought of Lonnie. "If I believe, he'll believe. He'll find the owner and get to the truth."

"I have to go, but I'll keep in touch. I feel a spiritual connection to you. There is an elderly woman who has appeared to me in my dreams on two occasions. Once the day you came into my shop, and again last night. That's when I made the decision to come here in person and try to convince you that danger is around you constantly. The woman in my dreams said to tell you to *keep your friends close and your enemies closer.*"

That could only be one person. "Grandma Carson." The thought of her sweet presence spread through me like warm maple syrup.

"I don't know who. I can only tell you what she said."

"Can you summon people or visions?"

"No, honey, it doesn't work that way. They come to me. I can't call them."

I'm sure my disappointment showed, because Garnet squeezed my hand. "I'm sorry. Just promise me you'll not stay alone in your house until the vicious monster is caught."

The fact that she used the singular form of the word *killer* stood out in my mind. "Do you believe the same person who killed Denise and Jake also killed David?"

Before Garnet could answer, the storeroom door burst open. To my surprise, Merrilee entered carrying a bag with paintbrushes sticking out of it.

She screeched to a halt. "I'm sorry, I didn't know you had someone in here."

"It's okay. We're through." I should have introduced Garnet and Merrilee, but I didn't want to take a chance on Garnet picking up something disturbing about the young girl. She appeared to have her emotions under control and was ready to start working on painting the Victorian Sampler's bags and boxes. I took that as a good sign.

"Look, you set up your stuff here, and I'll be right back."

Garnet and I left the storeroom, but stopped in front of the two fitting rooms before going on out into the flow of customers.

"Remember," Garnet said, "you must get the watch to the proper person and convince them that when they find who gave it to the dead woman, they will have the killer. And don't be alone in that big house until he is found." She gave me a hug and then headed to the door. "Now that I've talked to you, my dreams may stop, but if they don't and I receive any new information, I'll bring it straight to you since the state police aren't interested in what I have to say. Stay safe," she called and then left.

I stood there for a moment and then checked to see if Sandy needed my help with the customers circulating around the showroom.

"I'm doing fine," Sandy told me. "How about you? Everything okay?"

"It's been so long since things have been okay, I'm not sure I'd recognize it if it was."

I went back into the storeroom and found Merrilee with her paint supplies, brushes, paper towels, and a palette smeared with several piles of acrylic paints.

"How are you doing, sweetheart?" I gave her shoulder a gentle squeeze.

"Grandma and Aunt Sarah told me about my father. At first, I couldn't do anything but cry."

"Do you know why?" I tucked a strand of her long, blonde hair behind her ear.

"I guess because that was something I always wanted—a father. But to find out about mine, Mom had to die. I feel guilty that I can find happiness as a result of Mom's death." The beautiful teenager looked up at me. Her crystal blue eyes glistened. "Does that make sense, Evie?"

Particularly since nothing had been making sense, I could answer the bright young girl honestly. "That makes more sense than anything I've heard in a long time." A small amount of anger crept into my subconscious. How dare Denise withhold such valuable and life changing information from her daughter? And for depriving Lyle of giving Merrilee the love of which I knew he was capable.

"I'm sure your mom had her reasons for not telling you before she left us, but her dying had nothing to do with now having a father."

"I sorta came to that conclusion when I woke up this morning, but at first it was hard to take it all in. You know?"

"I can only imagine. Have you made plans to meet with him?"

"Not yet, but when I do meet him, will you be with me?"

My first instinct was to decline, but something in Merrilee's eyes told me how important her request was to her. "We'll see if that can be worked out. I just hope you do it soon because I know he very much wants to meet you."

I pulled a stack of bags from under the counter.

"I'll do two or three and then you can look at them to make sure we are on the same page." Merrilee smiled.

"Great." I went back out front to the showroom, closing the

door behind me.

Sandy was busy straightening a display of reversible tees. On the floor behind the counter, I found a big Victorian Sampler bag with white tissue paper sticking out the top of it.

I lifted it and guessed it held a couple of garments. "Did someone forget their package?"

"Ah, no," Sandy joined me behind the counter. "That belongs to Kitty Douglas. Her husband is going to come by and pick them up in a little while."

As if on cue, Lonnie came through the door.

"Good afternoon, ladies. Working hard or hardly working?" His wide smile made his blue eyes twinkle.

"You should be a comedian, Deputy Douglas." I leaned my elbows on the counter and waited until he crossed the room to us. "Lonnie, have you met Sandy McBride? I'm not sure what I would do without her around here."

"It's a pleasure to meet you. You're Lyle's sister, right?"

"That's right."

"Kitty said I was to come by here and pick up a package."

Sandy handed him the bag from the floor. "Actually, you're to pay for it, and then pick it up. She forgot her wallet, and she was running late for an appointment. She didn't have time to go home and get her money."

"She was in a big hurry when she called me. She's teaching a craft class at the nursing home."

"I gotta tell you, Lonnie, I'm very impressed with Kitty's community service. I've heard from customers a lot of good things about the work she does."

"Go ahead and say it. You can't believe that selfish teenager you knew way back when has turned out to have a good heart."

"You always could read my mind. By the way, when the investigation into Denise's murder first began, the state police took some things from her house just to see if they could find any clues. Did you get a chance to go through any of that stuff? It was pictures of you, me, Kitty, Denise, and a lot of old classmates." I started to mention the empty perfume bottle, but then decided against it since I now knew where that had come from, and I'd promised Neal he could have until the next morning to tell Lonnie about it. "Were you in on that part of the investigation?"

"No, I wasn't."

"When all of it was given back to Mrs. Farrell, she gave it to me because it was Denise's memories of our high school days. Mixed in with the pictures, newspaper clippings, and movie stubs I found a watch. No one seems to know who gave it to Denise. Anyway, I have a strong feeling it's connected to her murder. I tried to talk to you about it the other day, but we were interrupted and you didn't seem interested in listening to things I had uncovered in my own investigation."

"I told you not to get involved. I'm afraid you'll get hurt. Leave it to the people who know what they are doing, understand?"

"I understand, but I still want to talk to you about this."

"Okay, I have to serve a warrant out in your neck of the woods sometime this evening. I'll stop by your house."

"Good." That would work perfectly.

"Well, how much do I owe you?" Lonnie pulled his wallet from his pocket and handed a credit card to Sandy.

Before she could tell him, his radio interrupted. He stepped away to answer his call. When he turned back, Sandy had his receipt laid out for his signature. Lonnie signed it.

"It's good seeing you again, Sandy. I'm sure I'll see you around. I have to run. There's been an accident on the road to O'Brien." Lonnie grabbed the bag and hurried out the door.

"He seems very nice," Sandy said, and I noticed she had a slight lilt to her voice.

"He is. We've been best friends since we were kids."

"Cute, too."

Lonnie did have handsome features. Almost cherub-like with twinkling, blue eyes, rosy cheeks, and forever sporting a catchy smile. "I guess you're right. I just never think of him in that way."

I checked on Merrilee and was absolutely thrilled with her progress. She'd been at it for an hour and had done about a dozen bags. They were scattered around the room drying. The long-stemmed white bud and dark green leaves made a beautiful statement splashed across the pink background of the bags. I couldn't wait to use them. Her artistic touches would be appreciated by all who saw them.

"It's five o'clock. Why don't you get your things put away? Do you need a ride home, or did you drive your own car today?"

"I didn't go to get my license today. I'm walking to my friend Jennifer Nash's house over on the next block. Aunt Sarah will pick me up from there later tonight."

Out front, Sandy was behind the counter, closing out the register and removing the money from the till. "I've locked the front door," she said and then looked at me with a questioning gaze. "Does she know I'm her aunt?"

"I'm not sure. She hasn't mentioned it, and I thought it best to wait until she is ready to meet Lyle. Merrilee is smart beyond her years. She'll work it all out and be ready to meet the family she never knew she had. You'll see. She's going to love you all."

The front door jiggled. We both looked that way. It was Lyle. Sandy hurried to the door and unlocked it.

"Are you all right?" she asked her brother.

"Yeah, I'm fine. I need to talk to Evie." Lyle swiftly moved past her.

"Do you know a woman by the name of Garnet Windsor?" His face was pale and his breath short.

Things were happening so fast, I hesitated a second too long.

"Do you?" he asked again.

"Yes, yes, I do. Why? What's wrong?"

"She's been in a serious accident."

"Oh, no. What happened?"

"She ran off the road into the marsh on O'Brien Highway."

She'd just been there, telling me I was in danger. Now she was hurt. "Will she be okay?"

"I don't know. She's in really bad shape. They life-flighted her to Jacksonville."

Sandy had finished closing out the register and had been listening to her brother. When she looked at him, I noticed concern on her face. "Lyle, you seem more upset than usual about the accident."

She was right. "What's going on, Lyle? How did you connect this woman to me?" I asked.

"She was conscious for a few minutes when first responders arrived on the scene. She said the murderer had run her off the road and we had to protect Evie Carson. Who is Garnet Windsor? How do you know her?"

"She's a psychic from Atlanta. I met her when I was there a few weeks ago. She has worked with the police there on solving crimes. Evidently, she has tuned into me, and she came here today to tell me what she's seen."

"Psychic?" Lyle cocked his head slightly. "You mean she's a fortune-teller?"

"I believe she is a little more than that. I talked to a Detective Archer in Atlanta who vouched for her and her abilities to see the past and the future. She told me that the watch I'd shown you—the one Denise had in her keepsake box—that it's important to the case. And then she told me I was in danger and not to be at my home alone. She even gave me a message from my grandmother who died about six years ago."

Lyle looked dumbstruck. "That's crazy. Do you believe what she says?"

"I don't know what to believe. I've felt all along that the watch was important. You and Lt. Moore checked it out but didn't find anything special about it."

"Give it back to me, and I'll check it out again," he said as if that would make a difference.

I didn't feel that it would. "I don't have it with me. And besides, Lt. Moore made it clear to Garnet he didn't believe in her abilities, so he sent her away. He's not going to look into anything just because she says to." The watch had taken a position of high importance, and I didn't intend to put it back in the hands of people who couldn't see that.

"If it is evidence, you have to turn it over," he demanded.

"It was turned over, but it was given back. Now it's time to give someone else a crack at it." I didn't waver for a second.

"Okay. Okay. You and I don't need to argue about whether someone has the ability to read minds. You're right. Moore would reject anything to do with a psychic, but I want to have another look at it."

I didn't answer him.

"I'll tell you this—I do have enough faith in Ms. Windsor to heed her warning that you shouldn't be alone."

"What am I supposed to do? I can't stay with Lonnie's mom indefinitely. I want my life back to normal." By that time I was shaking from anger, frustration, and fear.

"The Windsor lady said she'd seen the killer. Now, I don't know if she meant in a vision or whatever it's called when she communicates with spirits, or if she saw the killer in real flesh and blood."

"Did you ask her what she meant?" I had to sit on a stool. My legs were threatening to drop me to my knees.

"I didn't get a chance to talk to her at all. The other officers who arrived before me questioned her as much as they could while the EMTs were working on her. She only said the murderer had run her off the road and you had to be protected. She lost consciousness shortly after that."

"I don't know what to do. Please tell me," I pleaded with him. "What should I do? Should I go to the hospital to see Garnet? Does she have family with her? As with so many other things, I feel responsible. If she hadn't come to see me, she wouldn't have been hurt."

Sandy stroked my back. "None of this is your fault. You have to stop thinking like that."

I knew she was right, but my insides were twisted into painful knots of guilt.

At that moment, the storeroom door opened and Merrilee entered the room.

Every part of me rebelled against dealing with another unsettling issue. Yet, it was thrust upon me, and I would handle it the best way possible. It wasn't every day that a father and daughter came face-to-face for the first time in their lives. The room buzzed with profound uneasiness. The color drained from Merrilee's face. She turned to escape the room and the adult eyes staring at her.

I took hold of her wrist and stopped her.

"Don't run away, honey. This is important."

She didn't resist, but she didn't face Lyle either. "Come on." Without a struggle, she followed me the few steps to where her father stood. "There really isn't any reason for you to put off the inevitable. I know this is awkward for you, but it's awkward for Lyle, too. Isn't it?" I looked to him for help.

"Yes, of course it is." I could tell he was struggling to keep his emotion-filled voice from cracking. "We do need to talk and try to get to know each other. At least a little bit."

When I was sure she wasn't going to bolt, I released my grip on Merrilee's arm. Her gaze scanned Lyle's face, as if taking in every bit of him would help her accept the fact that she had the father she'd prayed for all her life.

I stepped next to her and put my arm around her shoulder. "Merrilee, do you want to tell us what you're thinking?"

Pulling her bottom lip between her teeth, she nodded.

"Okay, what is it?" I edged her on.

She tilted her head to look into Lyle's eyes. "What should I call you?"

"Well, if Dad is a little uncomfortable for you, Lyle would work just fine."

"It's funny, but I've been thinking about you since the day Mom died. Something about you stuck in my mind. You came to the house and asked me and Grandma a bunch of questions. You wanted me to know that I could call if I ever needed anything. You were very kind to Grandma and to me. Did you know you were my father then, or are you always nice like that?"

"I learned the day before you did that you are my daughter. Your aunt said she told you everything about your mother and me, so you know I only met her one time. She never told me about you. If she had, I would have been in your life from the time you were born. Now that I know about you, I hope we can form a friendship and I can try to make up for the years we've lost."

"As for your question about his being nice all the time," I said, "I can answer that. Yes, he is. He's kind and considerate." I said those words with no hesitation. "It'll take time, but I know he wants to be part of your life."

"He's not the only one." Sandy spoke for the first time. "I'm Lyle's sister, and that makes me your aunt. My name is Sandy. I have a little boy named Scotty who is going to be excited about meeting his new cousin. I hope you'll be okay with spending time with us so you can get to know us." She smiled widely.

"It's just so weird. I don't know what I'm supposed to do or say." Merrilee's words were laced with concern, but the anxiety had vanished from the young girl's face. I believed I saw a shy smile quaking at the corners of her mouth.

"I'll tell you what," Lyle said. "Would it be okay if we go to the café across the street and talk for a little while? You can tell me all about yourself, like what your middle name is, what kind of ice cream you like, and when your birthday is. You know, stuff like that."

Merrilee nodded. "Okay. Oh, wait. I'm supposed to walk to my friend's house on the next block. Aunt Sarah is picking me up from there."

"If you want to go, I'll call your aunt and let her know that Lyle will bring you home. You can call Jennifer and tell her you aren't going to make it. How does that sound?"

"Will you go with us?" Merrilee asked.

"Yes, please do." Lyle urged.

Going with them would give me time to decide if I was going to the hospital, or to the house I'd been warned to stay away from. "Okay, I'll go for a few minutes, but I can't stay long."

"You come, too, Sandy," Lyle said to his sister.

While I called Sarah to tell her Lyle would be bringing Merrilee home shortly, she called her friend to let her know she was going to the café with her *dad.*

I'd stayed with them for about thirty minutes. They were doing fine on their own. I really didn't need to be there. But where did I need to be?

By the time Garnet had left the boutique, she had shaken me to the core. Then, after I learned the dreadful news that she'd been seriously hurt, I'd been slammed with intense fear. She had told the police it was the murderer who had forced her to wreck and I needed protection.

"I really hate to do this, but I need to go." I gathered my purse.

"Where are you going?" Lyle nearly jumped out of his seat.

"You can't go home alone."

My gaze snapped to Merrilee. Her eyes were wide with fear. "Is something wrong?" Her voice faltered.

"Nothing you need to be concerned with, honey. You stay here and visit with Lyle." I turned my attention to him. "I've decided to drive to Jacksonville and see if Garnet has regained consciousness."

Lyle rose, and we walked closer to the door where Merrilee couldn't hear us talking. "Evie, I can't let you go off by yourself. This Garnet person may be a impostor, but I can't take the chance that she isn't. I don't want you to be alone until we find the killer." He walked back to the table. "Sandy, I need a favor from you. Will you go with Evie to Jacksonville, to the hospital to check on Garnet Windsor? I'll feel better if she isn't traveling alone."

"Does this have something to do with the person who killed my mom?" Merrilee's concern plainly showed across her beautiful face.

"We really aren't sure, but I don't want Evie to be alone until we get some answers. She has been closely involved in the bad things that have been going on here in Hyattville. She wants to drive to Jacksonville, which is an hour away, to visit a sick friend in the hospital, and then she'll have to drive home late tonight by herself. I'll just feel better if she has someone with her." He turned back to Sandy. "I'll take Merrilee home. I'd like to spend a few minutes there with her and her grandmother. Then I'll go get Scotty from Nina's. He'll be home all tucked into bed when you get there." He then directed his attention to me. "When you bring Sandy home, you're to come in and spend the night at our house. You are not to go home alone. Do we understand each other?"

Silently I nodded, and then said, "Truthfully, I'm completely and utterly grateful I won't have to go traipsing through the scary darkness and go into my home alone. Thank you."

Sandy and I arrived at St. Vincent's Hospital in Jacksonville around eight o'clock. It came to my mind that I was supposed to meet Lonnie at my house about that time to give him the watch. I used my cell phone to call him. He answered right away.

"Helloooo," he sang.

"Hi. I'm in Jacksonville, hoping to see how Garnet Windsor is doing. Just wanted you to know I wouldn't be at the house tonight."

"That's okay. As it turns out, I don't have to deliver that summons out there."

"Darn," I said without thinking.

"Something wrong?"

"I was going to ask you to go by my house and feed my cat. I won't be home at all tonight, and since you still have the key I gave you when you put the alarm system in, I was hoping you could go by there and give Midnight his food."

"I can take care of that. Consider it done."

"I'll make it up to you."

"I'm thinking apple pie with sweet cider sauce."

"You're a glutton for punishment, but I'll certainly give it a try."

When I inquired at the ICU nurse's station where I could find Garnet, I was told she couldn't have visitors. I was then taken to a waiting room where a thirty-something-year-old woman sat staring at a television with the volume down low.

"Mrs. Carrey," the nurse said to the woman, "these ladies are here to see your mother."

Awkwardly, I crossed the room. "Hi. I'm Evie Carson, and this is Sandy McBride. I'm sorry about your mother's accident. How is she doing?"

"Not good. I haven't been here very long. I just came back from seeing her. I was allowed in there for only ten minutes. How do you know my mom?"

"I went into her shop a week ago. Today she came to my boutique in Hyattville, just outside of Brunswick." I hesitated, not sure how to describe my connection to Garnet.

"That's okay, you don't need to explain. She picked up vibes when you came into her shop, and then she felt compelled to try to convince you of what she'd seen. I know the drill. I've dealt with it all my life." Garnet's daughter didn't seem disturbed by the fact that her mother could possibly be dying because of her ability to see evil.

I, on the other hand, staggered under the devastation brought on because I'd ventured into Garnet's shop hoping to find a thread that might lead to my friend's killer. I truly believed that had I not gone there that day, Garnet would not be struggling for her life. My eyes burned as I fought back self-serving tears I had no right to shed.

I should have been comforting Garnet's daughter, but I wasn't sure how to do that. "Sandy's brother is a state trooper, and he was at the scene of the accident. He said Garnet tried to talk to them but lost consciousness. Has she awakened at all?"

"She hasn't come around since I've been here. The nurse said she's drifted in and out, but she's not been conscious enough to answer questions. She opened her eyes when I talked to her, so I think she knows I'm here." Her voice quivered.

"I'm sure she does." Sandy took her arm and led her to a chair. "Evie, why don't you two sit here, and I'll go get us a cup of coffee." She looked at the woman. "Mrs. Carrey, do you take cream or sugar?"

"Please, call me Pet," the woman said. "It's short for Petula. I'll have a little cream and one sugar. Thank you."

Sandy left on her mission to find coffee. I took Pet's hand and sat quietly for a few minutes.

"It's not your fault." She squeezed my hand and looked deeply into my eyes. "This isn't the first time Mom's gift has nearly cost her life. She possesses a tool to help bring closure to families who have lost loved ones.

"More than once she has out-and-out named a murderer only to have no one believe her. Then the killer has come after her. She knows there's a possibility she may die, but that doesn't stop her." Pet talked understatedly about her mother.

I wondered what her life must have been like with a psychic mom. "Why would she do that? If she doesn't think about herself, doesn't she think about the heartache for her family and friends?"

Pet smiled. "I know it's hard to understand, but it's because of us that she puts herself on the line to help anyone she can."

Sandy returned with coffee and muffins to sustain us until we could get something more substantial. Pet took the coffee but refused the sweet.

After taking a slow, thoughtful sip, she continued. "When my mother was a teenager, everyone ridiculed her because of her gift. She had a vision of a monster strangling her best friend. She dreamed it for several days but never told anyone else. My grandmother woke Mom one morning with the sad news that her friend had been killed by her stepfather. Mom blamed herself. She knew the man had been hurting her friend and he was going to kill her, but she didn't speak up. After that, mom never had a vision she didn't act on. And as I said, sometimes that puts her in harm's way."

A nurse came to the door. "Mrs. Carrey, your mom is becoming responsive. If you'd like to come in, you can."

Pet took my hand and pulled me with her. "I want her to go, too. Mom will want to see her."

For just a moment, the nurse stared and then led us to Garnet's cubicle. She had discoloration and swelling around her right eye, had an IV line in her arm, and was hooked up to a heart and blood pressure monitor. I'd imagined her looking much worse. Although I felt some relief, she looked weak and vulnerable, which only reminded me a killer was still on the loose and the savage person may be the reason for Garnet being where she was.

Pet took her mother's hand. "Mom, I'm here. Rubin is on his way. He should be here later tonight." She waited a moment. Garnet didn't respond. Pet motioned for me to come closer. "Let her know you're here."

Awkwardly, I went to the other side of the bed. "Garnet, it's Evie Carson." I started to grasp her hand but wondered if that was a good idea. Pet saw my hesitance and urged me on.

Garnet never opened her eyes, but she moved her fingers inside my hand. My gaze scanned her face, waiting to see any sign she was going to wake up or speak. When her mouth began to move, I thought I'd imagined it. But I hadn't. I heard her whisper my name.

I leaned closer. "Yes, Garnet. I'm here."

Her lips moved slowly, deliberately. "Watch the stars."

CHAPTER 15

EERIE SILENCE CLOAKED THE INTENSIVE CARE UNIT WHERE GARnet lay motionless, yet fighting for her life. Moments before, she'd tried to tell me something, but her weak voice had made it hard for me to understand. Instantly, I looked at her daughter, but Pet shrugged. To me, it had sounded like, "Watch the stars," but I couldn't be sure.

For another few minutes, Pet and I stood quietly beside Garnet's bed, looking for any sign she might wake up. But she didn't, and soon the nurse told us it was time to leave.

Once we were back in the waiting room, I told Sandy about my visit with Garnet. "I'm not exactly sure what she said. Did you understand her?"

Pet shook her head. "I think she said *watch the stars,* but I wouldn't swear to it."

I had to agree. "Yeah, that's what it sounded like to me, too. Do you think she could be referring to the watch?"

Pet shrugged.

A few quiet moments passed as we tried to understand what Garnet's words meant. "Could she mean reading horoscopes?" Sandy added her best guess.

Pet frowned. "Mom doesn't usually relate things as they pertain to horoscopes. She sees things in real time as they happen. Normally, everything she sees comes to light."

I was tired, hungry, and confused. But more than anything, I was heartsick for Garnet and her family. "Pet, is there anything I can do for you?" I couldn't imagine what that might be, but I'd do anything to help.

"No, nothing at all. My brother and his wife will be here in a couple of hours."

I pulled a piece of paper from my purse and scribbled my cell and shop phone number. "Here. Please call me if you need anything, and I'd appreciate knowing how she is doing."

"Of course, I'll let you know if anything changes or if she has any messages for you." Pet took my hand and squeezed it for a moment. "Be careful."

Leaving Pet was harder than I had expected, but Sandy and I had to get home. We had to be at work early in the morning, and I had to figure out what I was going to do about clean clothes since I couldn't go home to get anything.

I was just about to pull out of the parking lot onto the street when Sandy asked me to wait a minute. She hurriedly exited the car, deposited coins into the slot of a newspaper box, and pulled out a copy of Jacksonville's local paper. Once she was back in her seat, she turned on the dome light.

"What in the world are you doing?"

"I'm checking your horoscope." She scanned the front page index, then skipped directly to the appropriate section. "Here it is. 'You are in desperate need of R&R. Now is the time to dip into your savings and go somewhere exotic. Take a friend,'" she read.

There was a pregnant pause. Then, probably because we'd been absorbed in so much unfathomable sadness for so long that I couldn't allow myself to go any deeper, I began to laugh. Sandy stared at me for a moment, and then she joined me. We snorted and chuckled all the way to Interstate 95 North.

Suddenly I stopped. "Should we be carrying on like this with so much misery and sorrow surrounding us?"

Sandy looked my way. "Evie, you're not responsible for the things that have happened. A monster is on the loose, wreaking havoc on many lives. You can't quit living because others have died." She stared straight ahead. "I have a confession."

I stole a sideways glance at her. "Yes?"

The dash lights illuminated her face enough for me to see a smile tugging at her lips. "Your horoscope didn't say to take a friend. I threw that in just in case you decided to go somewhere exotic, so you might take me with you."

That was all it took to send us back into hysterical laughter. Despite the guilt I insisted on carrying, I welcomed the lighthearted relief Sandy and I were enjoying. It made the trip go by quickly.

Just before we reached the city limits of O'Brien where Lyle's house was located, Lonnie called. "Listen, we were slammed at the duty desk this evening, but I finally made it out to your house and fed the cat. Everything was locked up tight. I tried to call you, hoping you could tell me where the watch is that you wanted me to take a look at, but you didn't answer so I figured you were in the hospital and had your phone off."

"I'm sorry. Yes, I had to turn it off while I was in the hospital. Anyway, I have the watch locked away in Dad's gun closet."

"That's okay. I'll get it tomorrow. How was Garnet Windsor? Any change in her condition?"

"Not really. She did wake up while I was there. She told me to watch the stars."

"What does that mean?" Lonnie's cell phone crackled.

"I don't have a clue. I think I'm losing you. Thanks for taking care of Midnight for me."

"Sure thing," Lonnie said, and then hung up.

A few minutes before eleven, Sandy and I arrived at the home that she and her son shared with Lyle. Before we got out of the car, I reminded her I didn't have anything I would need to spend the night—no toothbrush or nightgown. And I didn't have any clothes to wear to work in the morning.

"Well, Lyle would kill me and you if we went to your house.

Let's go on in. I know I have nightclothes you can wear, and I'm sure I have a new toothbrush. If you can't find something in my closet for work in the morning, then Lyle will go with you to your house. How does that sound?"

"Good. Thanks for going with me to see Garnet. I'm not sure I could have made the trip without you."

Sandy gave me a hug. Any further words were lodged in my throat. We dragged our tired bodies into her house where Lyle waited with egg salad sandwiches and hot chocolate.

The next morning, since Sandy had left her car at the boutique, we rode into work together. She had me decked out in one of her stylish outfits, which luckily fit me very well.

My nerves were raw. Burning, unanswered questions twisted my stomach in knots. Each time the door opened or the phone rang, I jumped. For the umpteenth time, I glanced at the clock. Surely the hands had stopped.

By noon, I couldn't stand it any longer. It was time to start making calls.

My call to the sheriff's office didn't ease any of my anxiety. Lonnie was in a meeting and couldn't be disturbed. The duty desk deputy didn't know whom the meeting was with. I sincerely prayed it was with Neal Lancaster. I left a message for Lonnie to call as soon as he was free.

Next, I called the hospital for a report on Garnet. When I was transferred to the waiting room, Pet answered.

"How is your mom doing today?" If wishing could make it happen—

"The doctor said her vitals are all good, but it's still just a wait-and-see situation. He said it will probably be another twenty-four hours before we see any signs of improvement. That is, if we are going to."

"Has she awakened at all since I was there last night?" Although I was worried about Garnet and her recovery, I really wanted to know if she had said anything else.

"No, she's been resting comfortably. I really think your visit has helped her do that. She knows that you weren't hurt, too."

For some reason, I was fine. It was those around me who needed protected. Pet assured me she would call if there was any change.

As I hung up, Sandy returned from her trip to the bank and picking up lunch. I tried to eat, but everything threatened to come back up. Slowly, I sipped a diet soda, hoping for relief.

The phone rang, and before I answered I knew it was Lonnie.

"Hi, Evie." I didn't think Lonnie would be in a jovial state, but I didn't expect the distinct anguish that drifted through the receiver.

"I take it you've talked to Neal."

"Yes. The state police are taking his statement. He told me you convinced him to talk to me. Thanks."

"Are you okay, Lonnie?"

"I'm not sure." He sounded preoccupied. "I really need to have a look at that watch. Did you happen to bring it with you today?"

"No, it's at my house."

"I'd better have a look at it right away."

I could hear someone talking in the background. "Lonnie, are you still there?"

"Sure, I'm here. I have to go by to pick up Kitty. She and I have something we have to take care of in O'Brien. I hate to ask you to do this, but I'd need you to meet me at your house. If you wait fifteen minutes, that will give me plenty of time to get there before you do."

I didn't see anything wrong with going to my house in broad daylight, especially since Lonnie and Kitty would be waiting for me. Besides, it would be a perfect opportunity to pack a few things to take to Sandy's, where I would be staying for a couple of days.

And that reminded me I'd certainly been taking advantage of Sandy lately, but hopefully she would understand my leaving her alone in the boutique again. "If you're sure you'll be there, I'll meet you." I disconnected the call with Lonnie.

"Sandy," I called into the back room. She joined me behind the counter. "I have to go out for a while. I'll be back as soon as I can."

"Under normal circumstances, I wouldn't ask, but where are you going?"

"I'm going to meet Lonnie at my house." I grabbed my purse.

"Are you crazy? Where is he now?"

"At the sheriff's office. I know he's under a lot of pressure, but he sounded really strange. Anyway, he said if I waited fifteen minutes before I left he'd be waiting at my house for me."

"I don't think you should go there alone. We can close up early, and I'll go with you."

"I'll be fine. Honest. Lonnie will be waiting for me."

"Evie, please. You could be in real danger if you go alone."

I flashed an honest smile at Sandy. "Are you psychic, too?"

"No, but I now know one. She has advised you not to be by yourself, especially in your home."

"I'll tell you what—if Lonnie isn't there, I'll wait for him before I even get out of my car. Will that make you feel better?"

Sandy drew her lips together tightly. "Okay." Her tone had gone from frantic to calm a little too rapidly.

I left the boutique, but as I climbed into my car and started the engine, I had no doubt Sandy was calling her big brother.

All the frightening predictions aside, it was good to be home. The old house looked peaceful and quiet, but something was out of place. On second glance, I realized what it was. Midnight was out of the house, sitting on the porch waiting for me to let him inside, which is where he should have been.

Surely, Lonnie wouldn't have let him out when he fed him last night, or maybe, during the day someone broke in again and he escaped.

Neither scenario made any sense. Unexpectedly, Midnight skittered off the porch and raced around the house. In a matter of seconds, he reappeared inside on the living room windowsill. The back door had to be open.

"What the hell is going on?" I reached for my cell phone, but then I saw my front door open, and Kitty waved to me from inside.

I got out of the car. "Damn, Kitty, you scared the crap out of me." I climbed the porch steps.

She gave me a curt nod, and appeared a little angry.

I'd be mad too if I'd been dumped out there all alone. "Where's Lonnie?" I hurried into the house.

"I don't know."

I stopped short and turned to face her. "What do you mean, you don't know? Didn't he bring you out here?"

"No."

I stole a glance back out into the yard. "How did you get here? Where's your car?"

"What is this? Twenty questions?" Kitty virtually snarled.

"What are you doing here?" Her glare nearly burned a hole through me. I hurried to her. "Is something wrong? Are you sick?" I started to lead her to the sofa, but she pulled free. I held my hands up to assure her I wasn't going to touch her again. "What is it? What's wrong?"

"Give me the damn watch." Kitty's mouth moved, but the voice wasn't hers. It was deeper, harder, scarier.

I stepped back and landed in the chair on my ass. When I looked up, I was staring into the barrel of Dad's .38. My brain froze. I could not process what was happening.

"Kitty, I . . . I don't understand." My voice shook.

"You don't need to understand." She thrust the gun directly at me.

Although I shook violently, Kitty's hands were calm enough to do surgery. "You have the worst timing of anyone I know. I was getting ready to shoot the lock off the gun cabinet when I heard you pull up." Kitty's menacing laugh ripped through the hot, summer air. "Now *you* can open it for me."

Somehow I had to rationalize what was happening. Kitty was having a breakdown, and I was clueless as to what I could do. Certainly the whole town of Hyattville had been under tremendous pressure, but the killer hadn't threatened or tried to hurt her. Why was she acting that way?

I was there to get the watch so Lonnie could see if he could connect it to Denise's murder. Yet Kitty had gone to the extreme of using a gun to force me to give it to her.

"Get up from there, now. I want my watch." Her words thundered through my head.

"*Your* watch? I don't have your watch. I have Denise's watch."

Anger twisted Kitty's sweet face into a horrific demonstration of evil. "It's *my* watch, you stupid bitch."

I shivered but finally found the strength to stand. "Why did Denise have your watch?"

"I don't think that really makes any difference at this point, do you?"

"Yes, I do, and you damned well better tell me what this is all about."

Kitty laughed wickedly. "You always were slow on the uptake, Evie."

Maybe she was right, because I couldn't make any sense of the craziness going on around me. She shoved me toward the hallway. It was then I noticed shoe prints in the dust on the hardwood floors. The prints led to and from Dad's room. They were made by Kitty's J. Carmelito's and plainly showed the stars in the heels. They had to be the stars Garnet warned me about.

From behind, Kitty shoved me again. She stood close enough for me to smell her perfume.

Honeysuckle. Ray de Miel.

Anger and stupidity seethed through me. I clenched my fists at my side and stood toe to toe with Kitty. "You're the one." Of all the things I thought Kitty was, murderess wasn't one of them.

But I would have to add it, and sadly, believe it. With that realization, my heart took the sharpest blow yet. "You killed Denise and Jake, didn't you?" The words were so bitter, I thought I might throw up.

Kitty laughed again. The hair on the back of my neck stood up.

"Wow, you really are slow, but you need to move fast and give me the watch."

Suddenly, the fog was lifting. I had many questions for Kitty. Hopefully I could get some answers and perhaps stall for time. Someone—Lyle or Lonnie—would come looking for me. "How did you even know I had it?"

"The day of the funeral, I saw Denise's brat give you the watch, and I've been on a mission to get it back ever since."

"So it's you who has been coming into my house. You were looking for that watch. I knew it held clues to everything, but no one would listen. No one found it important. What happened to you? What made you bring this kind of pain to so many innocent people?"

Her expression held absolutely no remorse for the anguish her actions had caused.

When it was apparent she wasn't even contemplating an answer for me, I continued to stall for time. As I talked, I listened for the sound of a vehicle, but none came. "I thought you were afraid of guns. You even made me hide that one the other night because it frightened you so. What was that all about?"

Without taking a sighted aim, Kitty fired the pistol with skilled accuracy, hitting the combination lock. Shards of metal scattered. Instinctively, my hands went to my ears, and I believe I screamed. Kitty laughed and shoved me down on the bed.

She kept the gun trained on me, and with her free hand she pulled the gun case open and easily retrieved her watch. She clutched it to her chest and visibly sighed with relief. Did she think that was the end of all her problems?

"If you could do that, why didn't you do it weeks ago?"

"Until last night when you told Lonnie where it was hidden, I couldn't find it. Do you think I'd have kept coming back if I knew where it was?" She scoffed. "And you think I'm a nitwit. I guess you're thinking a little differently now."

I teetered between fear and anger. My stomach churned. I shoved my balled fist into it, hoping to stop the threatening motion. I was fairly sure Kitty would be even more upset if I puked on her J. Carmelito's. I wanted her out of my house. "You have your damn watch. Now get out of here."

Kitty scratched her temple with the barrel of the gun. Before I could move a muscle, she pointed it back at me. "Stay right where you are. I'm not leaving you here to tell the world my little secret. We have some things to settle."

"What does this have to do with me? And to think, I'd actually started liking you. Like everyone else in town, I've been very impressed with the charitable work you've been doing.

How can you be that way one minute—" *and be the monster who murders helpless people the next?* "Why would you do such terrible things?"

She showed no sign of answering my demanding question. Instead, she flashed that menacing grin.

"Why, Kitty? Did you find out Neal was also seeing Denise? Is that why you killed her?"

Her smile disappeared, replaced by a dark shroud of evil. "You have that all wrong, you stupid bitch. She found out that *I* was seeing Neal. She walked in on us at the motel. That's when everything went to hell in a handbasket.

"Neal told me to leave, and while I was getting back into my clothes, he literally begged that whore not to leave him. He had the nerve to tell her he loved her with me standing right there."

Disgust filled every fiber of my being. "You took her life because Neal chose her over you?"

"Of course not. What do you think I am?"

You're a very sick woman, Kitty. A woman with split personalities—and one of them is very evil.

"Kitty, you're just not making any sense."

"When I left the motel, I forgot this watch. Lonnie gave it to me for our twentieth anniversary last year. The next day, Denise came to my house and told me she had my watch, and if I ever had anything else to do with Neal, she would give it to Lonnie and tell him exactly where she'd gotten it." She pursed her lips as a pouting child would. "You understand, don't you, Evie, I couldn't let that happen. So, I decided to just get rid of her. I could then tell Lonnie I'd lost the watch, and that I was so very sorry. I could go back to my normal life."

Obviously deep in thought, Kitty lapsed into silence, which lasted only a moment. "I guess I should have given that a little more consideration. In hindsight, I should have forced her to give me the watch, and then killed her."

How could Kitty stand there displaying more remorse for not getting the watch beforehand than for killing Denise? I couldn't put rational thought to anything Kitty said. How had she gone from typical, teenage insecurities to being submerged in madness? How would Lonnie ever get over such a thing?

She paced a little, but continued her story in an eerie monotone. "I followed Denise to the motel. After I parked my car around the corner, I pulled Lonnie's nightstick from under the car seat, and then I waited until Neal crawled out the back window and slithered through the hole in the fence like the slime he is." Kitty stopped a moment as if to reflect on her thoughts of Neal. I had a few of my own, but then wasn't the time to cough them up.

"I went to the garage where Denise's car was and waited for her to come out of the room. About two hours passed, and she didn't come out. I figured the cow must have fallen asleep." Kitty smirked. "I went around back, and the window Neal had crawled out of was still opened. I looked inside. Denise was in the bathroom. I could hear water running, and I figured that would drown out any noise I'd make climbing into the room. I got a bucket from near the dumpster in the alley and climbed inside. I'd barely made it into the room when Denise came out of the bathroom. Her hair was wrapped in a towel, and she was naked as the day she was born. All I could figure out was that she heard me and came to see if Neal had come back. Boy, was she in for a surprise." Kitty stared off into the distance, a satisfied smile curving her lips.

I tried to gauge the chance of my taking the gun away from her. As if she'd read my mind, she pointed it directly at my heart and shook her head.

"Don't. It would be a shame if I had to kill you." Quickly she came back to her story of killing Denise.

"I hit her in the throat with the Billy club and crushed her pretty windpipe. I got the biggest charge out of watching her gurgle her way into death and letting her know I had the last word on the matter. I checked her purse to see if by some chance she had my watch with her. She didn't."

Vomit climbed high in my throat. I closed my eyes and swallowed several times to keep from losing it, but in the dark, images of Denise gasping for her last breath forced me to open my eyes again. Could any of this get any sicker? Suddenly it did.

"Kitty, did you kill my husband, too?"

Her gaze snapped to me. "Oh, don't act like that was someone you cared about. Don't forget you'd already thrown him out like last week's newspapers. I did you a favor, and I didn't make a mess in your house either."

She had killed David. Why? For God's sake, why? "How did you get him out there in the woods?"

She waved the gun at me and chuckled. "Easy. I was upstairs looking for the watch when he pulled up. I took your gun from your nightstand and concealed it with a towel. I couldn't allow him to tell you I had been in your house. I told him you were out in the woods with one of the officers investigating Denise's murder. He was happy to race out there to give you legal advice in case they were planning on arresting you."

I must have made an audible gasp, because Kitty abruptly stopped and stared at me.

"Oh, yeah, he actually said that. He hightailed it across the meadow. I almost had to run to keep up with him. He talked the whole way over there like I gave a shit about how much he could do to save you if they even thought about arresting you." Kitty rubbed her temple as if she had a headache.

I heard a car pull into the front yard, but evidently Kitty didn't. She continued to talk. "Once I got him out there, I shot him. I gotta tell you, Evie—he was so full of crap, I almost shot him on the way across the meadow just to shut him up."

I prayed whoever was outside would not just walk in and risk becoming another one of Kitty's victim. I heard slight creaks of the hardwood floors. Quietly and slowly, someone was walking down the hall. Hoping to distract her, I stood.

"Don't make me shoot you, Evie," she yelled.

My heart nearly stopped. Kitty had her back to the door, and I prayed help had arrived. With a casual stride, she walked up next to the bed where I sat, put her arm around my head, and tilted it upward. As she turned to face the door, she jabbed the barrel of Dad's gun sharply into my throat.

Lyle stepped into the opening, his gun drawn. He identified himself as a police officer. I could tell by the stark terror etched on his face, Lyle was as shocked as I had been that Kitty was on the business end of a gun.

"Put the gun down, Mrs. Douglas, and step away from Evie." His gaze never left Kitty's face—not even when she shoved the gun's barrel further into the tender flesh of my throat, pressing against my windpipe. I had to struggle to breathe.

"Do it now," Lyle demanded.

Kitty chortled. "You may shoot me, but are you sure you can hit just me? Are you sure I won't pull the trigger first and blow her throat away? Come on—I'll count to three, and we'll shoot."

Only then did Lyle look at me. I tried to signal with my eyes, but I'm sure their rapid movement confused him. I wanted to make him understand that if he shot her, I'd fight with all my might to push the gun away from my face before she could fire the weapon. Evidently, all I registered on my face was wide-eyed terror.

"Lay your gun down," Kitty demanded.

Lyle bent slightly and lowered his gun to the floor.

"Kick it over here like a good boy."

As he did, I felt the gun pressure release from my neck. Kitty had moved it away. Lyle took a step forward. A loud blast sounded near my head. A hole opened in Lyle's shirt, and blood instantly appeared. He fell to the floor with a resounding thud.

I screamed and pushed Kitty aside. Quickly, I dashed to Lyle and slumped at his side. Touching his neck, I felt for a pulse. I heard the gun click near my ear. I froze. My last cognizant thought was wondering why Kitty hadn't shot me. A fraction of a second later, excruciating pain exploded in my head. Darkness cloaked me like a thief and carried me into a hole I feared I'd never climb out of.

I fought a horrific battle to come out of the nightmare. The more I forced my mind to wake up, the more vivid the awful images became. Finally, I forced my eyes open. Surrounded by green walls and medical equipment, I lay on an uncomfortable gurney. Pain constricted every muscle up the back of my neck and deep inside my head. Slowly I shifted my position to look at the opposite wall. Lonnie sat with his head bent as if in prayer.

"What happened to me?" I barely eked out the words.

Quickly Lonnie raised his gaze to mine. His misty eyes startled me. Without hesitation, he rose and grasped my hand so tightly I flinched.

"God, Evie, I'm so sorry." He pressed his cheek against mine. The wetness of his tears seared against my skin. "It's entirely my fault. I shouldn't have sent you out there until I knew where Kitty was. I thought I'd pick her up, and we'd go to your house. I needed to know for sure if the watch you were talking about was the one I'd given to Kitty, but she claimed she'd lost it. But I couldn't find her, and then I couldn't get to you fast enough. I'm so sorry."

Slowly the kaleidoscope pieces fell away and left behind a perfect picture of the bedlam Kitty had rained down upon the town of Hyattville. The devastation she had unquestionably caused her husband. Yet, Lonnie felt the need to apologize to me.

"No, Lonnie, I'm the one who is sorry." I rubbed my free hand along his arm. "It'll be okay. We'll get Kitty the kind of help she needs. You'll see, it will all be okay." I knew my words were empty. I didn't have the power to make things right again, but I was at a loss for words and too confused to try to manufacture any.

A sharp pain stabbed through my head. I groaned and nearly screamed. Lonnie moved so he could look at me.

"Should I get the nurse?" He fumbled for the call button.

"No, I'm okay." Suddenly, I knew what I needed more than anything. "Where's Lyle?" As I said his name, I recalled the last time I'd seen him. I struggled to sit up, but dizziness forced me back onto the pillow. I took hold of Lonnie's shirt and pulled him closer to me. "Is Lyle dead?"

Lonnie stammered, but finally answered. "No, he's in surgery right now. Sandy's waiting for him to come out. She'll come directly here as soon as she hears anything."

"Where's Kitty?"

"I don't know."

The thought of Kitty being unaccounted for struck terror in my heart. "What do you mean?"

"When I showed up at your house, she was gone. I found Lyle shot and you unconscious from a blow to the head."

"You mean, she didn't shoot me? I heard the gun click, but I didn't hear the blast I was expecting. She's shot everyone else connected to me. She definitely had the chance. Why not me?"

Lonnie shook his head. His silence told me he had no more idea of what went on in Kitty's head than anyone else did. At that moment, his life was a train wreck and would remain so until his wife was found.

"Why are you here? Shouldn't you be out combing the countryside for Kitty?"

"I've been temporarily relieved of my badge and gun until they can decide how my wife could be a murderer and I, a Hyattville deputy, had no earthly idea. Actually, I'd like to know the answer to that myself."

"I was with her many times in the past few weeks, and I didn't pick up on anything that would lead me to conclude she was cra— I'm sorry. I shouldn't have said that."

"It's okay, Evie. The facts are what they are, and there is nothing we can do about it."

"If you didn't see her, then how did you know she was the one who shot Lyle and knocked me out?"

Lonnie went to the small sink, put a paper towel under the running water, and then wiped his face. "Neal told me the whole sordid story of his and Denise's affair and that he was the father of her unborn child. He told me you figured that out and forced him to confess it all to me. Since you reasoned your way through the other details, I assume you know he was also having an extra-extramarital affair with my loving wife."

"She's sick, Lonnie. She may not have cancer, or heart trouble, but she is just as sick. Do you have any idea where she would be?

Have they put out an APB on her and her car?"

He dropped the paper towel in the trash can and then sat again in the chair next to my bed. He looked deeply into my eyes. I could almost see the pain. "Oh, her car is parked at our house. I have no idea where she is or what she's driving. Evidently, I've never known her at all. I thought I did. I thought she truly loved me. How could I have been so stupid for so many years? What a mockery she's made of our life, our marriage—and what a complete fool I've been."

"I'm sorry you're hurting." I squeezed Lonnie's cold hand. "We'll get through this. By the way, what's going on with me? This looks like the emergency room, so I assume I've not been admitted to the hospital."

"No, you haven't. You've been here for several hours."

I touched the patch on the side of my head. The feeling had painfully returned. "Have I been out all that time? Or do I just not remember?"

"I don't know. I just got here about twenty minutes ago. They told me it took five stitches to close a gash above your right ear. Apparently, Kitty whacked you with the gun."

Instinctively, I felt the area surrounding the bandage. "Did they shave my head?"

"I'm sure they had to, at least some of it." His raspy voice raked over my sad heart. "You'd stopped bleeding by the time I got to your house, but your pretty red hair was matted with blood."

"Auburn," I corrected, partly from vanity and partly to direct his thoughts away from Kitty.

"What?"

"My hair is auburn. You know, brown with a rich tone." I tried to smile, but my face hurt.

"With all that blood in it, it looks as red as it was when you were twelve and I called you Strawberry Shortcake."

I managed to smile and hoped he would, too. But he didn't.

"Kitty killed Denise and your ex." Lonnie stared out the window, his eyes glazed with so much suffering. There was nothing I could do to help him. "She killed Jake, too."

After her confessing to the other two, I felt Jake's murder was a given. "I guess that is the most natural assumption we can come to."

"I didn't assume it. She told me she did it."

"You said she was gone. When did she tell you that?"

"She called me on my cell phone a little while after I found you and Lyle. The investigators had already been called in and were doing their jobs. My phone rang, and there she was telling me she'd gone away where no one would ever find her. I begged her to tell me where she was so I could go to her, but she wouldn't.

"I asked her why she had done such horrible things. She said she did it all for me. Do you believe that, Evie? She murdered three people, shot Lyle, and knocked you unconscious, and it was all for me. How can I ever face life again knowing my crazed wife did all that, swears it was for me, and I have no clue why?"

Poor Lonnie. How would his life ever be normal again? "She

didn't tell you why?"

He tried to answer, but sobs stifled his words. He buried his face in his folded arms on the edge of my bed, and his sounds gave way to a mournful cry I will never forget. This was a man tortured with *whys* and *what ifs* that would never go away. I had no words to ease his suffering. I stroked the back of his neck and let my old friend empty his soul of an unthinkable pain.

Would Lonnie's pain ever go away, or would it push him into a void leaving him as crazed as his wife?

Chapter 16

After Lonnie's tortured cries subsided, he kept his head buried in his folded arms. I continued to rub his tense shoulders. Gradually, his muscles relaxed, and I sensed he had returned from somewhere deep inside the dark hole of what his life had become. The small ER examining room had a sink where he splashed cold water on his face and then dried it with paper towels. Within a few minutes, he appeared to have it all together. He combed his hair, and magically the familiar, dependable Lonnie returned.

I waited for him to set the tone of what our discussion should be. "I have to go look for Kitty. I'll lose my mind doing nothing." Lonnie started to walk away, but turned back. "I'm really sorry."

"You have nothing to be sorry about. She fooled us all, Lonnie. Go find her, but be careful. She's sick, and there's no way to predict what she'll do."

Unexpectedly, Lonnie scooped me into his arms. "I couldn't

bare it if something happened to you, especially at the hands of Kitty. Please stay safe." He pulled back, and our gazes locked. "When they release you, call me. I'll come back and take you to Mom's." He pointed a warning finger at me. "I mean it this time, Eva Lynn. You cannot be alone until Kitty is taken into custody."

After Lonnie left, I struggled to a sitting position and waited until the room quit spinning. Just as I was about to slide off the gurney, a doctor entered the room.

"Miss Carson, I'm Dr. Lewis. Today is your lucky day. There's no fracture or concussion. The stitches we gave you shouldn't leave too much of a scar. If you have a regular doctor, see him in ten days to have the stitches removed. If not, come back to the ER, and we'll do it."

If my head hadn't already been spinning, it would have started to just from listening to Dr. Lewis run through his instructions for me. I hoped he'd written it all down, because I would never remember all that. And did that mean he was sending me home?

"You're releasing me?"

Dr. Lewis looked at me like I had two heads. Did he not realize I'd been knocked unconscious at the hands of a deranged woman with a gun? "Yes. Do you have someone to drive you home?"

"I guess so." I didn't want to go home. Bad things happened there. No one knew where Kitty was, and I didn't have the strength or the courage to face her.

"My nurse will be in shortly to help you get dressed and to take care of your discharge instructions." Dr. Lewis scribbled inside my chart, slammed it shut, and then left.

Thirty minutes later, I was dressed in my bloodstained clothes and discharged. It was then that I discovered I had a deputy stationed outside my room. He had been instructed to take me to Mrs. Douglas's house, where an investigator would come and take my statement. But I didn't want to go there. I wanted to find Sandy and find out if Lyle was out of surgery yet. Deputy Stone agreed to let me go to the waiting room, but he went with me. He told me he would call the station and let them know where I was, and then he waited by the door.

Sandy sat alone, rapidly flipping through a magazine. She couldn't possibly be reading or even looking at the pictures. Understandably, her mind would have been wholly on her brother. Exhaustion made her shoulders drop. She looked so small and fragile.

Not wanting to startle her, I spoke softly. "Sandy? Have you heard anything yet?"

She immediately raced to me, and we hugged for a long time.

"No, I haven't heard anything, but I'm glad you're up and moving around under your own steam. Are you okay?"

"Yes, I think that's what my attending physician said. He talked so fast I barely understood him." The room spun slightly. I stepped away from Sandy and wilted onto a red vinyl chair. "I'm just a little lightheaded, but I'll be fine."

Sandy joined me. "God, Evie, I've been so worried about you and Lyle. He's been in surgery for over an hour, and I haven't heard anything from his doctor."

Even though I'd been given a local anesthetic before they had sewn me up, my head throbbed, and I was having a little trouble reasoning things out. "Should we be worried because we haven't heard anything about Lyle?"

"They didn't have a prediction as to how long he'd be in there. They weren't sure what they were going to find once the surgery started. I didn't even know what questions to ask." Sandy took my hand. "Thanks for being here with me. This reminds me of another sad time."

I gave her hand a gentle squeeze. "I'm sure you must be thinking about your husband, but this is different. Lyle is going to be just fine." While I tried to convince Sandy, I was also trying to believe it myself. "There are so many unsaid things I want to be sure he knows."

"He already knows you love him," Sandy said. "That's a big part of what's keeping him alive, and I'm grateful to you."

I nodded so Sandy would know I understood, but words failed me. I appreciated her being in my life, and I wanted Lyle there, too. He had to be okay so I could tell him.

The silence closed around me. Just when I thought I'd possibly explode, Sandy spoke. "Do you have any idea what happened to cause Kitty Douglas to do the things she's done?"

That would probably be a major topic of discussion for a long time to come. "All I know is she was afraid Denise was going to tell Lonnie about Neal and Kitty's affair." I shook my head in disbelief at the meaning of my own words. "To snuff out lives over something like that . . . well, it just doesn't make any sense. She's always been self-centered and mean in a childish way, but I never dreamed her capable of murder."

Before she could comment a state trooper showed up and asked me a million questions. At least that's what it felt like. Finally, he finished. Deputy Stone remained stationed at the waiting room door.

A short time later, the automatic doors leading from the surgical wing opened, interrupting our futile discussion. A doctor dressed in green scrubs *swooshed* into the room. Sandy hurried to meet him.

"He's out of surgery. He did really well." The physician spaced his words calmly allowing us to absorb the vital information he passed on. "We got the bullet out. It did quite a bit of damage, but we were able to repair all of it. I'm expecting him to make a full recovery in a very short time."

"Can I see him?" Sandy's voice cracked and at the same time, my heart did, too. She was obviously relieved to hear her only brother was going to survive his part of the harrowing ordeal so many had been suffering through.

"They are just now taking him into recovery. It'll be a while before he's settled and enough of the anesthesia wears off for him to know you are there. That will probably take about an hour or so." Then the doctor reached out and laid his hand on Sandy's shoulder. "He's going to be just fine. You take a break. Go get some coffee. The nurse will come for you when it is time to go back." He smiled, and I could see Sandy visibly release the pent up pressure she'd been dealing with.

The doctor stopped beside the deputy stationed outside the waiting room. The men exchanged a few words. From the way they glanced in my direction from time to time, I had the strong feeling they were talking about me. I didn't have the strength to even imagine what they were saying.

For the next hour, Sandy and I chatted about the new shipment of merchandise for the Victorian Sampler, the different ways we could display the items, and when we should start selling the fall line. We talked about anything except the one thing on both our minds: Lyle.

When the door opened, we both jumped to our feet.

"Mr. Dickerson is awake and asking for Evie."

I couldn't move. His sister should be the first to go in, but Sandy grabbed my arm and shoved me in the direction of the nurse. "Go on, Evie. Tell him I'm here, and I'll see him a little later."

"Are you sure?" More than anything, I wanted to go to Lyle and see for myself that he was going to be okay, but by all rights, Sandy should have been the first to see her brother.

"Of course I'm sure. I wouldn't want it any other way."

"Thank you." I hurried away before I lost what little control I still had.

Other than being flat on his back with an IV drip going into his arm, Lyle looked wonderful. When I saw his dark eyes shining and his mouth sporting the most beautiful smile, the heavy load lifted from my heart. As long as he was okay, I could deal with everything else.

I rushed to his bedside and hugged him as tightly as I dared. His right arm wrapped around me and pulled me even closer. Nothing could ever feel as good as knowing Lyle was going to be good as new.

I pulled back to look at his beautiful, happy face. "You're going to be around for a long time, aren't you?"

He chuckled a little and squeezed me tighter. For a few moments, we didn't move. Suddenly, his breathing became soft, and I knew the anesthesia was still working and he was dozing. Slowly, I moved away and went back to the room where Sandy waited.

"He seems to be doing well. He was awake, smiling, even laughing. He nodded off, but I'm sure he'll be in and out until the medicine they used to put him to sleep completely wears off."

Sandy's bright smile made me grin. "The nurse came back while you were in there and said they would be moving him to a room in about an hour." She nodded to the sentry at the door. "Deputy Douglas is here."

I looked at the two officers, who were deep in conversation. I joined them.

"What's happening?"

"Nothing new. I had left orders with Deputy Stone to call me when you'd been released. I'm going to take you to Mom's, where you can rest."

I sensed I would meet with resistance if I told Lonnie I didn't want to go to his mother's just yet, so I'd wait until I said good-bye to Sandy. Once he and I were in the car I would tell him my wishes.

Once we were in the car, I relaxed a little. Lonnie, on the other hand, appeared to carry the weight of the world on his shoulder.

"Where are you going after you drop me off?"

"I don't know. I went back to the station, but Lt. Moore said he wanted me out of the way until he and his men could decide how much I knew and if I should be charged with aiding and abetting a murderer."

How could someone in Moore's position make such a stupid accusation? "You shouldn't be getting the brunt of this just because she's your wife. Have you tried talking to Moore about how unfair he's being?"

"No, Evie, that would have been the sensible thing to do. Instead, I tried to deck him. That was my mode of discussion. My fellow deputies had to pull me away. I'm sure that won't look good on the report he's compiling."

"Yeah, *that* was a good move. Take me to my house, Lonnie.

You can hang out there with me. I need to pack a few things and look around and, basically, feel grounded." More than anything, I just wanted to go home.

Without an argument, Lonnie drove me there. It was nearly four in the morning. The silver moon hung low on the horizon and graced the tips of the marsh grass swaying in the slight breeze. Somehow that brought Kitty to mind. She was like the marsh grass. It made a striking vision on the top, but beneath its surface lay unseen dangers—leeches, moccasins, gators, and quicksand. Beneath Kitty's beautiful surface lay the heart of a demented killer.

I stole a glance at Lonnie. He stared straight ahead with an intensity that told me his mind was anywhere but on the road ahead. "What about Beasley?" The sheriff's fate had also been on my mind. "Now that we know it was Kitty, he'll be exonerated. He should immediately go back to work, right? Maybe he can bring some balance back to the department."

"He'll return to work right away, but the state and GBI are still in charge. I'm not sure exactly what Johnston can do. I would think they would want me there in case Kitty calls again. They would be able to trace the call."

"Can they do that if she's on a cell?"

"They can narrow it down from which tower the call is coming. That would give them the general vicinity. They've checked all the trains, planes, and buses that have left in the last seven hours. I told Moore I could look at surveillance cameras at convenience and retail stores to see if she appears on any of the tapes. I'd be more likely to recognize her than anyone. Any information we could find that might tell us which direction she is headed would have to be a help." Lonnie gripped the steering wheel tightly. "But that horse's ass Moore won't agree to that."

"Did you say her car was at your house?"

"Yeah."

"Then maybe she rented one. Has that been checked out?"

"That was the first place they checked."

As we drove into my yard, Lonnie's cell rang. He looked at the digital number on the ID screen. "It's Kitty." He answered and put it on speakerphone. "Where are you?"

"You know I'm not going to tell you where I am. The important question is where are you? I called the station, and they said you'd been put on administrative leave. Why is that?"

"Did they know it was you calling?"

"Of course not. I disguised my voice," she said in a deep, hard tone, which sounded nothing like her own. "Pretty good, huh?" She didn't wait for him to answer. "Now why aren't you at work like you should be?"

"For some strange reason, they seem to think I know more about my psychotic wife than I really do. You have to give yourself up, Kitty, and put an end to this craziness. Where are you?"

"Where are you?" she asked him again.

"I am at Evie's. She has just been released from the hospital after having her head sewed up from where you split it open with what we assume was the barrel of her father's gun. Is that what you used to knock her out?" Disgust filled his every word.

Sadness for Lonnie choked me.

"Ah, must have been her lucky day. I tried to shoot her, but the gun misfired. Piece of crap."

That was the second time that day I'd been told it was my lucky day. I prayed I wouldn't have any more of them. I feared I wouldn't be lucky enough to survive.

After a short pause, Kitty continued. "I can't believe that watch was in the gun closet all the time. I made a copy of the key your mom had so I could get into Evie's house without breaking in. I went through every drawer and closet in that place except for the one with the guns. I even slept in that bedroom where it was locked away. That annoys the hell out of me."

"Why, Kitty? Please tell me why you've done these terrible things."

"I told you already. It was for you."

"How was it for me?" More anger than I'd ever heard from him strangled Lonnie's voice.

"You deserve to be the sheriff of Hyattville. You've worked hard. You've done all the work that Beasley takes credit for. I hadn't planned any of the things that happened, but I had to keep Denise from ruining our marriage."

"Don't you realize *you* had already done that by sleeping with Neal?"

"Not if Denise couldn't tell you about him. Then when I killed her, it all fell into place to make everyone believe Beasley was guilty. That would get rid of him and make room for you to be the sheriff. I'm not so stupid after all, am I?"

"You're beyond stupid—you're a murderer!" Lonnie shouted.

Somewhere in the background on Kitty's phone we heard a *ding* like a kitchen timer going off. The line went dead.

Lonnie and I looked at each other. "She's timing her calls. She thinks that will keep them from being traced." Lonnie flipped his phone closed.

I knew we were both stunned and heart-stricken by the things Kitty had said. She'd just piled even more guilt on her husband's shoulders. I felt sorry for Lonnie, but I knew someday he would be okay. Kitty, on the other hand, would never be free of the demons living in her world.

I was still baffled about one thing. "She's told us her reasons for killing Denise and David, but why Jake? How did he play into all this?" I opened the car door and got out.

Lonnie followed me up the porch steps. "You heard her just now. She keeps saying she did it all for me."

Before Lonnie and I went into my house, he called Lt. Moore to tell him about the recent phone call from the state's number one fugitive.

Inside my home, I touched everything I passed . . . the things that reminded me of Dad and Mom and Grandma Carson. I wanted to connect with them and to awaken the happiness they'd always brought me.

God, help me. My loved ones are all gone, but I hang onto their memories as if they are the air I breathe.

Lonnie went to the kitchen to get us something to drink. As I went down the hall to Dad's room, Midnight padded along behind me. Unsure of what kind of chaos had been left behind after Kitty's rampage, I readied myself for anything. Much to my surprise, there was only a small amount of blood where Lyle had lain. New footprints overlapped the ones made with Kitty's stars, almost to the point of obliterating them.

"I'll clean up this mess for you." Lonnie had walked up behind me. I hadn't heard a sound.

When I turned, he handed me a glass of ice water. "It really doesn't look too bad considering," he said.

"No, it doesn't."

"Why don't you gather your things? I'll take care of this in no time. If you need help, holler."

I took one more glance around the room and then went upstairs to pack. I didn't know how much to take with me. What was the appropriate time frame to catch a crazed murderer? We weren't talking about Rambo, who could disappear into a Georgia swamp, never to be heard of again. We were talking about Kitty, who wouldn't play softball because she might break a nail. If stung by a bee, Kitty Douglas would swell beyond recognition. Surely it wouldn't take long to find her.

I settled on four outfits and then gathered all the other things I would need for the next few days. Back downstairs, I found Lonnie sitting in the porch swing staring at the yellow streaks of sunlight breaking through the morning sky. The sun would be completely up in just a few minutes.

"What do you think I should do with Midnight? I don't know whether to lock him in the house and try to come out here every day, or leave him outside and hope he'll be safe."

"It won't hurt him to stay out. Our old cat, Punkinhead, stayed outside more than he ever stayed in. I'll bring you back tonight to check on him."

I agreed. Soon we were loaded into his car, headed back to town.

"Wasn't Punkinhead that big, old, orange cat you had when you graduated from high school?"

"Yeah, I still had him when Kitty and I were first married. She backed over it in the driveway shortly after we lost our baby. I loved that stupid cat."

"I know you did."

Lonnie had Punkinhead at least five years before he married Kitty. I remembered the cat lying on the porch swing looking like a big, round, fake fur pillow. About once a week, he would bring home an offering of a dead field mouse and drop it at their front door. This did not make Lonnie's mom very happy. Remembering her beating with a broom the already dead mouse, I had to smile.

"Evie, I just had a terrible thought." By the pale shade of green on his face, it had to be bad.

"What's that?"

"I always thought it was strange the way Punkinhead died. Kitty called to tell me she'd run over him. He had darted under the car, but when I came home to bury him, the tire tracks went over his back end from his spine to his feet, like he was in a lying position. His head was smashed in, but it looked like only his rear had made contact with the tire. I thought it was odd, and then a few days later, I took out the trash and noticed a coke bottle with something on it that looked like blood. I asked Kitty about it, but she said she had no idea where it had come from. I threw it away and never thought another thing about it until just now." Lonnie swallowed hard.

"I think Kitty beat the cat to death and then ran over him so I wouldn't know. It worked because I didn't suspect any foul play. She had to kill several people before I would think her capable of killing Punkinhead. How stupid am I?"

I laid my hand on his arm. "You aren't stupid at all. You love her. Actually, in my own way, I do, too. We just can't fathom how she could do the things she's done. It's not your fault."

"There is no rhyme or reason to her actions. She's killed all these people and Punkinhead. Yet, today, she told me she didn't want Jake's cat to starve to death, so she dropped it off at your house." Lonnie bent and scooped up Midnight, who had been resting on the porch. He stroked the cat's black fur. "This is Jake's cat. You wondered how he got here since you're so far away from your nearest neighbor. Now you know. Kitty had a random soft spot for this cat, and so she found it a home. How does that happen?"

"I don't know. I keep saying she's sick, but even that doesn't explain it away." Midnight crawled from Lonnie's lap to mine. His soft fur and gentle purr unruffled some of my frayed edges. At least Kitty had made one decision that I was happy for. She'd brought Midnight to me.

"How about your mom, Lonnie? How did she get along with Kitty? Did she ever find anything strange about your wife?" If she did, I doubted she would have said anything to Lonnie about it.

"No, she never interfered. Definitely not like Kitty's mom. June McGovern had her nose up our butts at every turn. But as long as I was happy, my mother was happy." He paused reflectively. "Apparently, Kitty was the only one who wasn't." Lonnie shook his head. "I must not have been much of a husband. I didn't have a clue."

Saying I was sorry again just didn't seem enough. Lonnie knew even in my silence, I felt his devastation, and nothing I could say would ease any of it. I was beside him then, and I always would be.

We parked in his mother's driveway. "You go on in. Mom may still be sleeping. She doesn't know about Kitty yet." He handed me a house key. "I'll bring in your things. I kinda want to regroup before I see Mom."

"I understand." Just as I got out of the car, Lonnie's phone rang. I waited to see if it was Kitty again.

"Okay. I'll be right there." Lonnie hopped out of the car,

grabbed my bags, and hurriedly slid them onto the porch. "Sorry. That was Stone. Moore wants me at the station PDQ. Go inside with Mom, and stay there until I get back. They have pinpointed the area where Kitty's calls are coming from."

As I looked into Lonnie's sad eyes, I saw something that hadn't registered with me until that moment. Lonnie was frightened out of his mind. Not for himself, but for the wife whom, in less than twenty-four hours, he had lost forever. I threw my arms around him and squeezed him tightly. "Please be careful, Lonnie. You are very important to me." I'd lost too many people close to me. Lonnie, the closest thing to a brother I would ever have, couldn't be added to the list of lost loved ones.

"I know. I love you, too." He hurried to the car.

I watched him speed away. He would pass the Victorian Sampler in about a minute. That started me thinking about the business I'd missed at the boutique that day. Later at the hospital, after I found out how much care Lyle would need, Sandy and I could work out the details of getting the boutique opened again. All of that could, and would, wait.

Once inside Mrs. Douglas's house, it appeared Lonnie was right. I didn't see his mom anywhere. She must have been sleeping still. My head hurt, and I was mentally, physically, and emotionally exhausted. I had to lie down before I fell down. I climbed the stairs to the guest room, where I'd been staying after David's death.

At the end of the hallway, the attic stairs were folded down.

From up there, soft music drifted to me. Balls of black lint were strewn on the long, narrow rug covering the shiny pine wood floors under the ladder. Evidently, Mrs. Douglas wasn't sleeping. When she'd taken me into the attic to find the pictures of my parents, she'd mentioned she was going to clean out some things. She hadn't been told about Kitty yet, so she must have figured today was as good a day as any to start the job.

I decided to call to her so I wouldn't scare her. "Mrs. Douglas, it's Evie. Lonnie dropped me off." I climbed the steps into the stifling hot attic. The only light in the room streamed through a wooden vent on either end of the house. I could barely see where to step. I was amazed Goldie Douglas could see anything at all. "Mrs. Douglas, are you here?"

I heard a movement to my right, but I could only make out stacks of boxes, which held Goldie Douglas's possessions amassed over the forty-two years she'd lived there. I remembered a bare lightbulb with a string directly above the opening where the ladder had been pulled down for access to the attic. I reached for the string. When it touched my hand, I pulled it and the cluttered, dusty room was bathed with harsh light. I had to blink a few times to focus clearly.

Suddenly, I realized the soft music playing through the attic was classical, just like what I'd heard in the background of my mysterious calls.

"Stay right where you are, Evie." Kitty's threatening tone sent shards of fear through me. I jumped and then stared into the shadows on my right.

Chapter 17

A crib made up with dingy sheets, a dressing table stacked neatly with diapers, and a playpen filled with stuffed animals had been arranged in a semicircle in the center of Mrs. Douglas's attic. In the center of the makeshift nursery, facing my way, Kitty sat in a rocking chair, protectively clutching a baby doll to her chest with one arm and pointing Dad's gun at me with her free hand.

"You must be quiet, Evie. You'll wake the baby."

By then my eyes had adjusted to the harsh light, and I could see Goldie Douglas, with bound hands and feet and a piece of duct tape covering her mouth, lying on the floor. She stared at me through fear-glazed eyes. I started to go to her.

"Stop, or I'll shoot you right there." Kitty thrust the gun out in front of her.

I stopped. With my insides twisted into knots of fear, I struggled to keep my voice even. "We've been friends way too long for you to shoot me. Besides, you don't want to wake your baby do you?" I wiped perspiration from my forehead.

Kitty looked down at the doll. "No," she said softly, but then looked back at me. "But that doesn't mean I wouldn't shoot you. I'm getting pretty good at doing that, aren't I? Did your boyfriend die?"

Though terror burrowed deep inside me, threatening my own sanity, I had to think rationally. Did she want him dead, or would it be better if she knew he was alive? I struggled for the right answer. "Why did you shoot him? He would have helped you, Kitty."

Her eyes narrowed, and her nostrils flared. "No one can help me. I saw a head doctor for several years. All he wanted was to get into my pants." She began to laugh out loud. "Lonnie paid Dr. Cabella one hundred dollars an hour to make my brain work better. Dr. Cabella paid me three hundred dollars to screw his brains out during that hour. Don't you think that's funny, Evie? Part of the money he gave me was the hundred Lonnie gave him. So if you think about it, Lonnie was paying for me to have sex with another man. Who's the crazy one?"

"Come on, Kitty." I held out my hand for the gun and stepped forward. She pointed it directly at my heart. I stopped. I knew she could shoot with precision. One more step, and I'd be dead.

Please let this nightmare end.

"You've done this because you wanted to be the wife of the town sheriff, and you were afraid if Lonnie found out you were having an affair with Neal, he would leave you. Is that right? Make me understand,

Kitty." Our only hope of survival was to keep her talking.

She placed the doll on her shoulder and rubbed its back gently. The gun never left its readied position. "That pretty much sums it up."

"Don't you know what a forgiving and loving man you're married to? Don't you know how much he truly loves you and would have forgiven you anything?"

Adamantly, she shook her head. Sweat-soaked strands of her blonde hair clung to her face. "No, it's out of his hands. He is a law enforcement officer, and he has a duty to bring me to justice. It's too late for forgiveness."

Perspiration soaked a major part of her clothing. The heat, the fear, and the out-and-out despair were taking a toll on me. My head ached ferociously. Weak-kneed, I longed to sit down, but I didn't dare. I needed to be prepared for a quick escape for both me and Mrs. Douglas, if at all possible. In the meantime, it was important that I kept Kitty's mind occupied. "Why did you kill Jake? He was so harmless. Why him?"

She shrugged. "Once it all started, I was like Casey Jones on that train going downhill with no brakes. I kept going faster and faster with no time to think, hitting whatever happened to be on the track. By the time I got to Jake, I magically saw my chance to get rid of Beasley, and then Lonnie would be the sheriff. Who knows? He might even have gone on to be the mayor of Hyattville. Wouldn't that have been something?" She actually flashed a brilliant smile, and pride softened the hard edges of her expression.

"But how did Jake get tangled up in this? He was such a gentle giant. He could never hurt anyone, yet you disposed of him with no remorse whatsoever. How did you get him to bury Denise?"

Her smile faded. "That part was easy. It was getting Jake to keep his mouth shut that wouldn't have worked. So I knew as soon as he was through, I'd have to get rid of him."

"But how did you get him to go along with your plan in the first place?"

Keep talking, Kitty. Please keep talking.

"It didn't seem like a bad idea at the time. I thought it was pretty brilliant." Kitty rocked the baby and slowly unraveled her tale of Jake's sad ending. "Jake was the in-between man for Neal. Every month, Jake paid Neal's rent in cash to Lockwood for the motel room. So between his closeness to Johnston Beasley, and my spending a lot of time at the sheriff's office, plus the few times he'd come to the motel for Neal to give him money, Jake and I got to be friends. Denise threatened to run her mouth to Lonnie. I thought it all out and rationalized that unless Neal was flat out asked about it, he would never admit he and Denise had been in the room before she died. I was afraid that if Jake was questioned about who he paid the room rent for, he would tell them about Neal and about me."

Appalled beyond belief, I needed answers. "But how could you possibly get Jake to go along with something so terrible?"

"I could get him to do anything as long as I promised him pizza. This time I also told him if he didn't tell anyone and did just what I asked, I'd take him to see his dad."

Poor Jake. I'm sure he never understood what his father being dead truly meant. He must have been ecstatic thinking he would see his dad again. I wanted to sink to the floor and weep with all my might for that dear, sweet childlike man. While I steeled myself for the next round of Kitty's devastating tale, she talked in hushed tones to her baby.

"Jake brought his truck to the alley behind the motel room and then helped me haul Denise's body out the window. I gave Jake precise instructions where to bury her. I even waited for him down at his house until he finished the task. Little did I know you were in the process of royally screwing up my plan."

Mrs. Douglas moved slightly. She, too, was soaking wet and looked close to passing out.

"We need to get her up from there, Kitty. You don't want to be responsible for Lonnie's mother, your baby's grandmother, dying, too. Do you?"

She looked at the elderly woman. Kitty waved the gun in Goldie's direction, and then glared at her. "I'm going to let Evie untie you. You better just sit there and be good."

While I freed Goldie, I continued to question Kitty, knowing our lives depended on it. "How did you get the sheriff's gun—the one you used to kill Jake?"

"First of all, I don't look at it as *killing* him. I promised Jake I would let him see his dad, and I did."

Her thinking was sick on so many levels. "How did you get the gun?"

"Jake was very capable of using his head for more than a hat rack when he wanted to. He told me up front he had to take his bills to Beasley so he could pay them for Jake."

Jake could barely write his name. He was never able to keep a checkbook.

"I gave him a tote bag to take his mail to the sheriff. I instructed him to ask for a Coke like I'd seen him do many times. I knew that Johnston would go to the lounge and get Jake a cold drink. I told him to take the sheriff's gun, put it in the tote bag, not to let anyone see him, then come back to his house. I promised he would see his dad as soon as he got back with the gun."

Good Lord, did all that really make sense to Kitty? I shuddered.

"And I was true to my promise. I'm pretty proud of my best laid plan. My part in making Sheriff Beasley appear to be the killer was using his gun, deliberately making sure the bullet lodged in the headliner as it passed through Jake's empty head."

Her agitation escalated. She rocked harder and faster. "I wanted it to be a long time before Denise's body was found, but you ruined that. But once I stood back and listened to you help stack evidence against Beasley, I felt it was worth it. With Beasley out of the way, Lonnie would be next in line. I would be the sheriff's wife. The next step would be the mayor's office. That would make me the first lady of Hyattville."

Throughout her whole life, Kitty's dream for recognition had remained steadfast, but her method for obtaining it had taken an insane path. The sickening reality of it all was, to reach her goal, others had to die. I couldn't sink any further into sadness without losing my own mind.

She continued. "Since Lonnie has been on evening shift, I've been going by to see him at the station every evening. You know, to break up his long hours for him. After Jake went to see his dad, I went by the station like I did every evening. Since Beasley was never there at that time, I figured I could sneak the gun back into his office without anyone seeing me.

"As it turned out, since most of the people who are usually at the office were out pondering over the body you had found, I had no trouble returning the gun to its rightful place. It was a stroke of genius that I saw the sheriff's service pen on the desk. I grabbed it and drove back to the alley behind the motel and threw the pen inside. I guess I threw it pretty hard. I heard they found it under the bed, but they found it nonetheless. Beasley was relieved of his duties until further notice. Lonnie was one step closer to being the sheriff."

Suddenly, Kitty cooed to the baby. "Hush now. It's okay. Momma's here," she whispered in sweet tones that tore my heart out.

"Is the baby okay?"

Kitty didn't appear to notice I'd stepped closer.

"She's been crying a lot. I've tried to keep her quiet, but she woke her grandma." Kitty nodded in Mrs. Douglas's direction.

"You know, Kitty, Lonnie's mom loves you very much. She's very hot up here. Maybe we should let her go downstairs where it's cooler."

"No, she may be old, but she's tricky. She tried to take the gun away from me, and I couldn't let her do that."

"I'm sure she's sorry. Aren't you, Mrs. Douglas?"

The elderly woman nodded.

"I can't let her go down there. We all have to stay here." Kitty waved the gun carelessly. I prayed it wouldn't accidentally go off and hit one of us.

"I have to go to the bathroom," Mrs. Douglas said.

"Here, let me help you." I slipped my arms beneath hers and lifted her to her feet.

I was in the process of leading her to the ladder when Kitty shouted, "Do you think I'm stupid? If I let her go down there, she'll call Lonnie, and then he'll be here to get me."

"No, I won't. I really have to go."

While Goldie tried to persuade Kitty to let her go down to the bathroom, I saw Lonnie and at least one state trooper near the ladder out of Kitty's line of sight. My heart raced, and I tried to stay focused on her and not attract attention to what was going on below us. How would they ever be able to get up the ladder without Kitty killing one or all of us?

"Kitty, is your baby still crying?" I had to keep her attention on something other than the opening to the attic. While she talked to the doll as if it were real, I rolled my eyes to let Mrs. Douglas see what was going on below us. The trooper, dressed in SWAT garb, appeared ready to do battle with a terrorist. When I looked back at Kitty, all I saw was a fragile woman with a cracked mind. Yet her destruction made a wide swath through Hyattville, and in all likelihood, it would constitute a battle to take her down.

Below the opening, Lonnie held up a sheet of paper with these words written on it: *Move my mom as far away from the floor opening as possible.*

"Mrs. Douglas, you're burning up. Come over here where you can get some air." I put my arm around her. Out of the corner of my eye, I watched Kitty. She didn't show any sign of resisting this movement. We were by the wooden vent that allowed air to circulate in the attic.

"Kitty, it's so hot up here. Wouldn't it be better for the baby downstairs in the air conditioning?" I hoped pleading might work, but to no avail.

Kitty wiped sweat from her forehead and then onto her shorts. "We're fine here."

My mind was spinning trying to come up with a sensible plan. Should I keep Kitty talking? Should I work my way nearer to her and try to take the gun? At least get it pointed toward the ceiling until the officers could capture her? Should I stay put and use my body to shield Goldie in case the SWAT team charged in? I didn't have a clue. The heat wasn't making it any easier.

I hadn't seen Lonnie below us for quite some time. Where was he?

Kitty looked up at me with tears in her eyes. "Why won't the baby quit crying, Evie? I've done everything I can for her."

A shadow slid past the sunlight coming through the wooden vent on the other side of the attic. Someone was outside that window. Gradually, my mind started working and I knew what had to be done.

"I know what. Come with me." I slowly walked in front of Kitty, keeping a safe distance so she didn't think I was going to attack her. I opened the slatted window. "Bring the baby over here so she can get some cool air. I bet she'll quit crying then."

I slowly returned to the other side of the room where Goldie stood shaking violently. I put my arm around her and pulled her close, and I used my other hand to cover her ear. I wasn't sure what was about to take place, but I was sure it would be loud and disturbing.

Finally, Kitty carried her imaginary, crying baby to the window, the gun still securely in her hand. Just as her gaze snapped to the opening, Lonnie latched onto the exposed two-by-four directly over the vent and swung his body through the open window. His boots collided hard against Kitty's upper arm, sending her sprawling to the floor with a loud thud.

The doll flew from her arms and landed near me. She screamed with all her might and tried to reach it. Lonnie regained his balance from his jump through the window and latched onto Kitty, who was reaching for her baby.

One SWAT team member scrambled up the ladder, while another one entered through the same vent window Lonnie had swung through. She fought and clawed Lonnie's face and then pounded her fist against his body. But he never let go. He held onto her until the fight was out of her and she lay crumbled in a sniveling mass.

One of the other officers pulled Lonnie away from Kitty. He scooted against the wall and pulled his knees to his chest. The officer roughly grabbed Kitty's upper arm and hoisted her to her feet.

"My baby." Kitty's heartrending screams pierced the chaotic space of the attic.

I snatched up the doll and rushed in their direction. "I have your baby. I'll take care of her."

She looked at the doll cradled in my arms, and her screams quieted. Even with all the suffering Kitty had left in her wake, I couldn't keep from feeling a spark of compassion for the lost woman. Her mind was broken, and I ached inside for her.

The officer proceeded with handcuffing her and reading her rights. Kitty was taken down the stairs, and then they helped Mrs. Douglas down, too.

I joined Lonnie on the floor, leaning against the wall. After putting my arm around his shoulders, I pulled his head against me.

The rungs of the ladder squeaked as someone else headed into the attic. Lt. Moore appeared in the opening.

"It takes quite a man to do what you just did, Deputy Douglas. I don't believe I could have done it. I'm sure Beasley will want you back on the job when you're ready, especially after I finish my report." Lt. Moore waited a moment for Lonnie to comprehend what he'd said. When Lonnie nodded, the trooper went back downstairs.

"Do you want to be alone?" I asked.

"No, I really don't. Let's go make sure Mom is all right."

Thankfully, Lonnie's mom hadn't suffered any ill effects from being held captive by her daughter-in-law.

Kitty had been sedated and taken to the hospital for a mental evaluation, and supposedly she would then be transferred to the county jail to face murder charges. Personally, I didn't see that happening for a long time, if ever. Kitty's problems wouldn't be fixed in a day or two, and with the depth of her deteriorated mental state, she might never find her way back to sanity again.

As the ambulance took her away, Lonnie was torn between going with Kitty and staying to make sure his mom was okay.

"You go with Kitty. I'm just fine. She's the one who needs you." Goldie Douglas wrapped her arms around her son and held him for a long time.

Finally, he pulled away. "Okay, I'll let you know how she's doing as soon as I can."

He gave me a quick, silent hug and then left.

While the police continued to gather information about our ordeal with Kitty, I sat with Mrs. Douglas and held her hand. Finally, well into the evening, I was allowed to shower and change, and then Deputy Stone drove me to the hospital to see Lyle.

I found Sandy in Lyle's room. He was sitting up, eating, and listening to the evening news on the television. Sandy raced to me, and we hugged as if our lives depended on it.

"Lt. Moore telephoned to let us know what had happened. Are you okay?" she asked.

"I have a major headache from everything that happened today, and from the stitches I got when Kitty whacked me yesterday. But I'm going to be fine."

When I got to Lyle's bedside, his arm snaked out and pulled me tightly against him. "Thank God you're all right. What about Lonnie?" Lyle's compassion warmed me completely.

"He's strong, but I'm not sure how he'll come out of this."

"Anything I can do, I will."

Lyle was a man of his word, and I knew he would do everything in his power to lighten Lonnie's load.

"I was just telling Sandy to go home. She needs some rest." Lyle shifted to a different position. I helped him adjust the pillow behind his head.

"I'm going. Evie don't worry about coming to the boutique tomorrow. I'll be there, and it will be fine for a couple days, until you get back on solid ground."

"Thanks. I appreciate that."

"The doctor says he wants to keep Lyle for a couple of days." Sandy gathered her purse and a bag of magazines.

"Yeah, but I don't need a babysitter here. They take good care of me."

"We'll decide that later." Sandy said her good-byes and left.

"I really don't need a babysitter, but if you want to come hang out with me, that would be fine and dandy."

Thank God the worst was over, and no more people had to die. "You sound like you're doing well."

"That's what they tell me. The doctor said the bullet didn't hit anything I'll need in the next fifty years."

Grateful for such wonderful news, I rested my head on his shoulder and asked, "Did it hit anything *I* might need in the next fifty years?"

He laughed out loud and then grabbed his side, where a bullet had been removed.

"Sorry about that," I said. "But it's good to hear you laugh. There's been so little of that lately."

He smiled and squeezed my hand. "Do you have any idea how much I love you?" He raised my hand to his lips and kissed it.

All the shadows of my heart were replaced with the sunshine of my life. "I love you, too, Lyle." Nothing could ever take that away.

He pulled me close to him, and I stayed there for a long time.

"Oh, I forgot to tell you." Appearing supercharged with excitement, Lyle released me from his hug. "Merrilee came to see me today." There was a gentle softness in Lyle's voice. "I think she was really worried about me and had to see for herself. She's quite a young lady, isn't she?"

"She reminds me of Denise at that age. We were very close, and I feel that same closeness to Merrilee."

"I'm going to work really hard to be a positive part of her life."

"And you will be."

I looked at my watch. It was almost seven o'clock. I still had time to go home before dark. Suddenly, I realized it didn't matter what time of day it was. I could go to my house and not be fearful for my life.

"I'm going home," I announced with confidence I'd been sure I'd lost forever.

"You go ahead, sweetheart. It's long overdue."

I slept late the next morning and awoke with sunshine warming my bedroom. I threw back the sheet and stretched, feeling every fiber of my being tingling with the kind of peace that had been missing since I watched Denise being buried.

There was a lot of healing ahead for so many people, but at least we didn't have to worry and wonder who would be the next to die. I made a mental checklist of the losses, including Denise, Jake, and David. And Lonnie had lost his wife. Neal's and Patsy's lives had been torn apart, and the jury was still out on whether their marriage would survive.

And then I made an even longer list of the good things. Merrilee and Lyle had found each other. I had found Lyle. My boutique was doing well. My newest best friend, Sandy, could handle the boutique without me. I was finally able to stay in my own home, wake up in my own bed, and not worry about a mysterious, dangerous person invading my space.

Of course, I had to think about the ones who were hurt in the wake of Kitty's demented onslaught. That would include me with five stitches, Lyle with a bullet wound to the abdomen, and Garnet.

"Oh, my God." I jumped out of bed and hurried to the shower. In the culmination of Kitty's capture, I'd forgotten all about Garnet. As soon as I was dressed, I called St. Vincent's Hospital in Jacksonville. The nurse told me Ms. Windsor was doing well and had been moved to a regular room.

I then called Lyle. "How are you doing today?"

"I guess I'm being a little wimpy. I didn't sleep well, but they removed the IV this morning, and now I feel like a new person." He sounded tired.

"I'm glad to hear that. Is there anything I can bring you?"

"Just you."

I smiled. "I'm going to stop by and check on you, and then I'm going to drive to Jacksonville and see Garnet."

"I think that's a good idea. I'm sure they've told her, but you can assure her that the deranged woman who ran her off the road is locked up. Go see her first, and then come by here. I'm doing fine."

After I hung up, I called Sandy at the boutique and told her I was going to see Garnet. "I'll only be gone a few hours."

She agreed that was a good idea. "Lyle will call me if he really needs something before you get back."

We started to hang up.

"Oh, wait," Sandy said. "You might want to give Lonnie Douglas a call, too. He was here earlier. That is one lost man. It hasn't been very busy this morning. He stayed and talked for about an hour. He's a kind person. He doesn't deserve the things that have happened to him."

"I know. I'll check on him when I get back. Thanks."

I went to see Garnet and was happy to find her son and daughter with her, talking and laughing like they were on a Sunday picnic.

"Evie, come in, sweetie." Garnet motioned frantically. "I understand you met Pet the other night, and this is my son, Rubin."

After a few minutes of introductions and exchanging pleasantries, Garnet asked Pet and Rubin if they would give us a few minutes alone. They excused themselves and went to get coffee.

"Garnet, I'm so sorry you were hurt. Do you know they have the woman in custody that caused you to wreck?"

"Yes, they told me this morning." She ran her ring-laden fingers through her red hair.

"I feel so responsible for your being hurt."

"You have no reason to. I caused it by confronting someone I knew was dangerous." Garnet tried to pour a glass of water, but was having some trouble.

"What do you mean?" I poured the water for her.

"Evidently, the woman was in one of the fitting rooms at your boutique while you and I were talking in the back room. I was already near the town of O'Brien when I stopped for gas. She approached me and asked me what time it was. I think she was trying to see if I was really psychic and if I would call her out and declare her the murderer." Shadows darkened Garnet's face.

"I knew instantly it was her, and I stupidly told her so. When I got back into my car, I decided to go back to Hyattville and tell you what I'd seen while I was talking to her. Maybe I could describe her enough that you would know who she was."

I went to the window and opened the blinds. The sunlight took away some of the hard lines on her face.

"Evidently, she figured that was what I was going to do. She followed me to the straight stretch along the marsh going into town. When there were no other cars on the road, she went around me and then pushed me over. Like a fool, I panicked and ran off the road. I jerked the wheel back. They told me I flipped about three times and landed upside down in the water. I don't remember anything after the car left the road."

Oh, Kitty. What a tormented mind you must have to have so little respect for human life! God help you.

I spent a good hour with Garnet. She had talent unsurpassed. She told me of people she'd found, both dead and alive. She told me of people who doubted her, of names she'd been called, ranging from *witch* on the bad side to *angel* when her words were proven true. By the time I left there, I considered Garnet Windsor a remarkable woman and a friend.

Epilogue

Ten Months Later

It's hard to believe a year has passed since Denise and Jake died, then David shortly thereafter.

Lyle's body has healed completely, and he is happy he'll be around to play with the grandkids Merrilee will hopefully give him. He and I are madly in love, but I'm still not ready for marriage.

Kitty was committed to the state mental hospital and will probably never be well enough to stand trial for three counts of murder. Johnston Beasley is still serving as the sheriff, but it's rumored he will be retiring soon. With his major part in bringing Kitty in, Deputy Lonnie Douglas will surely be the front runner in the next election.

My dear friend Lonnie is doing well. He and Sandy have recently started dating, but it will be years before he will be legally and emotionally ready to marry again. They make the cutest couple, and Scotty loves Lonnie. How ironic that in the end, Kitty's killing spree might get her what she wanted all along . . . to be the wife of

Hyattville's sheriff.

Garnet Windsor and I have become very good friends. It turns out I have a little bit of psychic ability. At least that's what she calls it. I call it good old common horse sense and woman's intuition, but who knows?

What I do know is that today we are all gathered together to celebrate Merrilee's seventeenth birthday. She had a special request for her present from Lyle, and he wholeheartedly agreed. As all of us near and dear to the teenager gathered around, we watched the paperwork being executed changing Merrilee's last name to that of her dad's.

From this day forward, she will be Merrilee Dickerson. Her huge smile moved me to tears. The only thing that would have made the day better would have been if Denise had been there to see how happy her daughter was.

At that moment Garnet leaned close to me and whispered in my ear, "Denise is here, Evie. She's happy that Merrilee has her rightful name, and she'll be happy when you become Evie Dickerson."

I killed my husband, a town hero, and then called the police and turned myself in. "He's dead as a doornail," I said to the officer and then spit on Harland Jeffers' bloody, dead body.

With my head held high, I allowed myself to be escorted to a squad car outside my house. A house which had been more of a prison than the cell I was headed for.

Cameras flashed.

"Why did you kill Harland?"

Because he needed killing. And I, Montana Ines Parsons-Jeffers did just that.

So begins the rest of what's left of Montana's life. Not that she ever really had one.

Now she's headed for prison. There's no escaping it. It was the ultimate destination in her Flight to Freedom.

But one man might be able to help . . .

Diary of a Confessions Queen

Kathy Carmichael

Seven years ago Amy Crosby's husband, Dan, disappeared under baffling circumstances in the little town of Independence, Kansas. No marital dispute. No warning. No suicide note. As bizarre as taking out the garbage and never coming back.

She has no hope of seeing him again and presumes he's dead. So Amy begins legal proceedings to have the inventor of unusual devices declared deceased. Simple . . . that is, it would be simple without his valuable patents and insurance money.

What starts as a normal procedure turns into a fiasco. With her take-it-in-stride, confessions queen sense of humor, she endures blackmail, threats on her life, and repeated burglaries. Then someone close to her is murdered, and she realizes that an enemy wants to do more than frighten her. Whoever has an interest in her husband, everyone from his business partners to his family members, isn't playing games.

Sexy police detective Brad Tyler is assigned to the case . . . in more ways than one. Amy teeters on a precarious line between convincing him of her innocence and seeking his protection. An overpowering attraction makes their relationship a high-stakes race against the clock to find the killer. Coffee, tea, or murder anyone?

ISBN# 978-160542095-0
Trade Paperback / Mystery
US $12.95 / CDN $14.95

STRESS FRACTURE

D.P. LYLE

Dub Walker, expert in evidence evaluation, crime scene analysis, and criminal psychology, has seen everything throughout his career—over a hundred cases of foul play and countless bloody remains of victims of rape, torture, and unthinkable mutilation. He's sure he's seen it all . . . until now.

When Dub's close friend Sheriff Mike Savage falls victim to a brutal serial killer terrorizing the county, he is dragged into the investigation. The killer—at times calm, cold, and calculating and at others maniacal and out of control—is like no other Dub has encountered. With widely divergent personalities, the killer taunts, threatens, and outmaneuvers Dub at every turn.

While hunting this maniacal predator, Dub uncovers a deadly conspiracy—one driven by unrestrained greed and corruption. Will he be able to stop the conspirators—and the killer—in their bloody tracks?

ISBN# 978-160542134-6
Hardcover / Thriller
US $24.95 / CDN $27.95

APRIL 2010

The Rock & Roll Queen of Bedlam

Marilee Brothers

Leggy, karaoke-singing Allegra Thome spends her days teaching dysfunctional teens and her nights with wealthy new boyfriend, Michael. The rough patch following Allegra's divorce is over, and life is grand. But when Allegra lands in the middle of a drug bust and meets Sloan, a rough-around-the edges DEA agent and, later that day, a throwaway kid from her class disappears, things quickly head south. Sloan, who has the tact of a roadside bomb, is attracted to Allegra and alienates Michael. To make matters worse, nobody seems to care that Allegra's student, Sara Stepanek, is missing.

Add to the mix a rural Washington State town under the spell of a charismatic minister who doesn't hesitate to use secrets of the rich and powerful to keep them in line, even while withholding his own dark past, and Allegra's search for Sara becomes a race against time with dead bodies piling up and her own life in peril. Under the circumstances, it's not surprising things come to a head at the WWJD (What Would Jesus Drink) Winery.

Dawn Schiller

The Road Through Wonderland is Dawn Schiller's chilling account of the childhood that molded her so perfectly to fall for the seduction of "the king of porn," John Holmes, and the bizarre twist of fate that brought them together. With painstaking honesty, Dawn uncovers the truth of her relationship with John, her father figure-turned-forbidden lover who hid her away from his porn movie world and welcomed her into his family along with his wife.

Within these pages, Dawn reveals the perilous road John led her down—from drugs and addiction to beatings, arrests, forced prostitution, and being sold to the drug underworld. Surviving the horrific Wonderland murders, this young innocent entered protective custody, ran from the FBI, endured a heart-wrenching escape from John, and ultimately turned him in to the police.

This is the true story of one of the most infamous of public figures and a young girl's struggle to survive unthinkable abuse. Readers will be left shaken but clutching to real hope at the end of this dark journey on *The Road Through Wonderland.*

Also check out the movie Wonderland (Lions Gate Entertainment, 2003) for a look into the past of Dawn Schiller and the Wonderland Murders.

ISBN# 978-160542083-7
Trade Paperback / Autobiography
US $15.95 / CDN $17.95
AUGUST 2010
www.dawn-schiller.com

Theater of Illusion

Kathy Steffen

Children of an abusive father who spiraled into madness and murder, Sarah and Tobias Perkins survived by holding to each other.

As adults, the siblings live and work on the Spirit of the River, the riverboat that saved their mother from their father's wrath. Yearning to pilot the riverboat herself, Sarah is forced by custom to stand by as her childhood rival, Jeremy Smith, becomes not only pilot but first officer. It is 1910, and the River Board has specific opinions about where a woman belongs—and it is not behind the wheel of a riverboat.

Tragedy strikes when Théâtre d'Illusion—a traveling theater extravaganza—comes aboard to entertain passengers during the journey downriver. One of the performers vanishes, and then one by one, the passengers and crewmembers on board the Spirit of the River fall victim to a mysterious and deadly illness.

Plagued by the voice of his murderous father, Tobias finds peace only during overnight drinking binges. But when he awakes each day to a trail of death and destruction, he begins to fear his father's spirit has possessed him. As the sins of the past threaten to destroy the future, Sarah races against time to stop a vengeful killer. Will she bring the Spirit of the River and the surviving passengers home, or is all hope of escape an illusion?

ISBN# 978-160542086-8
Trade Paperback / Historical Fiction
US $15.95 / CDN $17.95

AUGUST 2010
www.kathysteffen.com

SHAMROCK ALLEY

A NOVEL

RONALD DAMIEN MALFI

Secret Service agent John Mavio infiltrates the infamous Hell's Kitchen in New York to shut down a ring of organized crime leaders involved in an elaborate counterfeit money operation, perhaps the worst in history. Based on a true story, the Irish villains of Mickey O'Shay and Jimmy Kahn are real. These violent criminals, once known as the West Side Boys, terrorized the community and inflicted gruesome deaths on numerous victims by bludgeoning, stabbing, shooting, and cutting into pieces the bodies of those who got in their way or refused to cooperate with their treacherous schemes.

Mavio is the courageous agent who risked his life to stop what may have been the most sinister operation this country has ever endured—a hero based on Ronald Damien Malfi's own father. Every step closer to the drugs, the booze, and the blood brings him one step closer to his own demise, a risk he takes to save innocent citizens from ongoing torture. His life undercover is a gory, dangerous world far removed from his personal reality—his pregnant wife, Katie, and his terminally ill father wait for him to return from each threatening encounter alive.

Then one day . . . these two worlds meet. Mavio must implement every skill he has painfully learned to save himself and the people of New York. He cannot fail, for failure would mean the end of everything honorable, just, and right. And, above all, justice must prevail.

Daisy Lockhart is a searcher. She just doesn't know it yet.

Burdened with an unlikely name by her father, a preeminent Henry James scholar, Daisy is a tightly wound grad student on her way to fulfilling the American dream. When her boyfriend breaks up with her, though, Daisy succumbs to the vertigo of uncertainty for the first time in a scripted life.

Embracing the plunge, Daisy flees. Her namesake chose Rome; Daisy Lockhart settles on the celestial city: Paris.

There, Daisy finds a soft landing in the arms of Mathieu. An impassioned writer, Mathieu has been rocked by the recent death of his mother, who left him for her American dream when he was a boy. Reeling from the loss, he latches onto Daisy with a fierce commitment that exhilarates, and suffocates, her.

Over a golden autumn day, Daisy and Mathieu clash over religion, art, Iraq, food, the metaphysical possibilities of a good shoe, and the murky memories tunneling up from their pasts. Dancing along a razor's edge of desire and discretion, the lovers lie to one another in minor and meaningful ways, until finally the deceptions and passion explode.

Torn between her blossoming love for Mathieu and the family and dreams she's left behind, Daisy must discover if the flickering flame of her self can survive the vacuum of this brilliant, difficult man, who will always take her breath away.

ISBN# 978-160542126-1
Trade Paperback / Contemporary Romance
US $15.95 / CDN $17.95
JUNE 2010
www.sarahhina.blogspot.com

Sorrow Wood

a novel by Raymond L. Atkins

Reva Blackmon is a reluctant probate judge in the small town of Sand Valley, Alabama. She lives in a rock castle with turrets and a moat thanks to Franklin Roosevelt and the New Deal and walks on one leg thanks to a drunken railroad engineer on the Southern Pacific. She sings Wednesdays and Sundays in the choir at the Methodist Church and believes in reincarnation the rest of the time. Her husband, Wendell, is the love of her life, stretching back down the corridors of time.

Wendell Blackmon is the disgruntled policeman in this same small town. He rides herd on an unlikely collection of reprobates, rogues with names such as Deadhand Riley, Gilla Newman, Otter Price, and Blossom Hogan. Law enforcement in this venue consists of breaking up dog fights, investigating alien abductions, extinguishing truck fires, and spending endless hours riding the roads of Sand Valley. Unlike his wife, Wendell does not believe in reincarnation. Nor does he believe in Methodism, Buddhism, or Santa Claus. But he does believe in Reva, and that belief has been sufficient to his needs over their many years together.

But the routines of Sand Valley are about to change. A burned body has been discovered at a local farm named Sorrow Wood. The deceased is a promiscuous self-proclaimed witch with a checkered past. Wendell investigates the crime, and the list of suspects includes his deputy, the entire family of the richest man in town, and nearly everyone else who knew the departed. As the probe continues, a multitude of secrets are revealed, including one that reaches from the deep past all the way to the rock castle. Who was this woman who met her end at Sorrow Wood? Where did she come from? What were the mysterious circumstances surrounding her death, and what did her presence mean to Wendell, Reva, and the remainder of the inhabitants of Sand Valley?